Also by George V. Higgins

The Friends of Eddie Coyle (1972)
The Digger's Game (1973)
Cogan's Trade (1974)

*These are Borzoi Books
Published in New York
By Alfred A. Knopf*

A City On A Hill

A City On A Hill

George V. Higgins

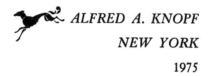 ALFRED A. KNOPF
NEW YORK
1975

THIS IS A BORZOI BOOK
PUBLISHED BY ALFRED A. KNOPF, INC.

Library of Congress Catalog Card Number: 74-21308
ISBN: 0-394-49540-3

MANUFACTURED IN THE UNITED STATES OF AMERICA
FIRST EDITION

Newly designated governor of the Massachusetts Bay Colony, John Winthrop of Groton, Suffolk, embarked for Boston aboard the *Arbella* in 1630, with other settlers. En route he gave a sermon: "A Modell of Christian Charity." He cautioned the colonists against the Lord's wrath.

Now the onely way to avoyde this shipwracke, and to provide for our posterity, is to followe the counsel of Micah, to doe justly, to love mercy, to walke humbly with our God. For this end, wee must be knitt together in this work as one man. . . . Soe shall wee keepe the unitie of the spirit in the bond of peace. . . . Wee shall finde that the God of Israell is among us, when tenn of us shall be able to resist a thousand of our enemies; when hee shall make us a prayse and glory that men shall say of succeeding plantations, "the lord make it like that of NEW ENGLAND." For wee must Consider that wee shall be as a Citty upon a hill. The eies of all people are uppon Us. . . .

Awaiting inauguration as President of the United States, John F. Kennedy on January 9, 1961, addressed a joint session of the Massachusetts legislature. He spoke of his affection for the Commonwealth: ". . . I am not here to bid farewell to Massachusetts. For forty-three years, whether I was in London, Washington, the South Pacific or elsewhere, this has been my home; and, God willing, wherever I serve, it will always be my home.

"It was here," he said, "my grandparents were born; it is here I hope my grandchildren will be born."

Carrying, he said, more than fond memories and fast friendships "from this state to that high office," he said:

"During the last sixty days, I have been engaged in the task of constructing an Administration. It has been a long and deliberate process. Some have counseled greater speed.

Others have counseled more expedient tests. But I have been guided by the standard John Winthrop set before his shipmates on the flagship *Arbella* 331 years ago, as they, too, faced the task of building a government on a new and perilous frontier. 'For we must consider,' he said, 'that we shall be as a city upon a hill—the eyes of all people are upon us.' "

Fond as he was of lists, he provided one:

"For of those to whom much is given, much is required. And when at some future date the high court of history sits in judgment on each of us recording whether in our brief span of service we fulfilled our responsibilities to the state, our success or failure, in whatever office we hold, will be measured by the answers to four questions:

"First, were we truly men of courage, with the courage to stand up to one's enemies, and the courage to stand up, when necessary, to one's associates, the courage to resist public pressure as well as private greed?

"Second, were we truly men of judgment, with perceptive judgment of the future as well as the past, of our own mistakes as well as the mistakes of others, with enough wisdom to know what we did not know, and enough candor to admit it?

"Third, were we truly men of integrity, men who never ran out on either the principles in which we believed or the people who believed in us, men whom neither financial gain nor political ambition could ever divert from the fulfillment of our sacred trust?

"Finally, were we truly men of dedication, with an honor mortgaged to no single individual or group, and compromised by no private obligation or aim, but devoted solely to serving the public good and the national interest?"

A City On A Hill

Shortly before two o'clock the blues began to work the baitfish in toward shore at Madaket. **1** One prospecting gull, high on the wind with his wings motionless, began to cry. Very soon other gulls came in from Cliffside, and the first dove toward the water to eat what was left of the slaughtered menhaden.

"That's planning for you," Richmond said. "I figured we had at least another couple of hours before they got hungry again, to sit here and drink some beer and pretend it was '60 again."

Six hundred feet up, a five-foot yellow-cloth butterfly, some child's present from the Nantucket KiteMan, floated out toward Portugal, trailing its broken string.

Up the sloping beach, two young men with beards took their rigs from the sand spikes, cocked the nine-foot Fiberglas poles at their waists, and ran down the sand into the water, arching the rods against the sky as they stopped, throwing the metal jigs out toward the gulls, far short.

"Well," Cavanaugh said, "there's no law I know about, says you've got to fish when you say you're going fishing. At least I didn't commit myself to anybody with that understanding. I'll sit in the sun if you want."

"It's not a matter of law," Richmond said. "It's a matter of what's permitted, and what's acceptable. This is an island. You have to tend to business on an island. You're not permitted to have no business unless you agree that having no business is not acceptable. Then you're a damned tourist. Off-islander. From America. Probably rich, and even if you're not, you're not allowed to deny that you are, because if you weren't you'd have something to do. Then they condescend to you. You're just a reliable source of income for the winter, if properly handled."

"How long've you been out here?" Cavanaugh said.

"I had some business," Richmond said. "You don't understand: it doesn't have to be a profit-making enterprise. It's a matter of going about something that you want to do, in an orderly fashion. Now those kids: what they're doing is running up and down the beach, waving their arms and going in the water. It's good for them and it feels good to them. But if they didn't have those rods in their hands, we'd start thinking they were nuts, or stoned on something, and we'd call up a reputable physician and have him come out here and take them away for a nice long rest.

"The same goes for us," Richmond said. "We're all right for now, just sitting here drinking beer and talking in the sun, because those fish are still way too far out to reach. But when they get closer, it may very well be necessary to get to work. The Mitchell reel was invented solely to justify being out on the beach here in August."

"Not September?" Cavanaugh said.

"September's fine," Richmond said. "We always left the day after Labor Day, so I developed habits of mind that made me assume that the place only existed in August. When I got here last year with my little project, I was mildly relieved to discover that the place has an existence of its own, even apart from the perceptions of the summer people. October, too: the weather's still beautiful, and all the people like me are long gone. Very nice. But the winter, boy, the winter you wear around your neck on a rope. It starts to improve around the middle of March, and when April comes, you really appreciate it. You've earned it. May is your reward, the nice time before the fogs start in June to punish all the people in the big boats who think they can duck the winter in Key West and come up here and just skim off the summer. Nature discourages windfall enjoyments. I didn't know that before."

"That's what comes of a lifetime of privilege," Cavanaugh said. "I could've told you that, if you'd asked me."

"It was more a matter of underestimating problems," Richmond said. "I've always had that deficiency. I expect to finish things much faster than I'm able. There was nothing in my expectations to cause me to think about getting through the winter. I didn't think I'd be out here to worry about it. I thought I was coming out here to take a month and get over Dee. Then I figured I'd start calling around, and I'd find something. When I found it, I'd leave, and go do it. What, I didn't know. But as soon as I felt better, I was going to go, and I thought that'd take about a month.

"Then," Richmond said, "I found myself in something close to an alcoholic stupor quite early one evening in November, muttering obscenities as I received the considered judgment of NBC's computers that Richard Milhous Nixon was winning the biggest landslide in American political history. CBS and ABC were saying the same thing. And it occurred to me that I was not only displeased, as I have been on a number of other election nights, I was hors de combat. There wasn't anybody with me, sweating whether he was going to win or lose and being brave about it. Then, on top of that, it came to me that if it was election night, it must be November, and if that was the case, I'd spent over two months making no progress at all on a one-month project. That rattled me as much as the vote."

"Now it's almost a year," Cavanaugh said.

"Now it's almost a year," Richmond said. "I've been tending seriously to my business for almost a year. I know."

"And how're you feeling now?" Cavanaugh said.

"Much better, thank you," Richmond said. "Oh, I've had my moments, my occasional relapses. Thanksgiving I called the boy, and Sandy came on and said how great she'd been doing, and now she understands, and actually it was the best thing for her. She doesn't hate me anymore. It was what inspired her to fulfill herself: that was what she said, and she wanted to thank me. The bitch." Richmond laughed. "Then I had dinner. A frozen turkey dinner that came in an aluminum foil pan. I don't remember if it had all the fixins. It was made of plywood. Then I went down to the Hub to see if they had anybody new that was dead. I looked at the index cards on the door, and my name wasn't listed, so I bought a magazine and went home and got drunk. Drunker."

"You been off at all?" Cavanaugh said.

"Christmas," Richmond said. "I went home. They called me up and told me that if I just stayed down here, all by myself, I'd get depressed, and that wouldn't be a good idea. I had a cousin who killed himself. He was a good deal older than I was, and he had very poor judgment. He used rat poison, the silly bastard. It took him about three months to get the dose right, and he was in agony. So we've always been very concerned about depression, and it never occurred to me that I came out here in the first place because I was depressed to start with. And I wasn't all by myself, as a matter of fact. But I didn't think of those things, which shows you what happens when you drink too much: you don't think of things when you should think of them.

"So I went home," Richmond said, "and that depressed me more. It also depressed my girl, I guess, because when I got back, she wasn't here. Then I was really depressed. I think if she'd been able to cook, I would've done away with myself when I got back and she was gone. Not with arsenic, though.

"But I drank myself out of it," he said. "I was all right by Easter. A little shaky in the mornings, perhaps, a bothersome tremor that caused whitecaps on the surface of the tooth glass of Smirnoff that I used as a phlegm-cutter on arising, but otherwise all right. Just before Easter. I could've left then, for good, but I wanted to taper down a bit, so my hands would be steady, and I also wanted to be sure. I didn't want to attempt too much in my weakened condition.

"I tried it out," he said. "I went home again, for Easter dinner, and I called up the boy from there. Sandy got on again and said: 'Went home to Mother, huh, Jess?' But I didn't have anything to lose, then. She described to me the astonishing sexual prowess of this graybeard loon that she visits in the hanging plants, and I thought it was pretty amusing.

"For me," Richmond said, "that was a considerable improvement. It was a funny thing. I was certain I'd get over Dee in a month or so, and look how long it took me."

"Maybe you were getting over something else at the same time," Cavanaugh said.

"I could've been," Richmond said. "The thought has occurred to me. It wasn't as though we'd gotten along together that well, or had been together that long. Or spent that much time together. I thought: 'The most it can be is that this time it's my pride that's hurt.' Which, I would assume, might be a lot different from somebody else's pride being hurt. Much easier to get over somebody else's hurt. But how can you miss somebody you probably never really got to like very much? I had to face facts: she didn't go off with him because we were getting along so wonderfully."

A Boston Whaler bounced through the rip at Smith's Point, the operator cushioning the shocks by crouching behind the wheel, the two passengers hanging on in the seats, the spinning rods whipping in the holders as the waves of the cross-currents whacked the planing hull. The boat left a broad white wake that vanished in the currents before the curve was complete. Four hundred yards offshore, the Whaler settled down abruptly and floated even-keeled as the men in it began casting into the water where the gulls swooped.

"Well," Richmond said, "the answer came to me: you can miss somebody like that quite a lot. Quite a goddamned lot, as a matter of fact, when you're sitting out here and thinking about how you screwed everything up to a fare-thee-well and there's nothing even in sight, let alone reach, that looks like it might work for repairs. I don't know. Maybe it was my pride, and I just had more of it'n I thought."

"You think it's permanent now, though," Cavanaugh said.

"Absolutely," Richmond said. "For a while the Steamship Authority was giving serious thought to an extra trip a day for the gleaming-white *Uncatena*, to provide enough Cutty for the fellow up on the Cliff whose wife ran away from him. But I switched to beer and wine quite a while ago, and by Easter I no longer had to get bombed; all I needed was a little edge on, all the time."

" 'Never drunk,' " Cavanaugh said.

" 'Seldom sober,' " Richmond said. "Right after Memorial Day I was back on the Senator's rule: nothing before noon, nothing between one thirty and five, easy-does-it after dinner. Of course the Senator and I might have some quarrel about what constitutes easy-does-it, but the way to survival is by flexibility and I've been pretty faithful to the principle of the thing. I did get stiff on the Fourth, but that was out of a sense of obligation. I always got stiff on the Fourth because it was the only way I could listen to all that crap about Glorious Independence. I think I'm all right now." Richmond squinted behind his Ray-Bans. The two fishermen made cast after cast. "They're still too far out to reach. We've got a real question about fishing here, I think."

" 'It is a problem,' " Cavanaugh said very slowly, " 'which requires, if indeed does not demand, the most careful reflection, and study, before any action is undertaken.' "

" 'Many sectors of the economy are potentially affected,' " Richmond said. " 'The coastal fisheries, our important vacation industry.' I forget what used to come next."

" 'The stake which we all have in the preservation of the ecology, and the environment in which we live,' " Cavanaugh said.

"I missed that one by at least a mile," Richmond said. "I thought it was the commotion around the Senator, everybody so anxious to catch him picking his nose that they didn't listen to what he had to say. I thought it was a dynamite issue, and I gave him all those excellent things to say, and several people went to sleep."

"I was just as wrong as you were," Cavanaugh said. "I didn't even know 1972 was over. I agreed with you. I was the jerk that talked you into retreading it, for Christ sake. I should've known better. When was the last time you saw a picture of a duck soaked in oil?"

Richmond drank Miller's and placed the can in the sand beside him. "It's the same old story," he said. "There aren't enough people in the Sierra Club to elect a President of the United States. There aren't enough, really, to keep a good issue alive. Not for long, anyway. Not long enough."

"It's the same way with everything," Cavanaugh said. "Sam's got very good foresight. He's got brains enough to see there's a guy working this side of the street and there's a guy working that side of the street, and what we better do is find another street with at least one side that's free. He stays current with what other guys're doing, and he still tries to work his own stuff up, and he does the best he can, not to waste his energy on something prime that somebody else is controlling. He backs it, but he doesn't compete."

"For a Congressman," Richmond said, "very sensible indeed. Very few of them can manage it. 'Economy of motion,' the Senator called it. 'Parsimony of effort. In a limited number of days there is a limited number of hours, no matter how few of them you sleep. Husband them.' And then, of course, he wouldn't."

"He was in a whirlwind," Cavanaugh said. "It's a lot

easier to remember things than it is to practice them, I guess, when you get into that kind of uproar."

"It's not easy at all," Richmond said. "None of it was easy. When I first went to work for him, the whole reason on both sides was that it was a natural. Then I started, and neither one of us was comfortable. He was used to being nice and keeping things back. If he wasn't nice, I'd nail him, and if he didn't keep things back, I'd print them, and somebody else'd nail him. I was used to being nice, because I wanted to worm things out, to print, and if I was nasty, no further worming. There was an awkwardness, and it lasted for about six months. Neither one of us really stopped to think about what must be going on. There wasn't time. But there were things that I really wanted to know, and needed to know, and should've known. When they came up, I reacted as usual, and I asked Jerry. If there was something he decided I should know about, instead of telling me he told Jerry. Jerry'd tell me. He was still leaking stuff to me, and I was still sourcing stuff out of him. It was silly, and there were the two of us, being silly without even thinking about it.

"Jerry noticed it," Richmond said. "What we both wanted out of my job with him was not happening. Jerry was sitting down with us one afternoon, and he was nagging me a little about this thing I'd given him for the NEA. The Senator. He didn't really like it. It was in line with what he'd said before—federal aid, vouchers for parochial schools, all that stuff—but he didn't really like it. Finally he said: 'Well, shouldn't we get something in there about public lease-backs on private schools? Don't you think that's important? I can't go up to the Shoreham and say all these things I've said before. These're teachers; they know when you're copying.'

" 'Senator,' I said," Richmond said, " 'the last I heard about that, it was a super-secret position paper that hadn't been adopted. I didn't know we had a go-ahead decision.' Well, Jerry had had Monroe and Terry working on it, and they were very close to having a draft bill ready. The Senator was right: it was time to balloon it and look at the response. The audience was perfect for it. But I hadn't known he was ready. Nobody told me, and I didn't ask.

" 'Jess doesn't work for the paper anymore, Senator,' Jerry said. Then he looked at me," Richmond said. " 'When'd you get so bashful about asking questions?' I didn't have an answer. 'Now look, you two,' Jerry said, 'this looked awful good, but it was just potential, and it's still just potential, and that's all it's ever going to be, unless we can stake things out far enough to hold the positions, and close enough so we can protect our butts getting to them. So I guess that means you and I've got to start talking, and you,' he said to the Senator, 'you've got to stop being cute with him.' "

"Did he?" Cavanaugh said.

"Most of the time," Richmond said. "He started to tell, more, but he never learned to ask. He'd listen, but he wouldn't ask."

"Yeah," Cavanaugh said. "Sam's the same way. Finding the new territory's easy enough, but getting those stakes out is murder. We can't move fast enough. There's plenty of stuff without paw marks on it, but then he has to learn about it, and that means somebody has to teach him, and he doesn't have the dough to hire the people to work it up for him. The guys that get on top of things and really ride them for all they're worth, they've got the horses."

"They also listen now and then to people who know

what they're talking about," Richmond said. "Even though they are lobbyists, and make their living that way."

"He's better about that," Cavanaugh said. "Steve told me when he left: 'Don't even bother trying to get him to listen to anybody from the manufacturers, or the oil people, or anybody like that. He'll see ADA, and ACLU, and the Quakers, and he'll listen to anybody from the churches even though he won't do a damned thing they tell him unless he was going to do it anyway. But forget about the private industry types.'

"Now I was coming off more'n a year with Senator Hammond," Cavanaugh said. "He wouldn't take an aspirin unless I called somebody from the AMA and they said it was all right. 'Steve,' I said, 'those guys can save a man a hell of a lot of work.' 'I know it,' he said, 'but Sam's different.'

"Then," Cavanaugh said, "Sanderson left ADA and went with the movie guys, and there was some lash-up one day and he came in to see Sam. And Sam let him in before he found out Sanderson'd given up being pure and started making a living for himself. So there's Sam expecting an uplifting sermon on the rights of the downtrodden and the theory of the leisure class, and Sanderson wants to talk about how if Birmingham wants to keep the skin flicks out, let Birmingham pass an ordinance, but keep the Congress out of the censorship business. Which gave Sam some pretty good information and he made a speech with it and got himself some ink. After that I said: 'Sam, if Sanderson can tell you something you don't know, when he's running around protecting our vital liberties, and he can tell you something new when he starts promoting blue movies, maybe there's some other guys you ought to start seeing.'

"You know Sam," Cavanaugh said. "He won't give up.

He just will not give up. He'll retreat, but he still fights. 'It's the same thing,' he said. 'It's still a matter of freedom of speech and civil rights.' So he kicks and screams, but he does it. When the Chamber of Commerce types come in, he gets very edgy, but he does it."

"The Senator played those guys like violins," Richmond said. "Personal calls, birthday cards, invitations to drinks, dinners, breakfasts: he was beautiful."

"He still is," Cavanaugh said. "Tidrow was in last week from the pipeline bunch. Sam was out. Really out: he was not in the goddamned office. Tidrow got pissed. Sam's evidently supposed to stay in his office every day, in case Tidrow wants to see him about something."

"Tidrow's an asshole," Richmond said. "He couldn't talk a whore into screwing. I could never understand why anybody ever hired that guy to do anything. I used to wonder if perhaps he was secretly retained by the people who opposed things, to go out banging the gong in favor of them. Talk about being personally obnoxious."

" 'I never have any trouble seeing any of them,' he said," Cavanaugh said. " 'I just came from seeing Senator Travis, but I can't see Sam Barry. I can't understand it.' So I said: 'They've got different problems in New Haven than we've got in New Bedford. They look at things differently.' But he was going to spend the rest of the week telling everybody what a great guy Travis is, and I knew it, and what a snotty bastard Sam Barry is, and I knew that, too, and there wasn't a damned thing I could do about it."

"There were times when I thought Travis might be too good at it," Richmond said. "Maybe he spent too much time with the Tidrows, and if he'd been just a little more ruthless with his schedule, and hadn't exhausted himself trying to get a valentine from every single voter in the

United States, he would've done better. If you told him there were people who would always dislike him, and never vote for him, he'd agree with you, and go along with the idea of putting his effort where it would do him some good. But the next thing I knew, he was committing himself to the Oklahoma State Convention of Federal Savings and Loan Incorporators for a keynote speech to a couple hundred people who loathed everything he stood for, and did not have friendly feelings about him, either. It was a waste of time."

"Yeah," Cavanaugh said, "but he had more of it to waste. He had you, he had Jerry, he had Eleanor, and he had two thirds of the wise men at Brookings, and he had enough telephone numbers in Cambridge and New Haven and Boston to get a full briefing on anything in the world at one o'clock in the morning. That night I called him at midnight about the Russian trawler? That was masterful. Get the guy out of bed in the middle of the night, forty-five minutes later he's back with a full treatise on the twelve-mile limit. That's when I knew Travis was serious."

"That was Churchill," Richmond said. "Visiting Fellow, Fletcher School, from Jesus College. We used to scavenge the papers every morning for names like that. When we got one, Senator Travis dropped an appreciative personal note to the scholar whose valuable paper on the Kerensky government had so enthralled the audience at the convention of American political scientists. A week later, Jerry telephoned about some minor issue that nevertheless troubled the Senator, because of its implications for strategic arms limitation, wondering if the professor had any views that might clarify things for him. The professor always did. Another personal note, this time of thanks, enclosing a tear sheet from the *Congressional Record*, reporting that

Senator Travis had consulted Professor Wisdom and believed his expert opinion ought to be considered by the Committee on Foreign Relations. After that, the professor volunteered material, batches of it, and when Senator Travis found himself with a speaking engagement at the University of California at Davis, Professor Thoughtful would be called for a private discussion in the Senator's suite at the Fairmont. You could've called any time of day or night to ask what the Senator had to say about temporary repairs to the Great Wall of China; somewhere at MIT we had a fellow who knew what the formula was for the mastic."

"Well," Cavanaugh said, "it's a little easier when you're a Presidential contender, I guess."

"There are ways in which it's easier," Richmond said. He drank beer. "There are ways in which it's harder. You get to be a contender partly because you started doing it when your candidacy was no healthier than the next man's. But the people you started with become confused about what was the cause and what was the effect. They respond because the man's a contender, but when he gets stronger, they commence to think he became a contender because they responded. Now there's a little bit of truth in that, so you can't deny it, and denying it would make them mad. Therefore you allow them to commit their private vanities, and thus encouraged, they develop a proprietary attitude about the man. After all, he's the trustee of their eventual appointments as ambassadors, and undersecretaries, and special advisors to the President. If he wants to behave recklessly with his chances to be President, very well, but he should acknowledge their rightful claim to rule the world without running for office, and unless he was more prudent, that claim was jeopardized. They acted like they thought it was lip-sync: he moved his lips while they talked, and the television cameras attributed what they said to him. They can be difficult."

"Yeah," Cavanaugh said, "I'd still take it. Congressmen don't get that kind of service, and they need it more. It's happened so often: we're collecting the detail, we're talking to the right people, we're making some progress, pretty soon he's going to be able to talk about it without making a damned fool of himself. Immediately somebody gets it in his head: close the shipyard. Phase out all the bases. The Russians start tearing up the trawler nets. And then, I'm not the guy anymore that calls up at midnight looking for fifteen thousand dollars' worth of research, free and at once: I'm the guy that *gets* called, and I haven't got that research because I've been spending all my time trying to stop Immigration from deporting somebody's half-assed cousin that sneaked in from Halifax nine years ago and then went and applied for a job with the General Services Administration. And that means Sam looks like a jerk when he could've scooped a whole flock of ink and looked like a genius, and it also means that somebody else beats us to something we were working on when the shit hit the fan."

"I always thought Sam's people had a great deal of confidence," Richmond said.

"Steve had a lot more'n I did," Cavanaugh said. "All the original ones did. 'We're small, but we're dedicated. We work our asses off, and we really care about things.' Virtue will prevail. I believed it. It's very appealing. I was used to Hammond's committee and Hammond's office. I once thought Utopia was just a matter of harnessing all the manpower and money that a fourth-term Senator pisses away. When you needed a fresh pad of paper in that office, somebody brought it to you, and another cup of coffee with it, without being asked. You could take somebody to lunch, if it'd help, and if you decided you didn't want to stay in Washington for the weekend after all, Senator Hammond's office could almost always get you on a plane without even mentioning that he was the ranking member of the Subcommittee on Aviation. 'Jesus,' I thought, 'here's where it's all put together. It's smaller, but it's working the way it's supposed to.'

"Well," Cavanaugh said, "it wasn't. Steve told me they'd spent the whole first term making up for Talbot. 'It served us right,' he said. 'We ran against Talbot on the war, and that he was lazy. Right on both counts, only we didn't know the half of it. We thought Talbot didn't do much; Talbot didn't do *any*thing. I think he spent six terms in Congress, asleep. We took him out by revving everybody up: "Things'll be different with Sam, boy, you just wait and see. Better service from your Congressman, your active representative in Washington," and a lot of people that didn't care squat about the war went with us on that point alone. So we got down here, and all of a sudden we had to deliver. We came in thinking we were going to have to make improvements. Hell, we had to start at Ground Zero. You think about it now, it was a lousy idea. They were used to Talbot, and we went and spoiled them, and since then they've been after us day and goddamned night.'

"Steve's got a tendency to look on the bright side of things," Cavanaugh said. " 'But it's mostly over now,' he said. Lying bastard. We do more constituent service than any other office in Congress, I bet, when you figure the actual population of the district. And while we're doing it, Muskie's snagging our issues and making headlines with a speech at Creighton University. Sam gets around to saying it on the floor a week later, and he's me-tooing."

"He lucked out on the war, though," Richmond said. "He did all right with that."

One of the young men reeled in his jig and hooked it to the lowest ferrule on the spinning rod, winding the line tight with the reel. He started toward Richmond and Cavanaugh. His companion continued to cast fruitlessly toward the water where the gulls wheeled.

"He did," Cavanaugh said. "Of course he started with that. He was prepared with the figures and the facts before anybody had any idea who the hell he was. And he didn't have anything else on his mind then: nobody was howling at him to do all the things that Talbot never did. They all had to catch up with him. The only thing that bothered him was Drinan getting all the national copy. 'If I'd've been from Indiana,' he said, and of course that was how come he was so nice to me all the time then: because it was the *Post* I was calling for, and not the Quincy *Patriot Ledger* or something, 'then they'd have room for me.'

" 'Sam,' I used to say to him," Cavanaugh said, " 'if you were from Indiana, you wouldn't be *from* Indiana, you'd still be in Indiana, and I wouldn't be calling you.'

" 'All right,' he said, 'then Drinan oughta be from Indiana, then. He's a priest. He doesn't need the job anyway.' "

"I thought about going back and working for him," Richmond said.

"What's he need?" Cavanaugh said. "Legislative or administrative?"

"I don't know if he needs either one," Richmond said. "I never actually did anything about it."

The young man with the beard walked past them, heading for the rip. He kept his eyes focused on the ground.

"You think about a lot of things, about doing a lot of things, when you stay out here by yourself for a long time," Richmond said. "You don't do any of them, but you think about them. One day in January, when Elliot was still at Defense, I found myself filled with energy, and I put in a call to Dick to ask if there was anything there. Then this great sense of purpose deserted me, and I was scared, and I didn't want . . . I went out, so if he called back, I wasn't there."

"Finley's leaving," Cavanaugh said.

"Booze finally get him?" Richmond said.

" 'Going back to Tucson,' is what he said," Cavanaugh said. "Said he's got the kids growing up and he's got to make some money now, because none of them're big enough to play football and it looks like he's going to have to pay tuition after all. 'That's what I get for marrying a pretty girl,' he said to me. 'I should've picked one with muscles. Then the kids could support me, instead of me supporting them, and I could do what I like.' "

"The booze got him," Richmond said. "If he believes that, he must be drunk all the time and unable to see straight. What the hell is it he likes to do, anyway? The son of a bitch never did anything but jam the gears every time we had anything to do with them. What he likes to do is stop progress. How the hell can you like that?"

"I think it's the hours, myself," Cavanaugh said. "Toby's forty-five or so, and he's been doing what he's doing now, with different titles, ever since he got out of law school. It takes it out of a man. I've thought it a good many times myself. 'I could take this job for the rest of my life, if I didn't think it was going to take the rest of my life just to finish what I've got on this week.' You get so damned tired. This is the first week I've had off in over a year. I told him, he was talking about using the Tuesday–Thursday plan, and I said to him: 'Fine. But plan also on not having me around down here, while you're up there smiling at people and pressing the flesh, because I need some time off.' This week and next was what I had in mind.

" 'No, you can't do that,' he said," Cavanaugh said. " 'If I'm going to be up there that much, you've got to be available here.' And I said: 'Look, I've got to do it. I'm bushed. I haven't seen my wife three consecutive nights in a year.' Louise's coming in, she's had the trip planned a long time. We'd meet up here and it was going to work nicely. But, no. He could see where I needed the vacation, but what about him? He wasn't taking one. There're all these things we've got to get started on. It's time. We're running behind. So finally he let me have a week, after I offered to quit altogether, and the only way I could get that out of him was by promising to see you."

"Uh huh," Richmond said.

The young man reached the point and began casting into the rip. Four hundred yards off the beach, one of the men in the Whaler bent over to boat a fish.

"You take what you can get in this world," Cavanaugh said. "I'm here, and the day after tomorrow I see my wife for three days, unless the boat sinks or something, or the fog comes in. Okay, I knew what I was getting into. I'd rather work for a guy who works too hard than work for a guy that doesn't work at all."

"I take it," Richmond said, "he's still hot for it, then."

"Oh, sure," Cavanaugh said. "When he gets down, when he's so exhausted from running around that he can't see straight, and he's popping Gelusil like candy, then he starts talking about how he hasn't done half of what he actually thought he'd do, no more'n a third of what he said he'd do, and less than a quarter of what he wanted to do, you've got to sit down and cheer him up and say: 'Look, somebody else wouldn't've done a tenth of it, and nobody else would've thought of the rest.' "

"He's a pretty good guy, actually," Richmond said.

"He really is," Cavanaugh said. "It was just a job when I took it. It was a damned good job, better'n the one I was losing. . . ."

"Even though that was my idea," Richmond said, "I had some reservations about it."

"Well," Cavanaugh said, "you give me a choice between getting along with a guy, and not eating, and you'll find me adaptable."

"He had a reputation," Richmond said. "So did you. I thought you might be a little too hard-nosed for the man. I'm glad it worked out."

"We both learned something," Cavanaugh said. "Finley came fishing around after it got out that he was leaving, did I want to go to work for Davidson? More money on the Senate side, and other good things. I turned him down. The last time they had an idea over there was the day Davidson came in and said nobody ever had any ideas. It's a terrible place. 'Save the goddamned bison, is what we've got to do, and no more wild ponies to the dog-food factory.' Someday it's going to register on Davidson's office that we had a regular war going on over there, west of Honolulu or something, whole bunch of our little yellow brothers running around shooting at people, and I think the shock's gonna kill him. Maybe not, though, if they didn't knock off any ponies."

The gulls moved in about a hundred yards, screaming.

"Howard Davidson always wanted to be a United States Senator," Richmond said. "He was lieutenant governor out there, he was governor, and he wasn't a bad governor, either. But he was good at things because he thought trying hard might make him a United States Senator, and he was right. That was the limit of his ambition. He didn't want to do anything in the Greatest Deliberative Body in the World. He just wanted to belong to it. He made it, twenty years ago, and subsided gratefully into it. When Howard Davidson meets his Maker, he'll be content to burn in hell, just as long as the Lord says: 'Senator Davidson, go to hell.' He'll go cheerfully. But he's a good man, and he plays a careful hand of poker, so they'll probably let him in on a point of personal privilege. There's an adequate supply of men, still ambitious, in Washington as it is."

"Among them," Cavanaugh said, "Sam Barry."

"I heard something," Richmond said. "Maybe I read it somewhere. Is he thinking about coming back up here next year instead, and running for AG?"

"For a little while, he was," Cavanaugh said. "It gets to him every so often. Sylvia calls it the Jesus Mood. If Sam'd been the one that went through all of that, and rose again on the third day, and these were the results he got, he'd probably hold another flood. Or a plague of toads or something. It hits him when he looks around for progress and doesn't find any. He starts talking about how he needs a job where he can be effective. Which is all right. It's good for him. It works out his aggressions.

"What Sam refuses to learn," Cavanaugh said, "is that it matters where you choose to work out your aggressions. For the Attorney General thing, he chose a party at the Thai Embassy, and for somebody to work it out on, instead of me or somebody else who's used to him, he took Tina DeRoche from the *Dispatch*. Now Tina's a hell of a girl, and she's not bad-looking at all, but she's a newspaperman, and he won't listen when I tell him that.

" 'I don't see what the hell interest they'd have in Topeka in what I'm doing,' he said. So I told him again: 'You've got to keep track of things.'

" 'I haven't got time for all the dirty gossip in this town,' he said.

" 'Then you have to keep your mouth shut,' I said, 'everywhere you go. You either keep track of the talk,' and he started telling me he didn't think half of it was true anyway, and I said: 'Yeah, but you don't know which half, and there's no way to find out unless you want to specialize in all that dirty gossip. So, you either don't talk, or you get in trouble because you keep forgetting that people that're going to bed with each other still have time to say something now and then, even though their clothes are off at the same time.'

"He didn't listen," Cavanaugh said. "Or else he didn't believe me, I dunno. So what I assume happened was, Tina told Gene, and Gene owed a guy a favor, and he dropped it where it'd do the most good, and the next thing you know, there's a nice dope story in the *Globe*."

"He's not still thinking about it?" Richmond said.

"He's full of contrition and repentance, if that's what you mean," Cavanaugh said. "No, not after what that kid Makris did to him. He absolutely creamed him. No experience as a prosecutor, except for three months in the DA's office, and his father's partner's got him in there and the only thing they let him handle was guys that were going to plead guilty anyway. And what was he going to do, deny it? He hated it. That was why he was teaching when he ran the first time, for God's sake. Sam Barry, putting guys in jail? If that professor thing hadn't come along, he would've taken the next offer, even if it was a monkey with a tin cup that was unemployed and had a hand organ and rights to a particular corner. Makris spiked him twenty-four hours out of the box."

"Tell Sam to sit tight," Richmond said. "If he wants to see something, all he has to do is wait for next fall, when they have the primary, and he can watch two or three of the pros do it to Makris. If that kid's serious, he's serious about getting murdered."

"How come?" Cavanaugh said. "He's not stupid. Not after what he did to us, he's not."

"Damned right, he's not," Richmond said. "He's worked more press out of cases in Salem than the whole of Garry Byrne's office makes out of ax murders in Suffolk. That kid has come out of nowhere."

"Somebody got a dirty file?" Cavanaugh said.

"Probably," Richmond said.

"My, my," Cavanaugh said. "Imagine that. He comes on like Crusader Rabbit."

"Well," Richmond said, "look at Sam if you want to see somebody that looks like a Boy Scout."

"I never believed that," Cavanaugh said.

"When I first heard it," Richmond said, "neither did I. Sam Barry? Oh, for Christ sake, tell me something I can believe. Then I started looking for things to believe. Reasons. Anything. Then I believed it. It didn't help me to believe it, but I believed it anyway. Now maybe I don't believe it. But it's there, just the same, and if Sam ever gets himself into a real knock-down, drag-out war with some intemperate little virgin with a hot attitude that wants the same job and never had his dick grabbed, it'll surface. And it'll hurt him, too."

" 'Booze and broads,' " Cavanaugh said, " 'never hurt a politician.' Look at that crummy thing they tried to do with that dame in Ohio or wherever it was that had the kid and put McGovern down on the birth certificate."

"Cav," Richmond said, "what happened to McGovern's no precedent for anything. It'll hurt Sam. The reverend clergy suspects they're losing their clout, and that makes them very protective of the clout they've got left, and at the same time, lustful to exercise it in a contest that they can't lose. If somebody can satisfy them that the candidate's been unzipping with a woman not his wife, the ones with white hair will go after him like it was a tong war. They won't do it to Makris, because Makris is Orthodox and they're not the guardians of his faith and morals. Unless the new Primate gives the Pope an engagement ring. But they'll do it to Sam, and they'll do it good, too, just to remind all the other rebellious harps of their origins. Makris'll get it from the big kids. He thinks he's pretty tough, but wait till some guy that's in Fogarty's pocket calls him up from the paper and asks him if it's true he got paid off to dump something in the DA's office. Or maybe they'll run a little time for somebody that's trying for county commissioner, nice testimonial cocktail party in the lounge at the Ship, fifty bucks a couple, and when he gets there the big item's how his wife runs around with the Fuller Brush man. He'll react. He's a hot-blooded kid anyway, thinks he's Zorba the Greek himself, and it'll massacre him. He's a lot like Sam, in his hip-shooting way. He's the kind of guy who shouldn't run for office. He's not that kind of guy. Does that make sense?"

"It does for Sam," Cavanaugh said. "He's doing something that his guts don't understand. You know what Sam wants to do, really wants to be? A philanthropist. Only he hasn't got any real money. So, if you want to do things for people, and you're not rich, what do you do? You run for Congress."

"There's so many of them," Richmond said. "So many; so plentiful, so attractive, and so infuriating. There was a night in San Diego: Travis was dog-tired when we got there, and he had to speak the next morning to the Public Power Convention. He was all primed to shove a whole lot of progressive stuff down their throats with the ham and eggs, and he really needed to be on top of his game. But he refused to go to bed. He wanted to stay up and worry.

"He didn't have any choice about what he was going to do," Richmond said. "What they were doing with depreciation was just as cute then as it is now, and if he didn't cut the legs out from under them, Muskie was going to get between us and McGovern with seven or eight governors and the people who read the *New York Times*. Still he preferred to have a choice, even when he didn't have one, so we had a late supper sent up and he said to me: 'Of course I can say anything I want, when it comes right down to it.'

" 'Not if you're serious about being President of the United States,' I said.

" 'Well,' he said, 'I'm serious, all right. I must be serious.' And he started telling me that it was all a matter of understanding that it wasn't only people who grew up. It was also understanding that you grew up. When you found yourself with a six-foot body, you needed to develop an outlook to go with it, different from the one you'd had when you were three feet tall and the choices were made by six-foot people who ran things and made choices. He said it was a matter of control, of comprehending that you, personally, controlled things. Not somebody else.

" 'There aren't any more United States Senators,' he said. 'When I was a boy, there were United States Senators. There were Presidents. Not anymore. Now there's

Ed Muskie and Barry Goldwater and Frank Church and the rest of us, behaving like Senators and looking like Senators and sitting in the chairs that held real Senators; I have to keep reminding myself that we have to be what we were elected to be, because Bob Taft is dead.

" 'I believed everything I read when I was a boy,' he said. 'I read about bears, and I dreamed about bears, and I woke up screaming and my father came in and turned on the light and scared the bears away. Now I wake up in the middle of the night, thinking about something at four o'clock in the morning, and I have to turn on my own light and do my own work with the bears.'

"In a way," Richmond said, "it's heartbreaking. Makris thinks he's bright and honest and he doesn't like crooks. He thinks a fellow like that would be a good Attorney General. He looks at Fogarty and does not see such a fellow. Therefore, he will go after it himself. 'I'm mean enough,' he told me, and in the courtroom, I guess, he is. So he plans to keep getting his name in the papers, and soon somebody with high ideals will arrive with three bushel baskets full of campaign money donated personally by the cardinal and the rector of Trinity Episcopal. He spends too much time with the Common Cause types. He thinks that's the way things happen. 'You are about to have a memorable experience,' I said."

"Tell him not to run?" Cavanaugh said.

"I did not," Richmond said. "I don't care if he runs. I don't find determination and human goodness offensive now, anymore than I did when the Senator was running. But I don't think anymore that it's essential that the good people run. Remember the way he said that? '*E*-ssential.' I simply told him that he was going to be steamrollered.

"He disliked the idea," Richmond said. " 'The least I

can do is drive everybody else closer to the issues.' Uh huh, and lift the level of politics generally. But I've seen the real dreamers at higher elevations, where you stumble over the carcasses of frozen snow leopards every twenty feet, and I'm not interested in compiling a bird book of dreamers. I expect that he'll get some help from that idea, while recovering from disaster and building a successful law practice. It won't pain him quite so much that Mike Fogarty became Secretary because the Secretary worked a judgeship out of the Governor and the other Reps took care of Speaker Fogarty the way they always do. Jimmy Makris thinks the voters will remember that when Fogarty runs for AG, but they won't, and he'll need whatever consolation he can get when they forget."

Out on the water, another of the men in the Whaler boated a fish. The young man at the point cast diligently into the rip. The young man up the beach put his rig in the sand spike and sat down.

"What did he want you to do?" Cavanaugh said.

"I was to be his 'link with the established wing of the party,'" Richmond said. "I said: 'Oh, come on. You're talking about primaries. The party's just the people who got out the Italian vote and the Jewish vote and the black vote and the mick vote in the last primary. I could tell you right now, almost, the fifteen percent of those people who aren't with Fogarty, and they're with Ianni. Not that they'll do him any good.

" 'None of that group finds me appealing,' " Richmond said. " 'I spent all my time in Washington. What little contact I had with them was the result of invitations to the Senator from Ted Kennedy, and they only snuggled up then to hedge their bets in case he made it and needed a federal highway administrator. In December he was hot, and they asked him to speak at Dorgan's, but it was March when the speech came around, and he was obviously in terrible trouble, and they looked at me like they smelled catshit. The next time you hear those guys saying nice things about somebody, you'll find you wandered into a wake, and the object of their affection is dead.'

"He didn't believe me," Richmond said. "He even suffered a mild annoyance. But they'll convince him. He'll understand."

Still about three hundred yards off the beach, the gulls climbed in the updrafts and headed off, most of them, toward Cisco. The men in the Whaler moved around in the boat. It reared suddenly in the water, coming up fast to planing speed and circling back toward the rip. At the point it leaped through the cross-currents, and one of the passengers displayed the two fish to the young man with the beard.

"Good," Cavanaugh said, "we didn't have to fish."

"We're not excused yet," Richmond said. "That was a snack. I think we'd better wait until evening. We still have our duty to the beer."

"Speaking of duties," Cavanaugh said.

"For those who enjoy that sort of thing," Richmond said.

"I have a little proposition which I think will interest you," Cavanaugh said.

"Most unlikely," Richmond said.

"Hear me out," Cavanaugh said. "As you may be aware, I work for Congressman Samuel Barry of Massachusetts."

"I did hear that," Richmond said.

"Personable fellow," Cavanaugh said. "Industrious, good family man, passionate believer in the ideals that made this nation great."

"Sort of a scrawny fellow," Richmond said. "Chicken-necked. He doesn't need a haircut. He does need a barber that won't white-sidewall him the way they used to when I was at Andover and Sam was at Cranwell. Might also consider changing tailors."

"That's the fellow," Cavanaugh said. "Sam represents a safe district. Harbors no real fear of defeat this time, but intends . . ."

". . . to campaign as vigorously as before," Richmond said, "in order . . ."

". . . to demonstrate to the voters of his constituency that his commitment to their needs and views remains as strong as it was when he first placed his candidacy before them," Cavanaugh said.

"You forgot 'undiminished,' " Richmond said. "It goes before 'commitment.' "

"Right," Cavanaugh said. "Nevertheless, it is possible that Sam may have a little more time on his hands in '74 than he had in '72. Thus, in the interest of a free and democratic society, he's looking to the future of the Democratic Party."

"Which, as we all know," Richmond said, "is the last best hope of mankind in these parlous times."

"Not necessarily," Cavanaugh said. "Sam thinks it all depends on who gets nominated in '76."

"A profound insight," Richmond said. "Congratulate Sam for me."

"Sam has a choice," Cavanaugh said.

"No *kidding*," Richmond said. "Has this gotten around at all in Washington?"

"We've been very discreet," Cavanaugh said. "Only a few trusted advisors have been consulted."

"Like, for example," Richmond said, "Mrs. Richmond's first husband, Steve Hamner."

"Mister Hamner's views have been solicited," Cavanaugh said.

"The Committee for a Democratic Choice," Richmond said.

"Did Steve get in touch with you?" Cavanaugh said.

"Not hardly," Richmond said. "Steve clings to the belief that I seduced Dee. We don't often have drinks together."

"No," Cavanaugh said. "Well, Congressman Barry is pleased to find himself in a position to call upon you to assist him in this exciting and challenging endeavor."

"Who's he got in mind, Hank?" Richmond said.

"Paul Travis," Cavanaugh said.

The young man at the point secured his jig to the bottom ferrule and started back along the beach toward his friend.

"The other day I was meditating," Richmond said. "I perceived that there's not very much going on this year, even for an off-year."

"There's something going on," Cavanaugh said.

"There are people who think there's something going on," Richmond said. "But there's a certain kind of people who think there's always something going on, just like at the Old Howard. They haven't been paying attention. This Watergate thing's going to take at least two years to sort out, and anybody who does anything now will have to start taking positions on it now. No serious person should do that. It'll haunt him."

"Even the Senator?" Cavanaugh said.

"Especially the Senator," Richmond said. "Let Senator Sam recite the Bible to people. Let them get into the soup. Mr. Richardson and the learned Professor Cox leaped into the gravy on their own, apparently under the impression it was a heated pool. Let them get out, if they can."

"In the meantime," Cavanaugh said, "what's a mother to do?"

"Look, Mother," Richmond said, "the Senator's possessed of an unfortunate receptivity toward ideas that will cause him trouble. In '70 we talked him into thinking he was Jesus Christ. In '73 you can probably convince him into thinking he's Lazarus. He's finished, Cav, if a lifetime death grip on a seat in the Senate of the United States amounts to being finished. And if it does, it's a great way to go. But people ought to leave him alone. You shouldn't get a man's hopes up. Sooner or later he'll start to look shopworn, even to himself. Leave the guy alone."

"It's not me, Jess," Cavanaugh said. "Keep that in mind, please. It's Sam. Sam thinks Paul Travis ought to be President of the United States."

"I forgot," Richmond said.

"Yeah," Cavanaugh said in the sunlight, "but at least you're starting to remember."

In the companionable dimness of the dining
room at Chanticleer, a waiter listened patiently
to a gray-haired man from New York who
shifted from side to side in his chair; his silver-blue double-
knit sportscoat was too large, and it remained motionless
with the chair while he complained with his voice and his
left hand that the duck was raw. His family looked on
with hopeful respect.

Louise, deeply tanned, leaned toward Cavanaugh, and,
buttering bread, said: "I didn't know who he was. He was
with another guy, and they both had dinner jackets on, and
those hideous lavender ruffled dress shirts with purple piping along the ruffles. Thin little purple piping, and narrow
black clip-on ties. Everybody else in the place was off a
boat. The really formal ones had blazers and ties. Most of

us had *jeans* on, for Christ sake, and sneakers. But they weren't bothering anybody. Well, you know how David gets."

"I have no idea how David gets," Cavanaugh said. "I think I met David once in my life, and he said his wife went to school with you, and I said that was all right with me, and that was the way we left it."

"The way I leave it," she said, "David must clear close to a hundred thousand dollars a year from that firm. He's a very successful guy."

"And he looks like Prince Valiant," Cavanaugh said. "How much does his father clear?"

"That much again, at least," she said.

"David's *father* is a very successful guy," Cavanaugh said. "David's *father* does a bit of work now and again for U.S. Steel. David had the good judgment to become his father's son. That's not success for David; that's primogeniture."

"A hundred thousand bucks," she said, "is a hundred thousand bucks."

"Not if you're talking to Maurice Stans," he said. "Then it's only about a third of what was really expected."

"I wouldn't talk to Maurice Stans with a megaphone," Louise said. "What David's got is his own American money."

"I don't see any way to quarrel with that," he said.

"That's a nice change," she said. "You've reformed, I guess."

In the lounge side of the ell, a man with a loud voice sang "Mademoiselle from Armentières," accompanied by a piano and cheering.

"On my way to Damascus," he said, "I was knocked from my horse. Then it was all clear to me."

"Jesus," she said, "does that mean you're going to start living with me?"

"No," he said, "I'm going to start living with Jesus."

"I hope you get along better with Him'n you do with me," she said. "Although considering your habits, it doesn't seem likely."

"Could it be worse?" he said.

"Probably not," she said. She wore a white silk dress with a deep halter neck, and the sides of her breasts were brown against the fabric. "You want to call this off right now?"

"Not especially," he said. "I haven't seen you in about six weeks."

"Which you seem to have survived pretty well," she said.

"I've been out on the beach with Jess," he said. "I've been drinking and sleeping and fishing and eating and getting a little sun. It's a nice change. Makes me feel good. I should've had my blood pressure taken before I came up here, and then again when I get back, so I'd know how good I feel. Very relaxing."

"I'll never understand," she said. "Why anybody pays any attention to that man, I will never understand."

"He's a nice guy," Cavanaugh said. "Partly, that. Mostly because he's very astute. He knows things."

In the lounge the man sang: "Hinky dinky parlez-vous." The cheering was thunderous.

"He doesn't know how to live with a woman," she said.

"If that's going to start disqualifying people," Cavanaugh said, "they can retire 'astute.' Hoist it up in the rafters with Cousy's home uniform shirt."

"He doesn't," she said. "He didn't know how to live with Sandra."

"Or else she didn't know how to live with him," Cavanaugh said.

"Sandra's a good, sensible girl," she said. "Very creative and very pretty, too."

"Very pretty, yes," he said. "Sensible? I dunno. The last I heard, she was duffing around Sausalito, doing acrylics nobody'd buy."

"She's having a one-woman show," Louise said.

"So'm I," Cavanaugh said.

"I'll let that pass," she said, "on your statement that you've been drinking."

"You guys got analysts," Cavanaugh said, "us guys got booze. Wouldn't do you any good to drink, wouldn't do me any good to see the wizard every Wednesday for eight or nine years."

"I have freed myself from my aggressions," she said.

"Hee hee hee," Cavanaugh said. "And we both know how you're doing *that* now, don't we, my dear?"

"You can be tiresome," she said.

"Or," he said, "I can be carefree and witty as all get-out. It all depends."

"On how drunk you are," she said.

"On that," he said, "and how come I got drunk. It all depends. Everything all depends. Sandy all depends, Jess all depends, everybody all depends. Like you being in touch with Sandy."

"I'm not in touch with Sandy," she said. "Tenley told me."

"Oh," Cavanaugh said. "How's old Tenley these days? Speaking of the bottle, as I think one of us was."

"Tenley was never on the bottle," Louise said. "Britt was, but then she had her thing out, and now she's all right. Tenley never was."

"Well," Cavanaugh said, "if she wasn't, she was on something else. Now there was a one-woman show for you."

"She's unconventional," Louise said, eating salad and smiling.

"That she is," Cavanaugh said. "Teach this kid to ask for regular coffee."

Louise laughed. She put her head back when she laughed. That tugged the halter tighter against her breasts. Cavanaugh could see the outlines of her nipples. "She was talking about that before I left, and was I going to see you. She asked me: Did you ever get over regular coffee?"

"No," Cavanaugh said, "I never did. Tell her that, the next time you see her. Tell her, I never saw a cup of black coffee since then, I didn't think first: 'Goddamnit, where's the cream?' and then get this instant replay of Tenley hiking up her sweater and squeezing her tit in the cup. I get it black now? I drink it black. Never can tell who's just had a baby these days."

"That was funny, though," Louise said.

The singer in the bar began "Lili Marlene."

"It's funnier now'n it was then," Cavanaugh said.

"Why?" Louise said.

"I don't know," Cavanaugh said. "At the time, she just did that to embarrass me, you know."

"Well," she said, "you *were* embarrassed."

"It worked," Cavanaugh said. "That's just another way of saying it worked. Of course it worked. That didn't make it funny."

"How'd it taste?" she said. "I never asked you that."

"And you'd have to ask," he said, "because you don't remember any you ever tasted, if you ever tasted any, and . . ."

"That's enough," she said. "We went through that a long time ago, and you were just as determined as I was."

"It was too sweet," he said. "I already had sugar in it. She didn't have to do that."

" 'My Lily of the *lamp*-light,' " the crowd in the lounge shouted, " 'my own Lil-lee Mar Lene.' "

"Have you got any idea why she did that?" Louise said.

"Click," Cavanaugh said. "No, I'll bite: was it to embarrass me?"

"No," Louise said. "Because she knows men. All you men ever think about's big tits, and she knows it, and she's got them, and she knows what you guys're thinking all the time, and she just wanted to show you. Big tits aren't everything."

"Nobody said they were," he said.

"Nobody said they were," she said. "Okay, being gullible, I'll accept that. But lots of people thought it."

"Not me," he said.

"It's not all you thought about," she said, "but it's always where you start, or else you get there pretty quick."

"That's so," he said.

"Well," she said, "that's why she embarrassed you. All you think about's tits, and all you think they're for, is, they're something for you to suck."

"They're also not bad to nibble," Cavanaugh said.

"Or that," she said. "The point of it is, they're to give milk to babies."

"The point of it is what you nibble," Cavanaugh said.

"And that," she said, "is why you bother with Jess. He thinks the same way you do."

"That's a pretty good compliment," Cavanaugh said. "For me, at least. For him, it's probably kind of an insult."

"I can live with that," she said. "Actually, for both of

you it's an insult, only neither one of you's got the sensitivity to know it. You know why he walked away from Sandy."

"As a matter of fact," he said, "I don't. I know he did, but I don't know why."

"Didn't you ever ask him?" she said. "Isn't that something you'd want to ask a friend about, when he was doing something of that magnitude?"

"No," Cavanaugh said, "it isn't. It'd never occur to me to ask a man a thing like that. If I heard something like that, and I ran into him a minute later. No, I wouldn't. If he wanted to tell me, I'd listen. But I'd never ask a man a thing like that."

"Well," Louise said, "then I'll tell you. Everybody else knew, anyway. It was simple. Dee wiggled her ass at him one night and he just *defected*. He decided, the hell with Sandy and the boy, and he went with Dee."

"He did go with her," Cavanaugh said. "Why, I'm not sure. I'm not sure he decided that."

"It's not that I don't like Dee," Louise said.

"I like Dee myself," Cavanaugh said.

"I like Dee a whole lot more now, as a matter of fact," Louise said. "Now that she gave the bastard what he deserved in the first place."

"You're awful good on what people deserve," Cavanaugh said. "I wish I was as good as you on that. What's your source?"

"Just looking at things," Louise said. "Just seeing what goes on, and seeing people get what they deserve."

"I can't follow that," Cavanaugh said. "I don't really think that's true, that he deserved that."

"It was the same thing he did to Sandy," she said.

"Jess was over thirty when he met Dee," Cavanaugh

said. "Dee was almost thirty herself. Sandy was about the same age as Jess. That was only two years ago that all happened, not quite two years. I don't think so."

"You don't think so, what?" she said.

"I don't know if she pulled his cock on a regular basis," Cavanaugh said. "I think it was more'n that, if she did. He's no kid. He had his balls tickled before. He was no kid then. If it was just ginch, it would've stayed ginch, and if it was, he wouldn't've done anything."

"If she could've stood it," Louise said.

"Stood what?" Cavanaugh said. "What the hell was there to stand? He's a nice guy. He's bright. He's polite. His grandfather bought a whole lot of Union Pacific stock before anybody ever heard of Leland Stanford, Senior. Maybe it was his great-grandfather, I dunno. His mother's side, anyway. And she was cheap. She still is. And his old man had to go out and match what she had before she'd let him have any of it, and he damned near did. Or after he did so much, it didn't matter, I dunno. So, Jess's rich, or he's going to be, and he's not dumb, he's discreet. He looks good, he's out in the weather all the time. You look at that guy and you see just what he is: a guy that didn't have to do a goddamned thing, and so he went to college and he did what he was supposed to and he always worked for a living and he's nice to people. What's the beef? What was there to stand?"

"Sam's right," Louise said.

"Now there's a new thing," he said. "Tell me, quick: what's Sam right about? I'll call up Ellen at home and get her out of bed and have her get a press release out extra fast. 'Sam Barry was right about something today.' AP'll run a bulletin on that, and analysis stuff on Sunday, too. 'How did Sam Barry get to be right?' "

"About you," she said. "He told me one night. You remember the night War Powers first went through?"

"Not a whole lot of it," Cavanaugh said. "The first part of it, yeah, but then it just sort of trails off into things I guess probably must've happened, but I don't remember them."

"No," she said. "I was wondering if you'd lie."

"I never lie," Cavanaugh said. "I don't necessarily go around telling everything I know, but I never lie. That kind of thing can get a man in trouble, if he's not careful, and sometimes it can get him in trouble even if he is. No, it was a hot night, and it'd been a hot day, and there was another hot day coming, and I was thirsty."

"Thirsty," she said. "Okay. Well, he told me, the trouble with you is, you should've gone to Exeter and then Harvard and then the family brokerage business. Maybe the B School. Then you would've been comfortable."

"Well," Cavanaugh said, "that just goes to show you, how much brighter Sam is'n I am. If I'd've had the benefit of his wisdom when I was a fetus, I wouldn't've picked a cop for a father. Fat lot of good it does me now."

"You could use some good, Hank," she said.

"That I could," he said. "So could we all, all honorable men."

"Sam said he thought if you didn't come to terms with yourself, you'd be in trouble," she said.

"I've got to speak to Sam again," Cavanaugh said. "He's too candid with people. It's always getting him in trouble. Sometimes it gets them in trouble."

"He won't listen," she said. "He thinks he's gone a pretty good distance, being candid. That's another thing he told me."

"He told that to John Clancy one night, too," Cavanaugh

said. "John was light, as usual. He's always light. Throw him a small bone and he'll worry it for three editions. Wrote up this giveaway long piece for Sunday, a dull Sunday. ' "Candor's What I Have to Offer the People," says ambitious, idealistic Sam Barry of Massachusetts.' Clancy thought he was doing the guy a favor. Made him look like a perfect asshole. I went in to him. I said: 'Sam, you can do this, I'm never going to understand how you can do this on just Pepsi, you know? Man's got to be drunk to do something like that. You're the only man I know in Washington that can get himself stiff on Pepsi. And people don't understand it. They think you're sober. You got to start drinking, that's all there is to it. You drink, and you talk like that, most of them've got enough problems of their own so they tell each other: "Hey, leave the guy alone, huh? He was so drunk he was pissing on his fingers." But you do it, and you're sober, and they figure you must mean it. I can't do anything about it.' No, you're right: he won't listen. Not to anybody. What he does best is talk."

"Can he survive that way?" she said.

"For a while, sure," Cavanaugh said. "As long as people see him as a straight shooter, and the Republicans're satisfied to screw around and put up a guy against him because the guy's been loyal, never mind whether he's strong opposition, *and* if some hot-shot doesn't decide to take him on and whip his ass in the primary, he's okay. But, well, Sam develops strong loyalties. The people who put him over are eager, and they work hard, and they don't seem to be like the people that get involved in national holy wars and forget about you as soon as *Time* gets them all upset about some new issue, and some new guy that's promoting it. Sam's people act like they've got a piece of Sam. He's important to them. He's not a symbol of anything to them. He's an example for them, an example of something they want the country to think about. As long as they outnumber the people somebody else can attract to work against Sam, Sam is all right."

"How long is that?" she said.

"It's something we don't have any control over," Cavanaugh said. "There's no way for us to get any real influence over the momentum of somebody else's campaign. Oh, we can keep the fences mended so maybe some guy that could recruit more troops and out-fund us gets himself involved in a bloodletting with another guy who has some pizzazz, and that leaves us cruising while they knock each other off. We can do that. But mostly we're passive. We—he was the beneficiary of Talbot's mistakes. The guy went to Congress, I guess he thought, because he deserved to, and then he picked up some kind of intellectual encephalitis, if he had any brain to start with, and he went down there and did a Rip Van Winkle and that's how Sam nailed him. Well, I can't see Sam going that route. But he's vulnerable. Not this time, but some time. He's vulnerable to anybody who can get up on a stump and wow the yeomen, and he'll last as long as somebody like that doesn't stick his head up. Then he's gonzo."

"He's a loser," she said.

"In the long run, yeah," Cavanaugh said. "In a way, I think he kind of wants to be. He was, the first time he went out. He expected to be, the second time, and then when it turned out he wasn't, he made himself a whole set of judgments. He decided God really is involved in these things. 'The significance of the New Politics,' he actually said this, now, he said it to Steve Hamner when Steve first went with him. He wanted Steve to be very sure he knew about the Mission, 'is the gradual transformation of people who practice politics, from politicians into a twentieth-century version of the clerisy.'

" 'I nodded politely,' Steve told me. 'You can nod politely too, if you want, because he'll tell you the same thing, I bet. I hadda go and look it up. I thought he was talking about priests or something. Here I am, all I ever did was scramble around looking for votes and keeping the lines open and trying to find a guy that could win. Any guy, anywhere, any job that was worth going after. I was in some brawls in Philadelphia that made your regular alley fight look like a tea party. I had two guys in a row that got wiped out in Harrisburg for vote fraud. And here's this guy telling me that we're heading for some kind of pure government, the reign of pure reason. He's a great guy, Hank,' Steve said, 'but part of the reason is he doesn't think like a lot of them, and every so often he'll come out with something that'll make you wonder if he shouldn't be off in a tower someplace, contemplating the universe.'

"Well," Cavanaugh said, "Steve was lagging behind the facts, which is a sad habit of Steve's, I since found out. Sam'd had a year down there by then. Maybe he went to Washington thinking that God sent him there because he was virtuous, and had the strength of ten, but Sam's not stupid, and I think he found out pretty fast that sure wasn't the explanation because he didn't even have the strength of one. The boys at the front desks shook hands, invited him to some paper-punching seminars, and ignored him. But he didn't ignore them; he watched them very closely, and he got very puzzled. Maybe he has it figured out now, I dunno. Mostly, I think, he doesn't think about it anymore, just sort of hustles along, trying to believe God sent him there for the vanguard, and if he can just survive until he gets some reinforcements, things'll maybe begin to work the way he wants them to work. But he doubts it. Then, when he feels bad, he thinks maybe God might've made a mistake with him, and maybe he ought to save God the embarrassment of correcting it, and just go back home nice and quiet, and lose, and that'll fix it. That'll make him feel better. A guy like Sam has to feel, has to have something to feel guilty about. Inadequate about. Sylvia gets exasperated with him. 'If only his nose was bigger, we could get him a long white plume and call him "Cyrano."' "

"How *is* your former playmate?" Louise said.

"Very well, actually," Cavanaugh said.

"Who's she bedding down with these days?" Louise said. "Does she still confide in you?"

"Constantly," Cavanaugh said, "and because they're confidences, I'm not going to tell you."

"I think that's sweet," Louise said. "It must be simply wonderful to be such good friends that you can stop going to bed together and still feel all warm and toasty about each other. It's cute, that's what it is: cuddly-bear cute. And so mature."

"Sylvia's a big girl from a small town," Cavanaugh said. "She's good enough to hold down any job on the Hill, and she knows it and she likes knowing it. When she gets on the horn and starts calling people, things start happening. If Sam didn't have Sylvia manipulating the donkeys by calling the people she knows that run their offices, he might as well go home. That girl can trade horses. If living in a pressure cooker makes her want to talk to somebody about her love life, that's all right with me."

"I'm glad it doesn't make you jealous, dear," Louise said, "hearing her talk about who she's banging now, and remembering the dear dead days when you were banging her. You're so well adjusted."

The waiter wheeled up the cart with the rack of lamb, carved it and served it, and refilled the bell glasses with Beaujolais.

"The guy in the stainless-steel suit over there," Cavanaugh said. "Why didn't you tell him, stick the duck up his ass?"

The waiter, pouring, smiled. "Do you know him, sir?"

"No," Cavanaugh said, "I don't. What does he do, tip thirty percent extra for being nasty?"

The waiter wrapped the bottle in a napkin. "I never saw him before, sir," he said. He put the bottle on the table. "But I've seen him before. There's a lot of him around. He's been coming here a long time, in large numbers, and he always brings his family. Long after they've grown up. It's a tradition. I'd say, no more than ten percent."

"So," Cavanaugh said, "why take it?"

"I'm in college," the waiter said. "It doesn't matter to me where I spend the summer, as long as it's a place I like and I can come out of it with twelve or fifteen hundred bucks. It could be here, it could be somewhere else. I'd feel just as good on the Vineyard, just as good as I did last summer when I was working at Méditerranée in Orleans. He wouldn't. People like him have to come here, because they've always come here. But now he can't really afford it anymore. Prices've gone up. He doesn't own a house here; he stays in a hotel. His family's bigger, because he's got those grandchildren to go with his daughters, and that means more rooms. He used to bring everybody up here for three weeks. Then it was two weeks. This year it's probably ten days. Maybe only a week. The kids get on his nerves. He's not having a very good time, and he thinks everybody knows it. This is very important to him. It's not important to me."

"I think I just got stuffed," Cavanaugh said.

"A little bit," the waiter said, and he laughed.

"So why do you stick with Sam?" Louise said, when the waiter had gone away.

"Ah," Cavanaugh said, "so we may enjoy dinner after all. Thank you. He hasn't lost yet, I suppose is the main reason."

"He's going to," she said.

"Not this time," Cavanaugh said. "There's a guy that's almost eighty, and he's been county commissioner since Millard Fillmore was President, and he acts like he's a hundred, and he thinks he's going to knock Sam off in the primary because Sam said he didn't believe a kid wearing a flag on his ass ought to go to prison for it. But there's not enough members of the American Legion and the VFW that vote on primary day for him to get very far, even if he did always hire everybody's indolent nephews to work on the roads in the summer.

"The Republicans have a nice guy that they should've let loose on Talbot about seven primaries ago. If they'd've done it then, Sam never would've gotten in, in the first place. But they didn't, and the guy was loyal, and besides, if he'd gone as a maverick, the Republican organization was probably strong enough then so he would've lost anyway. He's a very capable fellow. He doesn't beat his wife or anything, which if you saw his wife, and she was yours, you would beat her. He's good to kids and dogs. He's very, very conservative, which I guess happens to you if you spend twenty years of your life running the electric company, but Sam says he's straightforward about what he thinks, thoughtful, and he won't misrepresent anything. Sam likes him. Sam's going to beat his ass off."

"Two more years," Louise said.

"At thirty-seven thousand," Cavanaugh said.

"At thirty-seven thousand," she said.

"Look," he said, "it's not bad money."

"It's all right," she said.

"It's all right for you," he said, "because in Old Saybrook they spill more'n that. But you knew that when you married me, that I might think something was pretty damned fine that you had to cover a yawn about. When I got out of high school, my father told me: 'Don't waste your time.' Actually what he said was: 'Never mind all that shit. Take the exams.' He said it was secure. 'They'll always need cops.' Yeah, and my father's a brave man. He killed a man with a shotgun one night when the guy was coming out of a restaurant with a couple friends and three pistols, and my old man tried a warning shot first so they all had a clean shot at him before he stopped scattering gravel and started making holes in people. Well, they do need people like that. *I* need people like that, because I've got no desire to let people shoot at me so I can shoot back at them. 'I think I'll go to college anyway,' I said. 'It can't hurt.' No, I think thirty-seven's okay. I'm happy."

"It won't last, though," she said. "Not with Sam."

"Well," he said, "I thought about that a lot. The best year my father ever had was probably last year, because he had his pension plus eleven or twelve from the security job. Call it, oh, twenty-three thousand. But he always saved his money, and when the landlord died, they had enough to buy the house. We still lived upstairs, because the first floor rents better. But it was theirs, then, and nobody could throw them out anymore, and when they went to Ireland, there, they ate out of the pot, the same as everybody else. So, he was right for him, and maybe it'll turn out he was right for me, too. 'Only,' he said, 'I didn't *want* to wait all my life before I could go to Ireland.' Well, I don't particularly want to go to Ireland, now or in the future. I'm not Irish, I'm an American. But I don't mind being able to go to Vail, I don't object to seeing the Super Bowl, and it doesn't exactly piss me off that I can pay scalping prices when the Bruins play in Madison Square Garden. So, I'll take the thirty-seven as long as it's there, and in the meantime, I'll look for something."

"I figure," she said, "you've got two more years. No more. What are you going to look for?"

"I'm a lawyer," he said. "I can do that. It's just like the old man says about the post office and the cops, the post office was another thing he thought I might be interested in: 'It'll always be there.' If I don't come up with anything else, I can do that."

"It'll be there," she said, "but it'll be there for somebody else. Somebody who was there all the time. Not for you."

In the lounge the man with the loud voice led the crowd in "Bye Bye, Blackbird."

"I've got my ticket," he said. "There're people that know me in Washington. That never hurts."

"If you want to wither your life away in Washington," she said, "feast when you're in, famine when you're with the outs, worry, worry, worry all the time."

"Washington's where I ended up," he said. "If I'd done as I was told, I'd be where I want to be, but I'd be carrying mail in Dorchester or operating radar traps on the Massachusetts Turnpike, and that's not what I want to do. I made my choice. I think I made my choice, anyway. Maybe I didn't."

"The people you know in Washington," she said, "you think they're going to retain you?"

"No," he said, "other people. They're going to hire me.

People that know I know people in Washington. I've been around that town a long time."

"Who?" she said.

"Lots of people," he said. "People that need a lawyer that knows people in Washington."

"Who're they?" she said.

"People that've got business with the FCC," he said. "The CAB, the FAA, all of those things. HEW. DOT. Lots of people."

"Name two," she said.

"I don't know their names," he said. "I know they're there, though."

"They're not there for you," she said. "Those people have their lawyers."

"Look," he said, "nobody's eternal. Legal business moves around. It's got people in it, not statues and monuments. People change lawyers sometimes. It happens."

"Very slowly," she said, "and not very often. My father's worked his ass off for almost thirty years to put his practice together. It came right out of his hide. And he's still at it, too. My mother doesn't see any more of him now than she did when we were growing up, and when we were growing up he wouldn't buy us a watchdog because he said he didn't think he could get to know it well enough so he could be sure it wouldn't bite him when he finally did get home. He's been worrying about that goddamned office since before I was born, and he's still worrying about it. 'Every January first I get up,' he says, 'and I start thinking: "Well, I need a hundred and thirty-five thousand dollars to keep the thing operating for another year," ' or whatever it is, it's been going up every year, ' "and I wonder where I'm going to get it." ' "

"Probably where he got it last year," Cavanaugh said.

"Those airplane companies, the more they go bankrupt, the more business they make for bankruptcy lawyers."

"Sure," she said. "But you're still out there all by yourself. Nobody sends you a check every couple weeks, like the government does for you and Springer does for me, because you've been breathing fourteen days since you got the last one. You've got to go out there and scramble for it, one false step and you land on your ass, and that's the kind of thing you better start learning when you're young. A lot younger than thirty-three, I could say, but I won't. You go out on your own and you're going to enjoy a very good chance of starving to death."

In the lounge the man with the loud voice began "You're a Grand Old Flag." The crowd and the piano player drowned him out, singing "Show Me the Way to Go Home."

"It's always so pleasant, seeing you, Louise," Cavanaugh said. "I don't know why we don't do this more often."

"You just don't like facts, Hank," she said. "Nobody hires thirty-three-year-old associates for thirty thousand dollars a year; they hire twenty-four-year-old associates for sixteen or seventeen or eighteen thousand dollars a year, if they're real hotshots, and they work the butts off them and usher them right out the door, unless they're very indispensable indeed, when they start changing from eager little hard drivers into cagey savvy graspers looking for high-cost partnerships. You couldn't live on what they pay those kids, if you could get in front of one of them, and you couldn't stand what they have to stand if you could. And the reason why they put up with it is the same reason that you're not going anywhere if you go out on your own: because you can't even make fifteen doing that. You know what my father does? Do you think, when one of his clients needs something done in Washington, he goes down there himself, and does it? Not on your life. He has a man down there who handles all the Washington stuff. You think that guy started out working for a newspaper, and then started practicing law because the Congressman he was working for had his feet put to the fire? Uh uh. Former general counsels; retired undersecretaries; men who were special counsels whenever there was trouble that needed shooting, big, well-publicized trouble; former assistant attorneys general who were at Justice when Eisenhower was supposed to be running the show, not when Johnson and Kennedy were in: those are the people he calls. And so do all the rest of them. He'd as soon send the problem to the cab starter at Washington National as give it to somebody like you."

"Well," Cavanaugh said, "let me make one thing perfectly clear: I didn't mean I was expecting business from your father, and if I gave that impression, I misspoke myself."

She smiled. "Cav," she said, "I said I don't think you like facts. I didn't say you were suffering delusions."

"No," he said. "Well, there's that much, anyway. My wife works, and while she's got some reservations about me, which she will mention only under the most severe duress, such as seeing a hat dropped, she will concede that I am not hallucinating. In this life one learns to become grateful for minor courtesies."

"I work to support me," she said. "Not you. And I don't even have to do that much."

"Ah," he said, "but to get yourself supported by me, you'd have to come and live where I am. Could you kiss off twenty, *and* New York, for that bliss?"

"Or as Dad puts it," she said, " 'Your drawers were so hot for the guy you had to fly off and marry him, so how come you're not living with him, they're that hot?' "

"What'd you tell him, Louise?" Cavanaugh said. "Something about the spice of life?"

"I told him he ought to consider minding his own goddamn business," she said, "unless he really wanted me to stop talking Ruth out of it when she starts mumbling to me about that girl named Sunny who seemed to know him so well when she finally got him to take her to the Flagler Kennel Club. We understand each other."

"Understanding is a wonderful thing," Cavanaugh said.

"He doesn't run my life," she said. "I run my life. I work for Springer in New York because I like being in New York and working for Springer. I also like being married to you. In small doses."

"You know," Cavanaugh said, "I think I may have misjudged your father. Perhaps we have something in common after all. I think I'll call him up and tell him I'm coming to work for him. He'd probably jump at the chance to take me on as a partner, considering our shared concern for your welfare."

The man with the loud voice sang: ". . . a high-*fly*ing flag, and for*ev*er in *peace* may you *wave*. You're the em*blem* of, the land I *love*, the *home* of, the *free* and the, *brave*." The piano and the crowd roared along cooperatively.

"He'd probably jump at your throat," she said. "Or else you'd go for his, after about fifteen minutes. You'd have the rest of the partners taking out pistol permits, and a transit guard sitting in the reception room after the first week, if it lasted that long."

"I don't see why," Cavanaugh said. "I know that's one of the things he thought, that I was marrying you to get at his law practice. It usually gratifies a man to see his suspicions confirmed."

"Somehow, I don't think it would," she said. "Not this time, anyway, not this man."

" '*This* man?' " Cavanaugh said. "Whaddaya mean, '*this* man'? He could sit there with his two-handed watch, making the lights flash, and I could reform your dissolute life and regale him with stories of laughter and sadness that we Irish're so famous for."

"Watch it," she said, "I gave him that Pulsar, and that was before they cut the price ninety percent on those things. Besides, what'd happen'd be that you'd start participating in his dissolute life, and make him worse, and then I'd have to spend hours listening to Ruth. No, he wouldn't let you within a block of his place. Forget it. Sooner or later you're going to have to go to work. There's a limited number of brass rings, and you've used up your allotment."

"You *mean*," Cavanaugh said, "your father, sob, your father doesn't *like* me?"

"I think he's got reservations about you," she said. "Put it that way: he's got reservations."

"Gee," he said, "I wonder what caused that? You think it might've been when I told him I was for McGovern because he was going to take everything over twenty-five thousand a year from bastards like him and give it to the Welfare? Could that've been it?"

"Somehow," she said, "I think it goes back further'n that."

"Was it, you think," Cavanaugh said, "one of those times when he was talking about 'the coons' and 'the darkies' and 'the niggers,' and I said something that maybe hinted that I didn't *approve*?"

"Well," she said, "it didn't help, but I don't think it was that, either."

"Well," he said, "what could it've been, then? It can't

be, he just didn't like the idea of his princess hooking up with some night-school lawyer. John Mitchell went to law school nights, for Christ sake, and he's just a devil of a fellow. I know that's true, because Sidney Kafka told me so, and Ruth was sitting right there at the time, and now that I think of it, so were you. 'A patriot,' that's what John Mitchell is. You think it's maybe because he spent his whole life trying to make you into a Protestant and then you went out and married the same kind of commoner he always was himself, and a narrowback to boot?"

"Oh was he pissed when Mitchell got indicted," Louise said. "I never knew what 'pissed off' meant until I saw him and I said: 'Well, Sid, I see where the Attorney General got himself indicted.'

" 'Seymour hasn't got anything,' he started screaming, 'it's just political, it's nothing but the liberal vendetta all over again, they can't beat them fair, they beat them foul,' on and on and on. He was just about beside himself. No, it's not the narrowback," she said, "he doesn't know what a narrowback is."

"He knows what a mick is, though," Cavanaugh said. "He can spot one of them a mile off. I give you guys credit: when you're liberal, you're as liberal as hell, except if it's whether we oughta sell some more Phantoms to a warmongering nation that mongers with UJA money, but when you decide that you're gonna be bigots, there isn't another group in the world that can touch you for it. You're the best believers there is."

"Nobody gave him anything he's got," she said.

"Nobody gives anybody anything," Cavanaugh said. "Well, God probably will. Some morning he's going to wake up and find out his prayers've been answered and he's Low Church at long last. He's just like me. Maybe even one of dem Unitinarians dere. And then he'll be happy, come right downstairs and tell the old lady: 'Heave out the bagels, Ruth, where the neighbors can't see them. I'm trading the Calais on a '65 Merc that Leverett Saltonstall personally used to campaign in his last time, hasn't got no radio and it's kind of high mileage, but class all over the place. From now on your name's Amanda, and we don't eat nothin', already, that's been within a mile and six furlongs of a rabbi, no more.' "

"He still did it all by himself," she said. "He set out to do something in his life, and he worked like hell and he did it. That's not a bad thing in a man."

"I suppose," Cavanaugh said.

"He had dreams," she said, "and he had purpose. I happen to think they were the wrong kind of dreams. I've got some doubts about his purposes. But he had those things, and he really believed this was the greatest country in the world, and, and he took it at its word, and he got what he wanted. Most of it, anyway."

"He wanted you to marry David," Cavanaugh said.

"If he thought about it," she said. "A david. Some kind of david. A real david, a Catholic david, a Jewish david, almost any kind of david. Raise three kids in a Chrysler Town and Country."

"And money for Hadassah," Cavanaugh said.

"Or anything," she said. "He just didn't know. He's never had time enough to find out. He thought that was something else that you had available from the greatest country in the world. He still thinks so. It's my fault. You couldn't get him to emigrate to Israel if you had a gun to his head. He'll go there, but he'd no more live there'n he'd go to work naked and wave it at the governor. There's no way to tell him. The davids don't marry the me's. We're okay for Jennie's best friends from college, a little walk on the wild side to show you're not prejudiced, and when you get a few under your belt, it's okay to make some suggestive remarks to us, and if they pay off, well, fine. The jennies are very forgiving. Indulgent. But it's the jennies that the davids marry."

"I didn't say he was realistic," he said. "You were the one that was talking about the dreaminess of that iron-eyed horse trader."

In the lounge, the man with the loud voice and the crowd sang "Over There."

"There are some men that look a lot like davids, that do," she said, "counterfeit davids. The second-rate davids, the pale imitations, the ones with hemophilia and vague homosexual longings: they sometimes do. And then everybody spends the rest of their life being kind of *worried* about some funny feeling they really can't identify, except they know something's wrong. Not badly wrong. A little bit wrong. A little bit off-center. It's a good way to be unhappy.

"Your genuine *David*," she said, "knows better'n that. He knows the difference between a jenny and a louise. He's known it since he was two, at the latest; he probably was born with it. But they still train the genuine davids. And they develop this instinct about things. Dogs go up to them, but they never jump up or shed on them. They know exactly what they can do."

"My sympathy for your disappointments," he said.

"It's not my disappointment," she said. "It's his disappointment. He gets it off pretty well with the girls he pays, I guess, and if he can live with it, I can. I didn't want to be that anyway, what he wanted me to be. I don't know how Jenny does it. I suppose . . . I thought I knew Jenny pretty well. I never saw the girl upset. I still haven't. She went out with him every other week. He'd come up, or she'd take the train down there. She dreaded it. When she didn't date him, she had fun. As much fun as Jenny could have, at least, I suppose. But when she was going to see him, it was like *shiva*. It was nothing. It was just something she had to do. It was an obligation. It was dogshit. I said, 'Why do you do it?'

" 'Do what?' she said," Louise said. "I said: 'Nothing.' And that's what it was. I never used to be able to understand how she stood him. I used to think she did it because it was something she thought she was supposed to do, and that was it. But it was deeper than that, it goes deeper than that.

"Those guys had guns, Hank," she said, leaning toward him and taking his left hand. "When David started heckling them, they just didn't pay any attention. At first. They were very ostentatious about not paying any attention. They positively ignored him. But he pushed and he shoved, and this was Newport, and naturally everybody else in the place—I don't know what they were doing there, and I'd be surprised if they did, because they sure didn't belong there. . . ."

"Probably came in to have dinner," Cavanaugh said.

". . . probably," she said, "—was just like David, or wished they were, they were all off boats. The people that set the tone in there were davids, or would like to've been. And he just kept jeering at those two guys, and jeering at them, and jeering, and they kept their mouths shut, and they ate."

"Which is a hard thing to do," Cavanaugh said.

"They ignored him," Louise said. "And finally he went over to their table and he stood over them and said: 'I've been addressing my remarks to you gentlemen.'

"He was dead drunk," Louise said. "And the shortest

one—they were both short, and wide—looked at the other one, and said: 'Whaddaya think, John?' And John undid the one button on the coat and started to stand up, and the man that owns the place ran over and took David away, and David was laughing like hell. Then John sat down, and the other guy nodded at him, and they started eating again. And then everybody left them alone.

"They took David into the kitchen," Louise said. "Anybody could've seen the bulges under their coats. And Jenny was just as calm as she could be. He knows just how close he can get, and she knows he knows, and somebody always comes around to save him. Maybe it's instinct."

"Maybe it's God," Cavanaugh said, "watching over His assholes."

"It's as though he thought," she said reflectively, pausing over the last forkful of lamb, "no, he knew, he was never going to die. A private agreement or something. Very detailed. That if he behaves in a certain way, marries a jenny and does what he does, all of those things, it's complete in some way, and after that, outside of that, what he does is his own business."

"And no harm will come to him," Cavanaugh said.

"Right," she said. She put the lamb in her mouth, chewed it and swallowed it. "That's a very magnetic thing about a man. It's like a natural force. When he came back from the Onion Patch, everybody else on the boat had something broken. Last year. They got caught in terrible storms. He was crewing on *Nitro*, and they had broken legs and broken arms and had their teeth knocked out, and they had to leave one of the men down there because he got dashing when the spinnaker blew out and something happened, and instead of him saving it, he got a very bad concussion. They broke a mast. It was awful.

"David didn't get a scratch," Louise said. "He was out in the middle of it all the time and he didn't get a scratch. I asked Jenny: 'Are you going to let him do it again this year?'

"She looked at me," Louise said, "like she was wondering if I was a Martian. 'Nobody lets David do anything,' she said. She was amused with me. 'David does what he wants. He's done it every year he could, since he was fourteen. He's going to do it again this year.'"

"Does Jenny sweat?" Cavanaugh said.

"I'm not sure," Louise said very slowly.

The crowd and the piano player in the lounge led the man with the loud voice in "Harrigan."

"She might, on a very hot day, if it was appropriate. But she certainly doesn't go to the bathroom, and the only reason she has her period is that it's the responsible thing to do. Before I left, I had to run down to the bank and cover three checks," Louise said. "I had the money. I just didn't have it in my checking account, which of course was what I drew the checks on. The man at the bank's very nice: he calls me up, and I come down, and he doesn't bounce me. The cleaners lost my sweater. Springer called in, very nicely—he's in Barbados—to ask me how come Boudin never even got back to us about the idea for the show with the guy from Hudson, and of course the reason was that I got to the guy from Hudson, and told Springer about him, that he was agreeable, in spades was he agreeable, but then somebody called about something else, and I never did call Boudin. It slipped my mind. Jenny makes me feel very inadequate. She doesn't do anything, except be David's wife, but she does it so well. And she doesn't even do it on purpose, and that makes it worse."

"Then why do you hang around with them?" he said.

"Not when I'm with them," she said. "When you're with them, it's as though you were in the magic circle, and nothing can happen to you when—because—you're with them.

"It's not true, of course," she said. "Look what happened on *Nitro*, when everybody was with David. But it feels like it's true, and it's just so serene and uncomplicated and simple. Things work. Things go the way they're supposed to. If you're leaving Block Island today, you can use the radio and make reservations here tonight, or tomorrow, whenever you want. Edgartown after that. You'll be there, and have a nice hot shower, and the launch'll pick you up, right on time, and no water sloshing around in the bilge on your shoes, either. The sun'll come up and there'll be a nice fifteen knots, and you'll come all the way on a broad reach, with fresh limes that somehow appear for the gin and tonics. Things always work that way for them. It's marvelous."

"It must be," Cavanaugh said.

"It's some kind of magic charm," she said. "It follows them everywhere. Springer, my father, the bank, the dopes at the cleaners: nobody's ever mad at me when I make a mistake, and I more or less expect the people I'm dealing with to make mistakes and I don't get mad at them when they do. Just like I expected. But David and Jenny live in a world where there aren't any mistakes. It's just the opposite: everybody knows there won't be any mistakes, and when there aren't any, well, there aren't any. Nobody's particularly impressed. And I look at them, and I wonder what it is you have to do—be—to do that, and why I'm not."

" 'I'm, a Yankee Doodle, *Dan*dy,' " the man with the loud voice sang, " '*born* on, the *Fourth* of July.' "

"Then I look at you," she said, "and you're hacking around, not doing much, with a job and a lot of people that're not going to do you any permanent good, and it takes your whole life, and you seem to enjoy it all, somehow, just floating around and being careless."

"I do," Cavanaugh said, "and I don't."

" 'A real live nephew of my Uncle Sam,' " the loud voice sang.

"It probably doesn't matter," she said. "It's just a matter of curiosity, really. But I'd just like to know, as much for me as about you, really: we're living this way and we're doing these things, and where's it all come out?"

"For starters?" he said.

"For starters," she said.

"I don't know," he said.

"She went off again on *Celerity*," Cavanaugh said at the Jetties. He draped a towel around his neck. There was a heavy smell of rotten clams, dropped by the gulls to smash open on the macadam tennis courts but lost to decay in the sun.

"Uh huh," Richmond said.

"Look," Cavanaugh said, "you can't blame her. She works hard all year. She needs a vacation as much an anybody else."

"I'm not blaming her," Richmond said. "I gave that up. I don't blame anybody. For anything."

"They were going up to Boothbay," Cavanaugh said. "First Edgartown, then Cataumet, Hyannis, Scituate, Marblehead, and then up the coast. To Maine."

"Very nice," Richmond said. "Sounds like a very nice cruise. Where're you going?"

"For now," Cavanaugh said, "I'm not going anywhere. I'm on vacation. For the next four days or so, I'm on vacation. Nobody's calling me up, asking me questions and making me feel bad because I don't have any answers. Even dumb answers, let alone smart ones."

"Why didn't you go on the boat?" Richmond said.

"As a matter of fact," Cavanaugh said, "that's one question that I've actually got a genuine dumb answer for. Well, that and the fact that the invitation was a little weak, you know? A little weak. Just the slightest bit halfhearted. But I shouldn't complain. It wouldn't've made any difference if they tried to shanghai me. That chinless bastard. How come there's so many of you guys, haven't got any chins?"

"Beats me," Richmond said. "I'm fairly satisfied with my chin, actually. Nothing to brag about, but it's acceptable. But what the reason is for it, I don't know. Too fond of our own cousins, probably, way back there."

"Well," Cavanaugh said, "it doesn't matter. I wouldn't've gone anyway. I hate the goddamned things. They look nice. I give them that, all white and everything. And it's the wind they use to make them go, and I like the idea. I don't *think* that bastard can fuck up the wind. I may be wrong. If there's anybody that can do it, he's the one. But I don't think he can. I'm getting to the point where I like things that don't use anything up, and still go. So, the whole idea appeals to me. When I just think about it, it seems like a really nice thing. But when I do it, when I get on one of them, I think it eats it. I was never on one of them—I've been on, what, three or four of them, and the first time I got on one I thought to myself: 'Congratulations, Cavanaugh, you're living in *Sports Illustrated*, as I live and breathe'—that the son of a bitch that was running the thing didn't give out with the yo-ho-ho and lean the damned thing over on its side all the time, and I really hate that. They didn't tell me about what happens to your inner ear when everything gets moving on those things, and when the damned thing started to tip, I went nuts. I start to holler and then everybody looks at me and they get it up straight again, and we all spend the rest of the day with me miserable and them not having any fun, and being very nice about obviously not blaming me for it. 'Something he can't help, poor lad.' "

"You get sick?" Richmond said.

"Nah," Cavanaugh said. "I get scared. It scares the living bejesus out of me. I'm sure it's gonna tip over, and I'm the kind of guy that takes showers because when the water gets deep in the tub, it makes me nervous. I must be descended from cats."

"It's not," Richmond said. "It's almost impossible to tip one of them over. You'd need a hurricane to get all that lead into the air, and nobody with any sense's going to go out when there's wind around like that."

"Look," Cavanaugh said, "I know it's not. I've been out a few times. I had the lectures. I believe what they say. But it's in my head that I believe them. My head's not what I get scared in. I get scared in my guts. There's no way to talk to my guts. There's no way anybody's going to be able to convince my guts. They're in an uproar the whole time I'm on one. Don't tell me what's going to happen. Tell me about how I get over being scared about what's not going to happen and I think it is. That's what I need."

"I'll make a deal with you," Richmond said. "I'll cure you about heel if you can find a way to cure me of being afraid of what's going to happen, and does."

"Hell," Cavanaugh said, "you don't want that cured.

That's common sense. Take all you can get of that, and when you've got so much everybody can see it right off, call me up and we'll run you for President. You'll win easy."

"I mean it," Richmond said. "I had a premonition for a long time that sooner or later, Sandy and I were going to get divorced. It was always there, something that was coming. When I was with the kid, sometimes, it was like I could see a door opening on it. Someday I wouldn't be seeing him even as much as I was then; he'd be with her. I'd better make the most of it because it was something that I wasn't doing very well, and I didn't have an unlimited amount of time to practice doing it better.

"At first," he said, "at first I thought it was like that feeling of disaster you get, the time when it first registers on you that you are going to die."

"I got it when I was thirty," Cavanaugh said.

"Your birthday," Richmond said, "the traditional occasion for *Weltschmerz*. Can't you do anything original, for Christ sake?"

"I thought it was *Weltanschauung*," Cavanaugh said.

"I don't know what the hell it is," Richmond said. "I don't like it, though. I know that."

"Well, it wasn't my birthday," Cavanaugh said. "It was, I don't even remember what day it was, it was in the summer and I was taking a shower in that grungy little place in Foggy Bottom that I was living in with Sylvia, and I was dragging my ass. It just seemed like I couldn't get moving at all. Hammond was driving me like a mule, and it was all I could do to get my weary ass out of bed in the morning, let alone service her voracious appetite every night. Jesus, did that girl fuck. Talk about proving something. She should've shacked up with a machine, something with a big stainless-steel piston that ran on steam or something. And I looked, the shower had one of those glass doors which also scare the shit out of me, because I can see my naked body being cut to shreds as I fall through it, having lost my balance while stooping for the soap or something."

"They're usually tempered glass," Richmond said.

"It shall be understood," Cavanaugh said, "from now on, that when I discuss my irrational fears, I am not doing so in order for you to tell me they're irrational. They're my fears, goddamnit, and I ought to be able to have any kind of fears I want, and enjoy them like every other American citizen.

"The water was running down that rippled glass," Cavanaugh said. "Condensed steam, the water that bounced off me, running down the glass. And I just stood there. I took long showers then because Sylvia didn't like to get her hair wet and Hammond couldn't reach me when I was in the bathroom. It was just about the only way I could get any relaxation at all. So I was watching the water, and all of a sudden it occurred to me: *I am going to die.* Just like that. 'Someday I am going to die, and I am not going to exist anymore. I won't be here. I won't be anywhere. What's left they'll put in the ground. It'll all end, just *end.* No more food, no more drink, no more ginch, no more fun, no more of anything. Just nothing.' Jesus. Scared the shit out of me. Pissed me off pretty good, too. I hate feeling helpless. Sam kind of enjoys it, I think. I hate it."

"Well," Richmond said, "that's what it is, all right. You know what I'm talking about. It's those damned certainties. Except that I keep on adding, creating certainties. Like the thing with Sandy. Then after I added them, I made them come true. Self-fulfilling prophecies. I, being the prophet, make the prophecy come true. It didn't have to. There was no necessity for it. I made it necessary. To preserve my reputation as a prophet. When it happened, when *any*thing begins to happen with me, about the third thing I think of is that someday it'll be over. I believe in transience. I don't think I do it on purpose. I'm not sure, but I don't think I do. Still I knew, always knew that someday I wasn't going to be married to Sandy anymore. We'd be at a gallery, and Billy'd be getting restless, one of those overheated empty places with white walls and spotlights, and she'd be looking at something on a Saturday, and I felt like I could leave my body and go off somewhere and look at us, Sandy absolutely fascinated, Billy trusting us enough so when he felt cranky, he acted cranky, me standing there, just watching, and that instant was forever. It was always going to be there. But we weren't. Someday I would go away. So, I went away.

"And it was the same kind of thing with Dee," Richmond said. "The Senator, for that matter. I knew that someday she would go away. I knew that he would lose. Well, I knew he wouldn't win. I always knew it. I worked on everything I ever did like I didn't know things like that, but I did. I knew them. She screwed Sam. I know she screwed Sam. I always knew, before she did it, that she'd screw Sam. I didn't know it'd be Sam, but I knew she'd do it. With somebody."

"Jess," Cavanaugh said.

"Cav," Richmond said, "you've got your irrational, vague fears. I've got my irrational, vague behavior. And some of other people's, too. It doesn't matter, really, what she did. Why she did it. Bored, probably. Dee gets bored fast. Sandy's never bored. Sandy's fingertips are lively. I don't know why one's one way and another's the other way. With Dee it was probably the same reason for leaving that brought us together in the first place: she wanted to, and the guy wanted to; 'a maximum of temptation combined with a maximum of opportunity.' Why not? Jesus, he's a shit, you know that? An absolute shit."

"Well," Cavanaugh said.

"No," Richmond said, "I don't mean because of that. If that makes you a shit, then I'm a shit, and I'm not a shit. No, because he's a shit. He hangs paper."

"No kidding," Cavanaugh said.

"Yup," Richmond said, nodding. "He's got an actual record. They've arrested him in two states for writing bad checks. Never did any time, of course. He made restitution. It's not as though he needed the money. But he was convicted, and now he's running one of those fake ego-massage parlors for guys that think a felony conviction's some kind of distinction that makes them better human beings than us pedestrian types."

"How'd you find that out?" Cavanaugh said.

"I'm a taxpayer," Richmond said. "That's federal money he's distributing to retired bank robbers who make sandals and television interviews about Conditions in our Inadequate Corrections System. Pet convicts. I also wanted to know where the hell she went. I wasn't going to try to bring her back again, or anything like that. I mean, shit, if a woman wants to do something, she can't resist the guy and she wants to go, let her go. She's going to do what she wants to do anyway, no matter what you do. But what bothered me was: why'd she want to? That was what took me a long time. I was all right for quite a while, but that continued to bother me, and I think it still does. Now, I think I've got it figured out.

"Last month," Richmond said, "July, it rained almost

every single day. I'd go down to the White Elephant for a drink at night, and there'd be all those poor devils paying about a hundred and fifty dollars a day by the time they got through, to look at the rain and the fog. 'Nah, Mildred, we went to the Quiet Man last night. Tonight we're staying here.' You think I was drinking? You should've seen them. There was enough cranberry juice and vodka going through kidneys in that place to wipe out low tide if they all flushed at once. I sat there and thought about how Sandy and I might've sat there, twenty years from now, having a drink or ten, grouchy, dull, fifty-five or sixty, without the slightest interest in anything in the world. Except whether the guy that was singing was actually singing something that wasn't only clever but was also dirty. And Dee, too. The same thing. Every night the same old box for me, the same old dick for her, the same old thing and the same old thing and more of the same old thing. An orderly life. Where is my orderly life?

"That was what I decided. It was as close as I got. She missed doing things. I was out late, too late, too much. That's how I got mixed up with her in the first place, and I suppose it made her jumpy. My track record. She probably thought it was going to be like the campaign, but all it was was a guy with a job that he worked at too much, and that wasn't what she wanted. I don't know. I decided she wanted him because she didn't like what she had. She thought something else might be better, even if it was a crook. Which isn't very much to hang your hat on, but it'll do. I'll tell you what I think does it: time does it."

"What about the girl?" Cavanaugh said. "You don't have to tell me if you don't want to."

"Ahhh," Richmond said, "sure, I'll tell you. Another one of my, uh, well, actually, it wasn't a bad thing while it lasted, which is about all you can say of anything. She was eighteen. She was one of the chambermaids up at the Moby Dick, and I met her one night at the Brotherhood, and we got to talking and she was supposed to go back to drama school. Only, she didn't want to go back to drama school. 'Drama school is where they send nice girls now when they don't know what the hell's going on and they're afraid to find out.' So I said, they were closing up and I said: 'Why don't you move in with me?' And she didn't have anything else to do, so she did. She didn't take up much room. All she had was some sweatshirts and sweaters and some, I guess, three pairs of dungarees. She's the first woman I ever lived with, you could go into the bathroom in the morning to take a shower before she got up, and you didn't have to take a bra off the faucet handle before you could turn the thing on. She was pretty ordinary in bed, though. I think she thought she was doing it for room and board, and she didn't like it. Didn't like doing it for that. Used to talk to me about spontaneity all the time."

"Most kids that age," Cavanaugh said, "if they've got anything on the ball at all, it's not something they can see themselves as wanting. It's something that everybody else wants from them. I think."

"She wasn't really interested," Richmond said. "I guess she stayed as long as it took her to think of something to do, and then she did it. Fair enough. I'm almost thirty-six. You can't expect those things to be much more'n a roll in the hay, and you're lucky to get that. She's a nice kid. It'll all come out in some play where she's the experienced woman, I suppose, and I did my bit for the American theater. Look, I needed somebody then. I don't care if I did have to eat plywood turkey. I wouldn't've cared if she was twelve. It would've been all right with me."

In the sunlight men and women and children in whites and also blues and pinks and yellows hit tennis balls back and forth over the nets, between the green wind curtains on Cyclone fence. On the court closest to the manager's gray-shingled office, two married couples played mixed doubles with some acrimony between spouses.

"You got anybody now?" Cavanaugh said.

"Did I ever have anybody?" Richmond said.

"Well," Cavanaugh said, "if you're going to get morose . . ."

"I'm not getting morose," Richmond said. "I was born morose. I used to read *Winnie-the-Pooh* when I was a kid. You ever read that?"

"I think the deepest thing my father ever got into was *Mr. Wubbles and His Bubbles,*" Cavanaugh said. "He didn't do that on his own, either. Somebody gave it to me for Christmas when I was a kid, and I made the old bastard read it to me every night."

"Just as well," Richmond said. "Milne'd give a man diabetes if he wasn't careful. And of course you haven't had any kids yourself."

"Haven't had time," Cavanaugh said.

"The way you live," Richmond said, "I doubt if you've really had the chance."

"It only takes once," Cavanaugh said. "That's what a girl I used to know in college used to tell me when I was trying to get her to come across."

"The way you live . . . ," Richmond said, "no. You want to look out for those sailboats. What's she on?"

"She's all right," Cavanaugh said.

"I didn't say she wasn't all right," Richmond said. "What little I've seen of Louise, I like. When she was with *Newsweek* the only thing that bothered me was that she had the kind of intelligence that should've been out by itself, not all scrambled up with files put together by other people and written and edited and then written again. Not that she was right, but she was alive, and I bet it would've come through in what she did. What I asked you was what she's on."

"It's a friend of hers from college," Cavanaugh said. "Her husband's. A Pearson. I dunno. Thirty-nine?"

"A moderately big one," Richmond said. He nodded. He opened his duffel bag and brought out two cans of beer. Cavanaugh took one. They stripped off the ring openers and drank. "Those're the ones you've got to watch out for. The ones you've really got to watch out for are the Hinckleys and the Morgan Off-Islands, the Forty-ones. I don't know what it is about those boats, but everybody on them gets to drinking too much, and then the women all take off their tops, and pretty soon they're out there on a sea anchor beyond the channel markers, drunk as owls and screwing to beat the band, every one of them. They're worse'n mixed doubles for causing divorces."

"Well," Cavanaugh said, "thanks for that information, anyway."

"When I was a kid," Richmond said, "I hated this place. Every summer we came down here. God, how I hated it. My father would tell me how the people needed doctors, at least part of the year; that meant he was so damned tight he was swapping a real vacation that'd cost him money for a free vacation here, for taking out adenoids three days a week at the Cottage Hospital. They gave him the house for it. I wanted to stay home. I had my friends. I had what I thought were girl friends. When I was in college, I went to the Cape and screwed around because I was too big for him to make me come here anymore. It didn't occur to me that he was proud when he finally got his own place and he didn't have to spend August ripping out diseased tissue anymore. He could just go fishing. And now I love it, except during the winter, when I don't mind it, and I'm the only one in the family who does. But he's dead, from getting it, and he doesn't know it."

"That's too bad," Cavanaugh said.

"There's a lot of things that're too bad," Richmond said. "Doesn't do a damned bit of good to know it. He bought me a Star when I was old enough, and I wanted that boat. But he bought me the boat down here, which was not where I wanted the boat. He was tantalizing me, I thought. He was trying to make things nicer for me, so I'd like it better down here when I had to come. But I was too dumb to know that, of course, and I named it *Eeyore*.

"He's the horse whose tail comes off," Richmond said. "I was going to call it *The Knight of the Woeful Countenance*, but the man said the transom wasn't big enough. It pissed Dad off. That's nothing new."

"Tell me this," Cavanaugh said, "what're you going to do?"

"Well," Richmond said, "now that's an interesting question. What're *you* going to do?"

" 'I dunno, Angie,' " Cavanaugh said, " 'whadda you wanna do?' I don't know. I'm not going on any boats, I can tell you that."

"But you're going to drive that car like you thought it was an airplane," Richmond said.

"The plugs load up if you don't," Cavanaugh said.

"I think you're going to kill yourself," Richmond said. "That's what you're going to do. You'll stay away from boats that're perfectly safe, because you're afraid of them, and take your life in your hands twice a week on the Beltway. It's going to be a nice multiple some night, with a semi-trailer. And with your kind of luck, it won't be fatal. You'll be the best-informed paraplegic in the history of American politics."

"Look," Cavanaugh said, "you're forgetting something. I know what I can handle and what I can't. I was hauling flathead vees out of '49 Fords with a chain hoist and a maple tree when you were conjugating Latin verbs and having decorous teas with the headmaster's wife. And I had motorcycles when they weren't respectable. I always wanted one of those things. I knew what I was getting myself into."

"Then there's that delightful arrangement you've got with your wife," Richmond said.

"You're not going to tell me about women, are you, Jess?" Cavanaugh said.

"I shouldn't have to," Richmond said. "You know what I've been through, and you can see what it did to me. I shouldn't have to say a word. That ought to be enough to reform Attila the Hun. But apparently it isn't. You live in Washington and she lives in New York and you take her out to dinner a couple times a month, and you chew on each other a little and then go back to what you were doing before."

"We get along," Cavanaugh said. "It's the way we want to do things."

"We all get along," Richmond said. "But why pretend? Why stand around and tell yourself that you want things the way they are?"

"I don't," Cavanaugh said. "I seldom think about the way I want things, if you want the truth."

"Because they stink," Richmond said. "You shouldn't want them the way they are. You know it, too. The trouble with things that stink is that you can only stand them so long. Then you do something about them, without thinking it through. So you end up wrecking everything. You know why I walked out on Sandy?"

"Dee, I assume," Cavanaugh said.

"Sure," Richmond said. "That's what Steve assumed and that's what Sandy assumed, too. Or at least that's what she was telling people. Okay, Steve didn't know. But Sandy knew. I wasn't living with Sandy after the middle of April, and I didn't catch up with Dee until August. I didn't know she was on the earth until about four months after what was between me and Sandy was all over. It was very funny, the way Sandy behaved."

"Where the hell were you living?" Cavanaugh said.

"Until I got carry-on luggage," Richmond said, "at the baggage claim carrousels at various airports. After I stopped carrying everything I owned with me, at various hotels, motels, and some places that looked damned close to flophouses. I was on the road all the time. I went to the Governors' Conference for him. I was in New York a lot. We were way out in front then. We had a year to go before the convention, and I was doing preemptive fund-raising."

"I knew some people who were very pissed off about that when the time came," Cavanaugh said. "All that money locked up tight that they could've had. There's some as say you and the Senator had a lot to do with the way things finally turned out for him, grabbing all that dough before the nomination was decided and then holding on to it."

"Fuck 'em," Richmond said. "They were so busy running around and participating in everything that they never did get down to dealing with the nuts and bolts. They tried it too, in a kind of bungling way. They just weren't good at it.

"I was in Pittsburgh," he said, "for three weeks, on and off, getting things ready for the steel hearings. Dorsey had me running from smelter to smelter until I thought I was joining the union. Then, when I was in town, I was talking to him, and going off to Colorado Springs for the National Committee meetings. I stayed a few nights at the Carlton, a few nights at the Hay-Adams. Then I moved my stuff out of the house while Sandy was at Jackson Hole, telling her parents, and left it with Burns in Georgetown. When I was in town, I slept on his couch, but I wasn't there very much. Then it was late September, and things heated up. I was on the road all the time, and that was when Dee and I decided it was more'n just another one-night stand. When it was over, I moved in with her.

"So," Richmond said, "Sandy decided I left her for Dee, which just wasn't the way it was, and I'm damned if I can see what the hell good she got out of it. She knew why I did it. As well as I did, anyway. We were sick of each other, and sick of ourselves, and sick of that goddamned town and the way we lived.

"When we got there," Richmond said, "we loved it. We did the standard bitching and moaning, but this was high adventure. We were going to make something happen. The Washington *Post*. Senators' unlisted phones. A man of integrity who cared about what we thought. No more farting around remembering the Yale Game and who got stiff last week at Corinthian. Substance. Talent. Power. Ideals. Power. Nobility. Power.

"Power," Richmond said. "When we first got there, it was all right. Then, somehow, it wasn't all right. Sandy began to hate it. I didn't like it. 'It's so phony,' she said. She was wrong. The problem is that it's too real. You're always on, and you better know it, too. You don't get any practice serves in that town. Nobody ever goes ahead and says something for the decent hell of saying it, to see how it sounds. Nobody with any sense, because there's always some whore around that can't wait to call Maxine Cheshire or Betty Beale. Then the next day in the paper is your dirty crack about the President; the guy you're working for couldn't get a sewer grant for home if the place was floating in shit. I wasn't used to that. I like conversation. You can't have any of that down there. It's all public addresses. And that's just part of it.

"It grows on you," Richmond said, "like any other malignancy. Sandy liked it and then she hated it and then she said she still hated it, but she really liked it. She adapted to it. For me, of course, when I went to work for him. I'm not knocking her. But she adapted and she's as bright as hell, and so she got to be good at it. She likes being good at what she does and so she likes doing what she does well. All we ever seemed to talk about, when we were by ourselves, was calculation. It was all calculation. We never did anything just because we wanted to. We did things, or we didn't do things, because of what doing things would make somebody else think about us, and about him, and that was all the fun we had. It was like we lived all our lives in the bar at the Carroll Arms.

"I got sick of it," Richmond said. "It was exhausting. I figured, some night, for sure, we'll do it and then she'll roll over and call up somebody and tell them how it was, and the next morning I'll hear it on the radio: 'Travis Aide Still Gets It Up, Wife Says.' I don't think people down there've got enough to do. They need something to occupy their minds.

"So," he said, "I woke up one morning, and what I disliked most, hated, about my work, I had in bed with me. It was in the house with me. She had breakfast with me, and late beer and cheese with me when I got home after midnight, and it was always there, always with me. I didn't like it, so I left it. I still had the commitment to him, and I thought he was important, and besides, I still thought it was important. I thought he ought to be President. I thought he was going to be President. Walking down that long lonesome road, babe, I really thought he was. So I would do that, and as soon as he was, I was out."

"What were you going to do?" Cavanaugh said.

"I got to thinking," Richmond said. "I became a little sappy. I had a violent attack of nostalgia, for when I was chasing the liars around instead of writing the lies that the liars told. I was working for him, I was trying to put him across, and I was in this green funk. What I was really doing was trying to figure out why the hell—not whether, but why—you get through work and you start home, and you feel like you're going to work on some job you hate. And you start to think: Well, where was it that I felt good? On the job before this. So that was where I bitched it, you think. It was changing the job. See? That means it's nobody's fault. That means you're not a faulty human being who goes around screwing everything up, too dumb or mean to get things right. And that's exactly what you need, something like that. So you start thinking about going back to when you were happy. You decide it was the job you had then that made you happy, and you think about going back to the job because you're still sharp enough to know you can't go back to the time. I had calls in to the LA *Times* and I was supposed to talk to the *Tennessean* and the *Courier-Journal*. I had a little list, just like the Lord High Executioner. Only I missed all of them. But it was one of my rods and staffs, and it kept me going until I met Dee."

"Which was probably not one of the best things that ever happened to you," Cavanaugh said.

Richmond said: "At the time it wasn't bad at all. Everybody was more'n a little nutty by then. Jerry wouldn't talk about anything except in the corridor or in the men's room with all the hoppers flushing, and Toby had so many rumors about things that were supposed to be going on that I called him the Plot-of-the-Day Man. Of course all of them were right, Jerry particularly. But this was in '71, remember, and anybody who really knew the things that were going on had to be crazy. At the time I knew very damned right well that everybody in the whole wide world was nuts, except me. That was the problem: I was born with the gift of laughter, and the sense that the world was mad, and furthermore, I was *right*.

"Now when you think that," Richmond said, "you're more'n a little daffy yourself. Unless you know you're daffy and then it's all right. But I needed it too much. If I knew I was daffy, I suppressed it. I wanted to know I was right, not batty. You let yourself marinate in that long enough, wandering around with a straight face, snickering at all those assholes in your mind, then pretty soon you have to go off someplace and lie down and rest.

"Christ sake, man," Richmond said, "that stuff that was going around about spies and bugs and sabotage and all that shit? Jerry reached me one night when I was going to Houston for some input on the space program; he said to me: 'Now look, man, all right? You stay away from the tail, man, while you're down there, all right? That town's crawling with broads, and about half of them call CREEP every twenty-four hours, and they'd just love to have something good on the Senator's honcho. So you keep your knickers buttoned, man, at all times.' I laughed at him. I kept it dry while I was down there because I was so screwed up then I think I would've thrown up if a woman'd touched me. But I was humoring Jerry. I was home one weekend, visiting the kid and pretending I was still living there. Very nice, oh, very nice. Like having a tooth drilled. And my kid found something in the cereal box that you could use to send secret messages, which he was old enough to laugh at, and I took it and we wrapped it up and I gave it to Jerry. 'For confidential internal memorandum purposes.' "

"Haven't heard from Jerry lately, have you?" Cavanaugh said.

"Oh hell no," Richmond said, "not more'n, say, ten or twenty times. First he was calling me. Then he wrote letters. He was going to set up the Segretti Chair of Political Ethics at the Kennedy Institute, and I was to be the first professor to hold it. Then he was going to the Carnegie Institute and give them a million dollars to endow the Liddy Foundation for the Study of Technology in Politics, and I was going to be the director. 'You haven't got a million bucks, I think, Jerry,' I said. Most of my defenses were pretty feeble. 'Yes I have,' he said, 'I'm getting it from Maurice Stans. You know how he is about a good cause.' "

"You should've given him the Flatbed Trailer Speech Prize," Cavanaugh said.

"I thought of that," Richmond said. " 'One of a Series in the Great Ideas of Western Man.' But then I decided: he earned it. He let me up after Dean was through. But then Butterfield testified about the goddamned tape recorders, and he couldn't resist that and he called me up again. So I said something good and dumb: 'Jerry, I never said you weren't right. I said you were crazy. You're still crazy.' "

"He's all right now, though," Cavanaugh said. "He got over that a long time ago. I was talking to him yesterday on the phone and he was fine. He was all full of piss and vinegar. I said I was going to be here with you a few more days or so, and then I'd be up, and he said: 'Ask him when he's going to be ready to take his thumb out of his ass and start being a useful citizen again.' "

"Good," Richmond said. "Jerry's too good a guy to get used up. Jesus, he had so much invested in Travis, and then something happens on top of that and he hasn't got anything left to meet it with. What was it, Bell's palsy?"

"I guess so," Cavanaugh said. "The whole right side of his face collapsed. It was supposed to've been the cold that did it. He was skiing up at Loon and they had this freak cold or something, all of a sudden it was down to about twenty below and a wind-chill factor like Antarctica, and he didn't come in fast enough."

"Yeah," Richmond said. "Well, it probably was. It's always something that sets it off. But it has to be there to get set off. And it sure was for him. When his daughter got walloped, I thought: 'I hope Jerry can handle this.' "

"She was a beautiful kid," Cavanaugh said. "Jesus, what a beautiful kid. I went out there for the wake, and I thought he and Ann were standing up pretty well. But good Christ, what a thing to have to take. Fourteen years old. How do you make sense out of a thing like that?"

"You don't," Richmond said. "Tell yourself there're trucks on the road. They have to be there. There's a lot of them. It stands to reason: with that many trucks there's bound to be some people driving them who don't know what they're doing. You just hope you never meet up with one of them. There's nothing else you can do. Except cry, I guess."

"He didn't," Cavanaugh said. "Not that I could see any evidence of, anyway. Ann was standing there, supporting him, and he was supporting her, and Josh and Caleb were doing the same thing for each other, and for them."

"Seeing them all together was a great thing," Richmond said. "They're all so nice to each other. Nothing like the sloppy shit you see, all that elaborate crap people go through when they're faking it. The Abrahams really like each other.

"They were out in Minneapolis the day I ended up with Dee," Richmond said. "It was the first time I ever saw them all at once. 'As soon as you and Dad're through,' Josh told me, 'we're going to Mont Tremblant.' That was the night I went in the bar and there was Dee. It wasn't the first time I saw her. I'd met her a couple of times. It wasn't the first time I had the inclination, either. But I went in there after I left Jerry and his family, and there was room at her table, and all of a sudden everybody else'd gone to bed and we were just sitting there, smoking damned stale cigarettes that felt like somebody was dropping razor blades down your throat, and she said to me: 'The hell's the matter with you? You got trouble at home?'

"It cracked me up," Richmond said. "I felt happy that night. There's a short, fat guy named Dennison in Madison, and how the hell he keeps all those Swedes and Germans in line, I'll never know. But he does it. You don't get name, rank, and serial number from people in three states unless Dennison says you're all right. Well, he wouldn't say it was all right. He wouldn't budge. I was after him and I was after him, and I was getting nowhere just about as fast as anybody ever got nowhere. He was going to see the Senator, and talk to him personally, before he made any decision. 'I know he's a good man, Mister Richmond. I agree with you about his integrity. Of course you can talk to Rudolph Kohler. Mister Kohler is a man of his own mind.' And then you'd go and see Mister Kohler, or Mister Hess, or Mister Olson, who's a bright-eyed little man that runs a bright-eyed little bank in Iron Mountain, Michigan, and it was: 'What can I do for you, Mister Richmond? Senator Travis. I haven't really decided yet. Well, no, as a matter of fact.' And half an hour later—you could drink enough coffee to float a locomotive, talking to those people —he'd finally say to you, whoever it was: 'Have you seen Matt Dennison? I have a lot of respect for Matt Dennison.'

"Well," Richmond said, "this was three goddamned states that guy was controlling. I went to Jerry and I said: 'He's got to see Dennison, personally. We can talk to people till we turn cerulean blue, but we get abundant nothing until Dennison says: "Go." He's tough on crop quotas, and the only way he's going to go for anybody is if the Senator goes in and tells him what he's got in mind, and it's what he wants.'

"I was wrong," Richmond said. "The Senator went in and he told Dennison he was for eighty percent of parity on price supports, or whatever it was, and he was for this on that and the other thing on the other thing. And Dennison told him the only way he could sell that program to his people was if the Senator told him he was truly con- vinced it'd be best for the country. Because he didn't agree with it. The Senator was great at one-on-one: he looked him right in the eye and told him that was what he had in mind. And Dennison said: 'All right.'

"The Senator told me that afternoon," Richmond said. "At lunch. Interrupted at lunch. Page for Mister Rich- mond. I went to the phone. 'Mister Olson in Iron Moun- tain,' the man says. 'I just talked to Matt Dennison. Any time you want to come up, I'd be glad to see you.'

"So Dennison joined up," Richmond said.

"I bet he was glad he did that," Cavanaugh said.

"No hard feelings whatsoever," Richmond said. "He's a very big boy. He didn't get where he is, being a crybaby. Ellison saw him when McGovern was out there, trying to get him aboard, after it was all over for Travis, and I guess Ellison stuck it to him. Why the hell did they have so many guys like that?"

"They had the Faith," Cavanaugh said. "They were like the JFK-Before-LA types, except those guys were used to it, and smart and lucky, and they weren't. They were enthusiasts. Them guys didn't recognize luck. It was all burning zeal, and knowing more about the universe'n God did, more about the country'n Jefferson did. They were gonna do what was best for us if it killed us."

"Pain in the ass," Richmond said. "Ellison put it on him, and Dennison said: 'Nope. He was the best man then and he's the best man now. He's just not running. That's too bad for the country. The other guy's going to get in. But I was right then. The country can be wrong now, if it wants.' Then he told Ellison to get his ass moving, and Ellison, as always, fell back on it, when the spirituals didn't make anybody stand up: 'But you've got to back the candidate.'

" 'I won't,' Dennison said, 'piss on his boot and tell him it's rain,' " Richmond said. " 'I'll vote for him, and I won't tell my people what to do. But I don't have to do a damned thing more'n that, what I want to do, and that's all I want to do.' And that's what he did.

" 'He's not going to come back, you know,' Ellison said," Richmond said. "And Dennison said: 'That damned Arab killed Bobby, and he's not coming back, either. But that doesn't mean I was wrong about Bobby. Now, get out.' And Ellison got.

"She knocked me for a loop that night," Richmond said. "I didn't think it showed. I didn't think it showed at all. And anyway, I wasn't even thinking about it. You remember how things were then. The guy was so far out in front the only thing anybody even thought about was how come the other guys were bothering. And I thought, that night: 'Well, what we did today gave him another length or so on his lead.' I didn't feel bad at all. I felt good. That was probably the reason. If I'd've felt bad, which a lot of times, I did, she wouldn't've been able to catch me off-guard like that.

"I said: 'What do you mean?'" Richmond said. "See, I didn't know I was showing signs because I didn't know what the signs were. She did. Her father was her mother's second husband. She had another one after that, whom she divorced when Dee was about thirteen. Her father was married twice, otherwise, once before he married Dee's mother, once afterwards. Dee was married when she was twenty-two and was separated when she was twenty-six, before she married Steve. She was still married to Steve when she met me, and they hadn't lived together for almost three years.

"There's a lot of things you can fool Dee about: she's plain stupid about spending money; show her whatever it is you want to sell her, and she'll buy it. She'd buy a hydrant if you wanted to sell her one. And some of the things she's gullible about're pretty important. Like whether a guy's smart. Or honest. Or means what he says when he says it.

"Politically," Richmond said, "she's just a groupie. She's looking for bodies to snuggle up against; she's cold and she's trying to get warm. In a campaign year, she's in politics, and she has nice, uncomplicated attitudes. She thinks it'd be better if the poor people had nice places to live and good things to eat. When they get sick, they ought to get the same doctor and the same quality of treatment as anybody else. There's no way in the world that you can tell Dee that there aren't enough good people around to put Mass General into every crossroads hamlet in the United States. Well, there's a way to tell her, but she doesn't like hearing it, so it's a waste of time. She's against war and she thinks taxes're too high and black people and women ought to have the same opportunities as white men graduated from Yale."

"Sam'd love her," Cavanaugh said.

"For a while, he would," Richmond said. "Then he'd start to see. She's bright enough. She's not stupid, and she'll work her ass off for you if she thinks you believe the same starry-eyed mush that she does. She's great with strays like me. She collects birds with broken wings and dogs with broken legs, but the ones she collects are people. Then, when they're ready to go flying again, or knocking over garbage pails, when they're just getting back on their feet, *she* goes out and leaves them there. She can't handle any kind of permanent responsibility. She doesn't have any staying power. Looking at it now, that's why she ducked out on Steve. Why she ducked in on him, I don't know. But he was over Bobby in '71, and you could still get a few laughs at the National Committee, running against *Richard Milhous Nixon*, for Christ sake, and so he didn't need her anymore. She thinks people're supposed to be screwed up. That's the only kind of people she ever knew when she was growing up, and that's the kind of person she is, and . . . I think that's why she hangs around campaigns: high-stress atmospheres: people all keyed up and hooked on adrenaline, crack sooner and faster and more often. It's just a different kind of need. It's familiar to her, need. She's like a hospital with nice legs and not a bad body at all: as soon as you get better, you have to go home.

"I didn't know that, at the time," Richmond said. "I thought she was clairvoyant. She could see when some-body needed to be hugged."

"Come on," Cavanaugh said.

"I mean it," Richmond said. "I was like a little kid. 'Well, yes,' he admitted manfully, 'there is a bit of, well, you could call it, um, ah, yeah, things're fouled up at home.' Choking back a tear. She blindsided me. 'Poor dear.' Poor dear, shit. She's not a bad-looking woman. I was in a mood. I had a notion. I wouldn't've minded getting laid. If that was the way you did it, getting poor-deared, fine. Poor-dear me. And I could see she didn't mind, either. There's all kinds of ways in the world of horsing around. There's some that do it because they want to, same as everybody else, but they justify it in other ways. You don't have to be out there very long to realize: a fair number of those people that get laid when they're drunk, get drunk so they can get laid without feeling maximum guilt for getting laid.

"The funny part of it was," Richmond said, "that it was also true. Isn't that something? I was all dented in and banged up and sore and hurting. I did want to be soothed, as well as screwed. She soothed me and she screwed me, and then when I was soothed, she screwed. That's probably the explanation for the paper-hanger: he's challenging, a challenging case. He's *all* fucked up, and that's her hobby: fucked-up guys that she can fuck. I dunno. But she did me a hell of a lot of good when I needed all the good I could get done, and never mind who. 'At that point in time I came away with the impression' that she was the best thing in the world for me. And I was right, too. She was.

"My mistake," Richmond said, "—and it's also going to be your mistake, too, if you're not careful, and you're not —was thinking I had something permanently repaired when it was only temporary, and I didn't know it. But still, it was Dee's plain simplemindedness that unstuck me from the flypaper I was in with Sandy, and I stopped thinking I was worthless, and *bad*, and all the rest of that stuff that makes your stomach churn and your head ache. How much're you drinking, these days?"

"For Christ sake, Jess," Cavanaugh said.

"I'm not telling you how much you should drink," Richmond said. "I can tell you how much you can drink, before you're drinking so much that it's all you're doing because you haven't got time for anything else. But how much're you drinking, and do you know why?"

"Snakes and the shakes, if I don't," Cavanaugh said.

"No," Richmond said. "That'll come, if you keep it up, and it's a funny thing, but the people that get 'em don't think snakes and shakes're anywhere near as funny as the people that haven't got 'em. But probably not for a while, yet. When I was drinking everything that wouldn't drink me, that was where I was headed. It wouldn't be the first time, either, that my family had something like that happen. My mother's uncle lived at the Hartford Retreat for a good many years, and a couple cousins sort of alternate there now, keeping the suite in the family.

"But at least I knew why I was doing it," Richmond said. "That didn't make it good for me, but I knew it, and when I got to the point of getting over Dee, I stopped the real serious stuff. 'It's not medicine, son,' my father told me, but he was wrong. It's medicine. It's bad medicine, but it's medicine, and that's a hell of a lot better'n no medicine at all."

"I'm using it for medicine, then," Cavanaugh said. "Nerve medicine. I got bad nerves."

"Did you know that, before?" Richmond said. "I bet this's the first time you even thought about it."

"No," Cavanaugh said. "I've thought about it. I noticed, I used to get drunk more. Not a lot. Maybe once or twice a month. Well, in college, every goddamned weekend, I was drunk. It was like it was an obligation in college. Everybody got drunk, every weekend. You meant to. You did it on purpose. But without meaning to, I used to get drunk every so often. I'd be out having a good time, and I'd just go ahead and drink too much. And I'd get these enormous heads on me.

"Then about four years ago," Cavanaugh said, "I noticed all of a sudden that I wasn't getting drunk so much anymore. 'Good,' I thought, 'I finally grew up.' I thought I learned how to hold my liquor. Then I noticed, I've had this really bad sinus trouble, and when there's a day that for some reason or other I haven't the time, or I stay in the office so damned late I don't want to go out and see if there's anybody around, or I've got to get up early on top of it, the next day, I just go home, have one beer and go to bed. And the next day, I don't have the sinus trouble. That's what started me thinking about it. I think about it."

"You're using it for dope," Richmond said. "You're using it because you don't want to think."

"That's what you said you were doing," Cavanaugh said.

"I never said that," Richmond said. "I was using it because I didn't want to feel. I didn't want to feel bad, and it seemed like there were an awful lot of things to feel bad about.

"I knew what I thought. I'd finished thinking. That's why I came down here: I screwed everything up once, and then I thought I had it fixed, and I was wrong, and I had to face that. Twice, I did it. I didn't want to face that. I felt lousy, and I didn't want to feel lousy until I got my strength up. You don't feel lousy."

"I haven't got time," Cavanaugh said. "I feel pretty good, actually."

"You feel pretty good," Richmond said, "because you keep going so fast, and drinking so much. You've been able to keep yourself from thinking about things. That's what you're using the booze for."

"Well," Cavanaugh said, "as long as you feel good . . ."

"It's temporary," Richmond said.

"Hell," Cavanaugh said, "everything's temporary. I'll take temporary feeling good to temporary feeling shitty, any time I get the choice."

"Getting the choice is also temporary," Richmond said. "That's what I mean. The longer you duck it, the worse it finally is when you get yourself cornered. That's the position I was in. Then you have to think about it. Something happens, and it makes you feel lousy, and you'll stay feeling lousy because you used up all the booze you can stand and you can't have any more. That tolerance you're building up means you're setting yourself up. That's when they have to put you away and start giving you something stronger'n you could get by going down to the store and buying some for yourself. Because if you could, people'd go down and get it and use it to kill themselves, accidentally on purpose. When they have to do that, you stay in a long time. Sometimes you never come out."

"Jesus," Cavanaugh said, "you're a cheery bastard."

"I am," Richmond said. "I'm well traveled in hell this year. I've got my feet burned, and I've got blisters on my arse, but I went through it and I licked it. I know what I'm talking about. I've been there. I know what there is, and I know how people go about using it. Some of them use the stuff to help themselves, and some of them use the stuff so they don't have to do what they ought to do: sit down and help themselves. And some of them're hopeless. It's the difference that counts."

"What's the difference?" Cavanaugh said.

"I didn't mean that," Richmond said. "It's knowing the difference that counts."

"And I know where you got that piece of wisdom too, my friend," Cavanaugh said. "Was it really that bad?"

"I went to a couple of meetings right after Christmas," Richmond said. "I was getting worried. Didn't seem to be making much progress, you know? I went as much as anything else to find out if it was happening. Well, they had a fellow there who stood up and said for years he used to come home from work and have a beer. Then he graduated to king-size. Then two king-size. Then, and this was when he joined up, he sort of eased himself up to the point where he was having three king-sized beers a night. Three of them. 'My dear wife talked me into coming here,' he said, and I thought to myself: 'I can make a pretty good guess about how much help I'm going to get from this group.' I didn't go back. It's cold and lonely here in the winter. A lot of people go, I think, because there's no bingo that night. I drink. They talk about drinking. Either way, I get a headache. Look, that thing you've got: what do they call that thing, anyway?"

"It's a Vette," Cavanaugh said. "A four-fifty-four Vette."

"Is that the Shark?" Richmond said.

"It's the Shark," Cavanaugh said.

"And it goes about nine hundred miles an hour," Richmond said. "So you drive it that fast."

"Not quite that," Cavanaugh said. "Dollar for dollar it goes faster'n anything else you can buy. The Jag and the Porsche and the Ferraris and the Masers and the Bee-Em-Vey're faster, but if they cost what the Vette cost, they'd be slower, or else the Vette would go nine hundred miles an hour. It's a hell of a car. Inside it looks like a tractor, but it goes and goes."

"You'll kill yourself in it," Richmond said.

"No," Cavanaugh said, "I don't think I'm gonna do that. I haven't finished yet. I got things to do."

"You're going to kill yourself with the booze, then," Richmond said.

"Wrong again," Cavanaugh said.

"You're going to kill yourself with the car and the booze," Richmond said, "the combination."

"I don't think so," Cavanaugh said. "When I'm really in the wrapper, I don't drive it. And when I drive it, I'm not in the wrapper."

"John Clancy used to decide when he was going to get drunk," Richmond said.

"And get up," Cavanaugh said, "and go outside and drop the car keys down the catch basin, and come back inside and drink till he fell off the stool. He's still doing it. He did it, must've been three weeks ago now, I guess, down at the Class Reunion. 'I am so fuckin' sick of this Watergate thing I could shit,' he said. 'I am going to get myself good and drunk and maybe when I come to, it'll all be over with.' He was working about fifteen hours a day. It was driving him nuts."

"And then when he passed out, somebody had to take

him home, and get him a new set of keys," Richmond said.

"Same thing," Cavanaugh said.

"Who decides when you're in the wrapper?" Richmond said.

"I do," Cavanaugh said.

"Which is what I was getting to," Richmond said. "John Clancy's got more brains'n you have."

"Of course he has," Cavanaugh said. "He's got a steady job, for one thing. Want one?"

"Probably not," Richmond said. "I'm still resting."

"What about your investment?" Cavanaugh said. "The one you had with Jerry. You just writing that off?"

"Jerry and I had different investments," Richmond said. "His was the Senator. Mine was in abstract stuff. Part of it was my commitment to him, but that's just the way it all came out. Most of it was just a kind of arrogance. I knew what was best for people. I was going to use the Senator to persuade them to let people like me do what was best for them. It didn't pan out very well. I thought somebody told you that."

"Ever hear of salvage?" Cavanaugh said.

"I've heard about it a lot," Richmond said. "I even knew a couple of people who tried it. But I never saw it work."

"How about the nation's Chief Executive?" Cavanaugh said. "Seemed to work with him."

"That was not a project," Richmond said, "which I wholeheartedly favored at the time. In fact, I was very much opposed to it."

"Okay," Cavanaugh said, "tell me this: what're you going to do?"

"I thought a lot about that," Richmond said. "The first thing I thought of was: 'I don't have to do anything.'"

"Uh uh," Cavanaugh said.

"No," Richmond said. "Even if that was what I was going to do, which I may be, I'd lie to you out of self-defense and say it wasn't. Because you'd have people calling me up, wouldn't you?"

"Maybe," Cavanaugh said. "There's a shortage of people that know what they're doing, and things need to be done. But not, for sure, coming down here to see you."

"I didn't say you had anything to do with Makris," Richmond said.

"I didn't say you did," Cavanaugh said. "I didn't, but it wouldn't make any difference anyway. I didn't have anything to do with him. He's just a guy that made Sam look bad because Sam took advantage of his own ignorance to give the kid a chance to make him look bad. Which doesn't let you out, by the way."

" 'Of those to whom much is given,' " Richmond said, " 'much will be required.' You think that's so? There's so much bullshit around these days. You accept something like that without thinking about it, and I wonder if you're not just making yourself into a champion sucker."

"More or less," Cavanaugh said. "It's more or less true."

"Does inheriting count?" Richmond said.

"Yup," Cavanaugh said. "Education, brains, everything. It all counts."

"Look," Richmond said, "I don't like the direction this conversation's taking. Let's go back and get cleaned up; we've earned a little gin and tonic with three sets, instead of beer that makes a man so fat. Then we'll go down to the Opera House and see if we can pick up some girls."

"Oh for Christ sake," Cavanaugh said. "I told you: I came up here, from Washington, for a vacation."

"You're going to be a big pain in the ass, then," Richmond said.

"Let me put it this way," Cavanaugh said. "Right now, no. Tomorrow, no. Next week, next month, sometime between now and, say, Halloween, probably."

"I'll give it some thought," Richmond said. "I'm going to have to start doing that again anyway, sooner or later."

"I never actually put it to him," Cavanaugh
said. "He knows what's on my mind, but if
I'd've asked him, flat out, I think he probably
would've said no. Jess'll talk himself into things if you
give him time to think about them."

"Well," Sam Barry said, "of course that's the beauty of
starting so early. You have a little time to play with, when
you need some."

They sat in red leather chairs in Barry's office in the
Cannon Building. They had their feet on the coffee table,
between stacks of papers and committee reports in green
bindings. Sam Barry drank from a can of Tab.

"You told me to use my own judgment," Cavanaugh
said. "Jess is like the rest of the horses: they're getting
thirsty, but they won't drink till they're ready."

4

"You had a nice vacation, did you?" Barry said.

"Look," Cavanaugh said, "my vacations are when I do the same things with people on Nantucket and in Boston that I do here. Yeah, it was all right. Matter of actual fact, it could've lasted a while longer, and I wouldn't've complained about it."

Barry got up. His gray suit pants were too short, and his shoes needed shining. "Yeah," he said. He went behind the desk and stared out into the courtyard. "Jesus," he said, "it's been like a Chinese fire drill around here, though. I'm getting hell from Charlie because I didn't come up right away, and I told him if I didn't get some work done down here, I was going to go under. Good Lord, I spent most of the daylight hours Friday with Masterson on the phone at Social Security. You realize how many of those things I had backed up? Seventy-eight. Of which probably twenty, twenty-one were legitimate beefs. Thursday I was after Kreski at the VA for a good hour on that old Italian guy from East Bridgewater."

"The one with with the plate in his head?" Cavanaugh said. "They still didn't give him his card?"

"They still didn't give him his card," Barry said. "He's sick. He's alone. He needs a doctor. He can't afford a doctor. He called three times while you were away."

"Kreski told me himself, before I left," Cavanaugh said. " 'As soon as we locate his jacket, we'll give him the card.' He had it all down. World War I, all the information just like the old guy gave it to us."

"Well," Barry said, "they couldn't locate his jacket. 'What's his serial number?' 'He can't remember his serial number.' 'Where're his discharge papers?' 'He lost them.' 'Well, Jesus Christ, man, how the hell're we supposed to locate somebody with nothing to go on?' 'The guy's on the earth,' I said. 'You want, I'll take you up to the rest home and show him to you. I'll have somebody take his picture. He didn't get that plate in his head by mail. He wants his pension.' 'Has he got a birth certificate?' 'I don't think so. He's an immigrant.' 'Get me his papers, then.'

"I called him up," Barry said. "He was pitifully grateful. 'Oh, Mister Congressman, thank you so much.' 'You're very welcome, Mister DiLupo. Now, have you at least got your papers?' No, he's-ah no got-tah his papers. He's-ah-lose-ah his papers. 'Long time ago, when they take my house.' Back to Kreski. 'Lost his papers.' 'Oh for Christ sake,' Kreski said. 'Well, call Immigration. Call him first and find out when he came to this country, and then call Immigration and see if they can give us a fix on the guy so we can give the old bastard his pension.'

" 'Hello again, Mister DiLupo,' this is your friendly neighborhood Congressman calling," Barry said, "for the ninth time today and what ever gave you the idea I was elected to spend all my time chatting with you? 'If you give me the date when you entered the country, and the place, I'll get you some new papers and then maybe we can get things moving along for you. Incidentally, are you a registered voter?' Of course not, they never are. 'It was at Ellis-ah Island,' he's-ah tell me," Barry said. " 'I'm-ah never forget-ah the day. June the twenty-three.'

" 'What year?' I said to him. 'Nineteen-and-a-twenty-six,' " Barry said.

"How the hell," Cavanaugh said.

"He fought for the king," Barry said. "He was in the Italian army. You were in the war, you get a pension and you can go in the hospital. That's all he knows. He was in the war. He's not getting any pension. He wants to go to the hospital where his daughter and his two boys don't have to pay for it. They got little kids. They can't afford it. He feels guilty."

"What'd you do?" Cavanaugh said.

"Well," Barry said, "I did call Kreski and absolve him and his agency of any blundering. 'At least in this one, Dale.' And then I got mad. 'I'm-ah pay-ah my taxes, all-ah these years, Mister Congressman.' 'I know you did, Mister DiLupo.' 'So how come, I'm-ah sick, I can't go anyplace where I can get better?'

"Which is," Barry said, turning around, his hands in his pockets, "a very fine question. How come, indeed? He worked all his life. He never made much money. He took care of his family. 'I'm-ah never go on relief.' He just didn't have a lot left when he got old. He's got Social Security and probably a hundred and fifty bucks in the bank, and digging didn't offer a profit-sharing plan or stock options when he was shoveling rocks for the gas company. So how come he lives in a country where we've got doctors who can practically rebuild a rich kidney patient, and he can't find a guy who's able to give him the kind of care he deserves. Just because he's a human being."

"Did you make another speech, Sam?" Cavanaugh said.

"I was going to," Barry said. "I was going to go over there and holler good and loud. But I didn't."

"I'm proud of you, Sam," Cavanaugh said.

"Instead I called Harold Mahoney," Barry said. "You've got to see Harold, incidentally."

"If I stayed up to see Harold," Cavanaugh said, "I wouldn't be here now."

"That seems to make sense," Barry said. "Anyway, I called Harold, and yes, he's still on the board of trustees at College Hospital, and yes, he will get Mister DiLupo admitted as a special patient, and of course I understand, the result of this is going to be either Harold's going to get stuck for the bill or else I'm going to have to come up with a government grant for a new gadget that'll separate corpuscles from platelets and costs six hundred million dollars, that they don't need anyway because you only use those things twice a year and there's already three of them twenty miles away in Boston, and I said: 'Yeah, Harold, yeah.' So the old fuselier, or whatever he was, is getting his treatment, and that's another one off our backs. But Jesus, what a sideshow. And then Charlie tells me if I don't get up pretty quick, I'm not going to be down here where I *can* go under.

"Charlie also had some very impolite things to say about our little project," Barry said. " 'Yeah,' he said. You know how Charlie says: 'Yeah.' Like he was Mother Superior getting Mary Magdalene's application to the convent. 'Well, if you got that much time to waste, come on up here and waste it at clambakes, willya? So I can keep some people behind us that sent us checks before and might even be dumb enough to do it again in a year or so, if they thought we remembered them from the last time and still gave a shit about what they had to say. Instead of fooling around pretending Travis is alive. He's not. He's nationally dead.' "

"Charlie may have something, you know," Cavanaugh said. "Jess's gotten kind of aloof, but the other people, I didn't notice any spontaneous expressions of delight and support. There isn't what you could call a groundswell of support for the guy."

"Well," Barry said, "it's not exactly a public celebration yet, you know."

"I know," Cavanaugh said. "But the people that know about it, there isn't that excitement, you know? It's not there. Even Steve. I saw him before I went up. Hamner's one of the true believers. At least I think he is. But he's going through the motions."

"Steve's all right," Barry said. "He's no Jerry, but he's all right. It's the beginning. It's the happy few, the little band of brothers, when you first start up."

"They're not happy," Cavanaugh said. "They're just few. I'm not even sure Jerry's Jerry anymore."

"I've got hopes for Jerry," Barry said. "I think when a little more time's gone by, and he's had a chance to assimilate all the bad things that've happened to him, he'll come back. Jerry is one tough Jew. I think Jerry's going to be all right again."

"Jerry's all right, right now," Cavanaugh said. "I had lunch with him in Boston, at Locke's."

"I've got to put Linda to work," Barry said. "Forget all this fooling around with having babies and go out there and make some money so I can eat at Locke's with Cavanaugh. I haven't been in there since the night we got through with the statement for Bobby and we went in there about nine thirty or ten o'clock or so, and had dinner. That was the last time I was in Locke's. I was going to win, and Bobby was going to grab the nomination, and if God wasn't in His heaven, things were operating satisfactorily during his absence. I had scallops, and Jerry paid, and that's the last time I was in there. Scallops with bacon on them. Tony Restic was with us, and he was going down to Rhode Island the next day—they were announcing their engagement—and Tony ordered Lobster Savannah, and then he got himself so worked up he couldn't finish it. I thought he was going to have an attack, he was so excited."

"Now there's one," Cavanaugh said. "Is Tony in, this time around?"

"There's problems there," Barry said. "The mayor's up next year, and I gather he's licking his lips about running for governor, and he doesn't want Tony out taking sides nationally this early. He's still fighting with Morrissette, and Morrissette . . ."

"Is he the skinny bastard from Woonsocket that always looks like his stomach's bothering him, or for nine days he's been trying to take a shit or something?" Cavanaugh said.

"Yeah," Barry said. "The moralist. He went up to Jack in '60, when we were in Providence, and this guy, now mind you, all he ever did was sit in the Rhode Island legislature for about twenty years and sulk because the Speaker used to laugh at him, and besides, somewhere in the state there was somebody having fun, and Morrissette couldn't figure out a law they could pass that'd put a stop to it. So here he was, the next President of the United States, for sure as far as Rhode Island's concerned, and Morrissette went up to him and said: 'Senator, when're you going to get your family life straightened out? My con-stit-u-ents want to know. They depend on me for advice.' And Jack just turned his back on him.

"That was the trip," Barry said, "when some guy that wore suspenders, came from Coventry and he was a shrewd old bastard, was hounding him about his farm program. That's wild country down there, between West Warwick south to Narragansett. URI's down in Kingston, and that sort of throws you off. You get to thinking: 'There's suburbs in East Greenwich and there's summer places in Watch Hill, and it's all the same.' Well, it's not. You go in from the coast a ways and that back country's full of swamp Yankees, guys with three elbows that impregnate their own daughters, and shoot at strangers if it suits them right. We didn't do a day's business in that underbrush until we brought Damon up from the middle district of Tennessee, and I remember Steve saying: 'The hell're we gonna do with a moonshine prosecutor?' And Jerry said: 'The man says the guy won every still case he ever prosecuted, and if he did that, there, he must know how to talk to that kind of people, and that's exactly what we got here.' And Damon went in there and when he came out, they were all in line behind him. They didn't know how they liked his accent. 'Talks too slow. Sounds like he's feeble-minded. Sure he ain't feeble-minded?' Pretty soon, they were sure. He ain't feeble-minded. 'Mean as barbed wire, that fella,' they said. He's not. He's a pussycat.

"So this guy from down there," Barry said, "he asks JFK about his farm program. And Jack asked the guy how many states there were, where the farmers were controlling the votes. The guy really knew his stuff. He had all the figures. And then Jack asked him if he thought any kind of farm policy was going to get those states away from Nixon, and the guy was honest, too. He said: 'No.' And Jack said: 'That's what I think, too. So fuck the farmers.' And the guy threw his head back, and laughed and laughed and laughed. You should've seen Morrissette. He looked like he had goiter, he needed more iodine in his diet, his eyes were bugged out so far. 'That's what I mean. That's exactly what I mean.' Oh, he's an awful man.

"Tony made a speech up in Cumberland one night, for the mayor," Barry said, "and some freaky kid asked him about pot, and you know Tony: he's got this way of saying what's on his mind. 'Let 'em have it,' he said. 'Treat it like booze.'

"Well," Barry said, "Morrissette took that down to the *Journal* and he was beating the mayor over the head with it for about two weeks. Tony called me up one night, he was in a very good mood, and we talked, and I invited him down here for the softball game or any other excuse he could think of, and he said: 'Can't do it. Have to stay in the house. He's got me restricted to quarters.' He was mad as hell at Tony. Course he hates marijuana too. He'll drink a couple kegs of beer before he says it, but that doesn't mean he isn't firmly opposed to people dulling their palates or their senses, or something. No, I don't think he's going to let Tony get very far off the reservation, nationally, until he sees where people're lining up in the state, and then he'll go where the power is."

"Because Tony's not a bad guy to have around," Cavanaugh said. "There's a fellow who can do things and do them right, the first time."

"Steve can do that too," Barry said. "You underestimate Steve. Jerry spoiled you. Steve just doesn't come on as strong as Jerry."

"He's no good at kicking ass and cracking heads, Sam," Cavanaugh said. "Don't get me wrong: I like Steve, and I respect his dedication. But he lets people get away with doing about half they could do, and a third of what somebody like Jerry'd get out of them."

"I don't think so," Barry said. "He's got a different style. He doesn't need to crack as many heads as Jerry, just because of that. Steve's only real problem is that he doesn't delegate as ruthlessly as he should. He ends up trying to do too many things himself."

"That's the same thing I'm saying," Cavanaugh said. "He doesn't know how to get people to perform up to their limits, and he knows it, so he takes it all on himself, and that's why things don't get done when they should."

"But outside of that," Barry said, "in many respects,

he's better than Jerry. At least for the situation we're in now. Maybe later, after Teddy makes up his mind, we'll decide we need someone different. But right now we need a nice low profile so we don't give anybody else any ideas."

"He's gonna go," Cavanaugh said.

"Well," Barry said, "that'd be all right. That wouldn't bother me in the slightest. But, in case he doesn't, we've got to be ready."

"Jerry says we're kidding ourselves," Cavanaugh said.

"Also all right," Barry said, "even if he's correct. It's a hell of a lot better'n kidding the country, which is what these other bastards've been doing ever since they got in. I'll take that chance. Hell, I'd take the Senator from Boeing if he was the only alternative to that pack of crooks. Did you hear what Thornton said the other night on 'Comment'? 'Ali Baba should've gone to the White House. He could've found a quorum there in five minutes.' "

"And thus was another VHF license made available to competing interests more likely to serve the public with a wider variety of programming representing all voices in the community," Cavanaugh said.

"No," Barry said. "They just got renewed. They're good until '78, and if things don't work right, they can always fire Thornton in '77 and act repentant until they get it back and then rehire him. He's the best thing they have, as far as the ratings're concerned."

"Jerry's been on Channel Two a lot lately, he was telling me," Cavanaugh said.

"I heard that," Barry said. "He had some nice things to say about me a couple weeks ago, I guess. The National Seashore stuff about the islands."

"He told me about it," Cavanaugh said. "I told him:

'Jerry, there's a maximum of fifteen people in the whole district that ever saw Channel Two in their lives, and they all vote for Sam anyway. Now if you want to do something, you've either got to get the Speaker to put Cambridge and Brookline into the district, or else you've got to say those nice things in a newspaper, where people can read them.'

" 'I don't know,' he said," Cavanaugh said. " 'They all watch the auction every year. We sell at least ten stuffed alligators and a couple dozen quilts every year in the Seventeenth.' "

"Sure," Barry said, "they're looking for bargains. I had a guy in here Thursday, when I was going around and around with Kreski the first time, came down from the Cape, all the way down here on the Greyhound. He's not used to talking. A sentence or two every five or ten minutes. He'd say something and you didn't know at first whether he expected you to answer. He thought he was telling me something I already knew. Cranberries. He was upset about cranberries. Started off: 'We'll probably get a frost by the end of September.'

"Well, it seemed like he probably had something there, but what I could do about it wasn't exactly clear to me, so I agreed with him. 'Water,' he said. 'there'll have to be water in the bogs by then.' I was tempted to tell him that was why I sold all my bogs, because I never did know when to let the water in. 'Frost,' he said. 'When we get the frost, we'll have to have the water in the bogs.' He still had me. Kreski kept calling, and interrupting. Sylvia came in with a guy from the Bureau of National Affairs that I should've seen because they're putting out this new service on something and maybe, well anyway, I didn't know how the hell they got the water in the bogs. When

I've driven by them, sometimes they had water in them and sometimes they didn't. I dunno, I assumed they just opened a gate or something and let the water in. 'Pumps,' he said. 'Gasoline for the pumps.' "

"I knew they had pumps," Cavanaugh said. "I thought, I guess I just assumed they were electric. Electric pumps."

"Some of them apparently are," Barry said. "A lot of them're too far out for electric pumps, no lines. They use gasoline. The things they use to pick them, the machines, use gasoline. 'Going to be difficult,' he said. He liked that. 'Difficult.' He said it three times. 'Nobody's going to be able to bring in any cranberries this year. No gas. Plants're gonna die. Help, what'll we do with the help, eh? That's why I'm here.' "

"He's probably right," Cavanaugh said.

"Of course he's right," Barry said. "I never thought of it. He was telling me something I didn't know, and he was way out in front on it."

"We ought to get ahold of Clayton down at Atlantic Spray," Cavanaugh said. "They all sell to Atlantic. See if we can get some statistics out of the guy for a change."

"That," Barry said, "and have Ellen start calling around pronto and see if there's anybody else that's going to get hurt and doesn't know it yet. Yesterday'd be good. Somebody's going to take a fearful beating on this, when the nor'easters start coming in again and they're sitting there shivering their asses off, and I'd rather be the guy with the stick than the guy that's getting the stick laid on him. The Administration's to blame for this screw-up and I want to be damned sure I do everything I can to make sure they have to eat all the crow they're responsible for. I sure don't want any."

"Put it in the newsletter, too," Cavanaugh said. "We

can probably find enough stuff that's already around for that, by the end of the week."

"Hank," Barry said, "nobody reads the goddamned newsletter."

"It'll get you on the record, at least," Cavanaugh said. "Then if they come after you, you can wave it in their faces."

"Hank," Barry said, "that's not going to get anybody any goddamned oil and gas. People're going to get cold, and the newsletter and being on the record against people being cold isn't going to make people warm. We're going to have people standing around out of work. We'll never get anywhere on things that'll do people some good. We'll be right back where we've been all along, trying to shovel shit against the tide and put out fires and fight off a depression. Never mind how good you can make me look with no work. Not very good anyway, I think. *Do* some work and see if we can't find a way to make things a little better instead of spending all our time just floundering around, trying to stop them from getting worse."

"Sam," Cavanaugh said, "you keep right on ignoring Charlie's advice. You stay away from those clambakes. He thinks you've changed a little since you got elected. He thinks you got smart. He told me that. 'All right, he's not still trying to save the goddamned world. Actually sounds like he's getting sensible, he's going to save the Seventeenth.' Don't go up there and spoil it all for him. Let him think you changed, and you're thinking about getting re-elected and raising money and all those things. 'Screw it,' he said, 'grab the guy by the ear, willya? I got a dame that's ready to write a check for ten thousand dollars if she can get him to listen to her once in a while. It's American money. Any reason why Sam shouldn't have it, instead of some bastard that'll use it to buy a Cadillac for his fuckin' girl friend?' 'No reason at all, Charlie,' I told him."

"Who is it?" Barry said. "Dagmar Bloom?"

"Ingrid, I think he said," Cavanaugh said.

"Ingrid Bloom," Barry said, "from Cohasset. Lovely lady. Big strong blond girl. "The Heart of UNICEF on the South Shore.' She called Talbot on the war one day and let him have it with both barrels. 'Talbot wants money for planes and bombs, and we want money for children. Throw Talbot out. Those bombs're hitting children we're trying to save.' Oh, it was beautiful. Talbot was absolutely speechless."

"So," Cavanaugh said, "let's give her a couple hours. We're going to have to spend a month up there and eat a ton of cheese and drink a hundred gallons of cheap red wine to snatch that kind of dough away otherwise."

"Her husband's name's either Leo or Jesse," Barry said. "I forget which. Mister Bloom enjoys a well-deserved reputation as a loanshark."

"Oh," Cavanaugh said.

"It was two thousand, the first time," Barry said. "The first time I ran against Talbot, the check came in. It was easily the biggest check we'd seen, and since the only people up till then who supported me were rather, uh, well, they were fine people, but short of cash. So here I was with this nice note from Ingrid Bloom, and a check that had her name and his name on it, and I thought to myself that Mister Bloom was sure awful impressed with me, for a guy I didn't think I'd ever met. So I called up Jack Sweeney in the DA's office, and I said to him: 'Who the hell is Leo Bloom?' Or whatever his name is. And he told me. Bloom's a gangster, very impure and not simple at all, and he's got a collection of politicians that he wears on a charm bracelet.

Ingrid's the front. Is she ever the front. But he doesn't live with her. He lives with his honey in Brookline. They're still married, and they're good friends, and she likes having power and he likes having her happy so he can live with his honey, so he gives her the cash that makes people listen to her and then, when and if he should need them, they find out that it's him they're going to be listening to from now on, and he's nowhere near as nice or as lovable as feisty old Dagmar, or whatever her name is. She can't understand it. She really means what she says, and she can't understand why people in my position avoid her."

"What's he want?" Cavanaugh said.

"Oh," Barry said, "right now he probably doesn't want anything, and maybe he never will. He just wants to be on the safe side, get himself a Congressman or three to go with the other people he's got, rather spend their time reviewing large issues with leaders of industry and intellect than getting constipated on wine and cheese and listening to what the people think. And then, six or eight years down the road, if Mister Bloom conceives a plan to improve the value of some wetlands that he got cheap by building a gaudy motel there, which'd do a lot more business if the government decided to run an interstate highway past the place and put a cloverleaf a couple hundred yards away, well, he's got somebody in Washington that can call up the Department of Transportation and explain that his support for certain mass transportation legislation doesn't mean he's given up on roads. Quite the opposite, in fact. His support for trains and subways is conditioned upon adequate improvements in our system of interstate highways, especially this one that could be shifted fifteen miles or so from its projected route to a place that just happens to be right next to Bloom's land.

"May never happen. But it might happen, and if it does happen, Bloom's got his guy in place, and the guy stays in place because he got fat and now he needs Bloom so bad he's got to do what Bloom says. Besides, Mister Bloom knows a lot about the stock market, particularly the market in over-the-counter, low-price issues, and letter stock that isn't even over-the-counter yet, and a prudent Congressman, mindful of the precariousness of political life, is often receptive to advice that he purchase, for a dime a share, a buck at the most, a hatful of options or stock itself in a new corporation being formed to build a motel in the wetlands. After all, if it does a good business, that stock can be sold, and who's to know that the registered owner was actually some dummy for the Congressman, huh? People that aren't very careful have been known to assemble large nest eggs that way. It's the spirit of free enterprise, and the open marketplace."

"Does Charlie know this?" Cavanaugh said.

"Charlie's been around for a long time," Barry said. "He gets out the vote, he really didn't like the war, and besides, that other bastard was a Republican, which offends his deepest sense of the proprieties of life. He thought, when he moved out to Hanover, as long as there weren't any of those damned spades in his hair, playing with his grandchildren and eating watermelon where he could see them, he could stand the indignity of being represented in Washington by a goddamned Republican. Also, he thought he could retire. But it got to him. Charlie's been around a long time, which can accustom a man to being around. He's as straight as he can be, himself, but Charlie Fraley studied under Beefsteak McCarthy, and when Beefsteak got Handsome John Flanagan thrown into jail for voting twice by voting in Ward Four as Handsome John, while Handsome

John was voting in Ward Five as Flanagan, so they arrested him when he got to Four as trying to vote again when he already voted there, Charlie thought it was not only fun, but perfectly all right. He has a high tolerance for dishonesty in others, and you have to keep that right at the front of things when he starts telling you about a way to do something quicker and easier. Some of them may be felonies."

" 'Ten big ones,' he said to me," Cavanaugh said. " 'All he's got to do is listen to the broad. He doesn't even have to say anything. Ten big ones. Just like apples on a tree.' "

"Sneaky," Barry said, "very sneaky. He looks so charming, and open, and guileless. It's easy to forget. You have to watch him all the time. He talks funny. When he was in the General Court he stood up one day and said that if they, they, 'The *Great* and General Court, should pass this bill, our forefathers if they were alive today would roll *over* in their *graves,* to see what we have done.' Of course what he was opposing was the bill to repeal the teachers' loyalty oath, but nobody remembers that because of Charlie's Irish Bull. I remember my father telling me about 'utter chowss,' which was what Charlie predicted to follow the annual effort by three or four guys that're so secure in their seats they can afford to do anything, even propose repeal of the sex laws so the homosexuals can get their cookies without committing felonies: 'The order of society is grounded upon the preservation of the family, and these vile practices threaten the very fabric of the family. If we should legalize, instead of recoiling from, the abominable and detestable act against nature, then the social order will col*lapse,* and utter chowss will en*sue.*' He's good and he's tough and he's smart, and he knows everything and everyone. But I went through this twice with him before, and he's not blowing it past me this easily, the crafty old son of a bitch. 'Look,' I said, 'you know what's he doing. He's out to purchase a piece of the government, and the piece he wants is me.'

" 'Leave him do it,' Charlie said," Barry said. " 'And then when he comes around, look at him like you never saw the bastard before in your life. You're not making no deals with him. I'm not telling you, give him your word. He's dumb enough, thinks he can get something nobody ever mentioned, let him be dumb. Complain? Let him complain. Guys do it all the time.'

" 'Charlie,' I said to him," Barry said, " 'the papers? If the papers get me being financed by the Mob, I'm so dead I was never even alive.'

" 'Deny it,' he said. 'What'd you know? It's the broad that give you the dough. Take the dough. It'll never happen. It does happen, you get out there and say: "I got it from the broad. How'd I know?" It's ten grand. You think that's pocket money? I know guys that'd kill children for ten grand.' Charlie just couldn't understand it when I said: 'No.' He still can't, so he's working through you."

"Well," Cavanaugh said, "it's your ass, I guess. If you think it's ice cream, I suppose it must be ice cream."

"Vanilla," Barry said. "What else did Jerry say?"

"Well," Cavanaugh said, "I don't know as I ought to tell you this, but he thinks you're going to win unless Bobby Orr gets naturalized and moves into the Seventeenth to try his hand at politics."

"If the election was held tomorrow," Barry said.

" 'If the election were to be held tomorrow,' " Cavanaugh said, " 'Sam would win easily.' "

"Now," Barry said, "what plans does he have for holding the election tomorrow?"

"He didn't mention any," Cavanaugh said. "Look, that's

the way they all talk. How many times's he been wrong?
Once?"

"Twice," Barry said. "He started out thinking Linsky
had Drinan, but he hedged that back before the actual fact,
and he thought I had Talbot the first time."

"And he's been using that outfit for ten or fifteen years,"
Cavanaugh said.

" 'It doesn't matter which one you use,' " Barry said.
" 'Any damned fool can ask questions and check off
answers. What you need're the right questions, and then
you're not asking questions, you're putting ideas in people's
heads.' "

"I'm always surprised you go along with that," Cavanaugh said.

"My job is to get people thinking about things once in
a while," Barry said, "that they're really not very interested
in thinking about. They'd rather think about getting laid
and keeping the kids in shoes and the Bruins and the Red
Sox and the Patriots and the Celtics, and their jobs and
who's cheating on whose spouse. They don't care about
tariffs and prisoners of war unless they import things or
their husbands're POWs. If there was another way to
remind them, every so often, that I'm tending the store
and there's a store to be tended—and incite them into ap-
proving of me because when somebody asks you if you
approve of your Congressman, it sounds dumb to say you
don't know the guy's name, so you say it, and then you
do it—I'd take it. But there isn't any other way to keep
people even sporadically aware of the fact that I represent
them in the Congress of the United States. I don't make
them vote for me, you know. If I did, the damned things
wouldn't be up in the air for three days after the election
while those bastards on the Cape that hate me count them

over and over, trying to make it come out strong enough in Barnstable to wipe out what I've got in Plymouth and Norfolk. Someday, when they finally whip me, I'm going to go down there and I'm going to start in Wellfleet, rubbing gravestones and getting the names of all the people who voted against me every year I ever ran. They've got the most active cadavers in the world on the Cape. At least the rummies that swing it in Dorchester're *alive*. My father more or less intimated to Charlie, once, that he thought maybe Beefsteak might've bused in a few voters that were residents of certain doorways on Dover Street and filled their pants with newspapers when it was cold, instead of using blankets and sleeping inside, and Beefsteak was outraged: 'I got to,' he said. 'If I don't, those horse-faced bastards'll get a hundred percent turn-out from the Old Granary Burying Ground that'll be enough to beat us. Sam Adams and John Hancock voted for governor the last time, and they never miss an election, dead as they are.' "

"Jerry also said," Cavanaugh said, "he's not sure, but he thinks if you took a reading now, 'the right kind of reading, you know,' he says, you might be able to line yourself up for something else the next time around."

"Not '74," Barry said.

"In '78," Cavanaugh said.

"Five years away, I start taking polls," Barry said. "Has Jerry got anything in that outfit?"

"No money of his own," Cavanaugh said. "I don't think he has, anyway."

"It's his brother-in-law, isn't it?" Barry said.

"Yeah," Cavanaugh said. "But, I'm not saying Jerry doesn't like the idea of his brother-in-law turning an honest dollar. He trusts Fulton, and Fulton runs Massindex, and that's what he's after. If he trusted somebody else, he'd use them, if he thought they were better'n Massindex."

"It's still his brother-in-law," Barry said. "It still costs a lot of money. It's still Jerry that wants a poll every time the sun goes behind a cloud. Charlie's always after me about the way we spend money, and an awful lot of the money we spend goes to Fulton."

"It seems to work," Cavanaugh said.

"Something works," Barry said. "I'm here, and I was here before, and I guess that's a good thing. But it's hard for me to be sure it was Fulton and Jerry that got me here. Maybe it was me that worked, and worked damned hard, too, along with a lot of other people."

"Next time," Cavanaugh said, "could I ask you to maybe work a little harder? Not that I've got anything against squeakers and cliffhangers, but you have to admit that fifty-point-three and fifty-one-point-two're kind of thin percentages, as pluralities go."

"Oh sure," Barry said. "When you're as near as I am, everything's important. But those margins'll get bigger the longer I'm here, just like they do for every old codger that got lucky and snatched the thing from some older codger when he got vague, or grabbed a district that was changing from an incumbent that didn't spend enough time in it to know it. All I really have to do now is start sending out the crabgrass leaflets around the first of the year and nail down a new grant to dredge Island Grove, and keep breathing, and if I do it enough times, someday I'll be an old codger and some fresh kid'll see the district's changed on me and come in and knock me off."

"I liked Island Grove," Cavanaugh said. "I used to catch perch there. I didn't care if it was polluted. I wasn't going to eat the damned things anyway."

"I'll do the best I can for Island Grove," Barry said. "If I cain't do nuffin', I won't do nuffin', and me and Br'er Fox, we won't *say* nuffin', we jes lie low."

"Be sure and say that at the NAACP," Cavanaugh said. "Then you really won't have to say nuffin', and there won't be a way in the world I can save your hopeless ass."

"What else does Jerry say?" Barry said. "Besides telling me to wait five years? Who paid for lunch, by the way?"

"Channel Two, I think," Cavanaugh said. "Jerry said he was paying, and I didn't take the check. I don't know."

"The poor put-upon taxpayers again," Barry said. "Well, better them'n me. At least they don't have to listen to Charlie when the chits come in."

"Jerry says Fogarty's got early foot on Ianni for AG. 'Mike'll have to do something extremely stupid to give everybody the excuse that most of them'd probably like to have to stick it to him, and Mike doesn't do anything even slightly stupid because Mike doesn't really do anything. Ianni's been holding testimonials for himself so long, he's got to run for something, but I don't think even he thinks he's going to shunt Fogarty. Either one of them beats Miller, no sweat,' " Cavanaugh said.

"What about Makris?" Barry said.

"The kid's quick," Cavanaugh said.

"Oh shut up," Barry said. "What about Makris? He got any strength up there, out in left field or wherever the hell he's coming from?"

"Jerry thinks: no," Cavanaugh said. "Jerry says the kid's all noise, no support, and less money. He mostly thinks the kid's out to get his name up on billboards so everybody'll know he's a lawyer and come to him when they get busted for driving under."

"By the great horn spoon," Barry said, "I hope that's it.

If he wins, we're gonna get indicted for sure. The whole world's gonna get indicted. There won't be anybody left to sit on juries, for God's sake, the way that guy comes out of the blocks."

"Richmond thinks he's mostly an asshole," Cavanaugh said.

"Jess saw him?" Barry said.

"He went down there to see Richmond," Cavanaugh said.

"Son of a bitch," Barry said. "The kid's really not stupid, is he? Up there in Essex County, clattering around, how the hell did he find out Jess was at loose ends?"

"Somebody told him," Cavanaugh said.

"Somebody who knows a little bit about things," Barry said, "and that means, somebody he was bright enough to know, knew about things, and he asked him."

"What I got from Jess," Cavanaugh said, "I'd say he knows what he's got to do, but he really doesn't know how to do it. He hasn't got the money to do it. He doesn't know anybody that can do it for him. Jerry thinks Fogarty's people are going to devour the son of a bitch. Nobody but Ianni's mother's going to take him seriously, and if the primary falls on the day when she's making raviolis, she won't go out either. He's got money up the gazoo, and he's sick of being a Rep, so run against Fogarty, get his ass whipped, and devote full time to his undertaking business. Forget the law practice. Jerry says Fogarty runs against Ianni, doesn't even notice Makris, and Fogarty wins. Which also means Mulcahy can retire from being Speaker and run for Secretary, and that means Fulginitti wins as usual and goes from Whip to Speaker, and that's why Ianni hasn't even got the kind of ethnic support you'd expect. And Makris retires from public life to devote full time to the private practice of law. 'What the hell is this "full time" everybody's always talking about?' Jerry says. 'Does that mean they're gonna loaf all the time in their own offices, instead of loafing all the time in their State House offices? They'll all be on relief by the end of the year.'"

"I don't like that stuff about Makris going down to see Richmond," Barry said. "I don't like that at all."

"Jess isn't with him," Cavanaugh said.

"Jess is all right," Barry said. "I just didn't think Makris was that smart. That's what bothers me. He's going to do the same thing I did, if I'm not careful. He's going to run once, when it's hopeless, and accept his trouncing with a boyish grin and a kind word for all the ferocious bastards that he didn't have any business challenging anyway, and it'll give him that kind of spurious legitimacy. Four or five years from now, I'll have a lot of trouble overcoming that, if I decide I'd like to go back. That bothers me. I thought he dusted me off because I said what I said. Now I'm beginning to think he's more'n just lucky, and fast enough to take advantage of an incautious statement. Maybe he also knows what he's doing. How the hell am I going to get turned around so I can go back there and do something if that guy that looks like he's just running around all over the place turns out to know what he's doing?"

"Well," Cavanaugh said, "that's a long way off, no matter how you look at it."

"What's Jerry say about that?" Barry said. "Do I take myself out, or don't I?"

"Jerry says no," Cavanaugh said. "Fogarty's careful. He doesn't know Makris that well. That makes him worry about him more'n he'd worry if he did know him, because that's what Fogarty does, and he hasn't done bad at it, either."

"I despise people like that," Barry said.

"Do it on your own time, then," Cavanaugh said. "Jerry says, right now, the best thing for you is the best thing for Fogarty, and the best thing for Fogarty is if you're still thinking about it, because that makes two harps and that keeps the other harps out. That shakes it down to him and Ianni and Makris, and Makris's out and Fogarty beats Ianni for fifty thousand bucks and a lot of signs that'll go just as good when he runs against Miller."

"Miller's got to be the coldest man that ever spent a whole lifetime trying to make compassion into a political program," Barry said.

"I know it," Cavanaugh said. "He's got everything in the world going for him, except he's a Republican where that's an endangered species, and he's as warm as a plastic toilet seat. Why the hell is it that the first thing you do, if you're a Wasp and you got principles, is scowl all the time?"

"I dunno," Barry said. "And he's not even like that. He just looks like he's like that. I wish there was some way to help a guy like that."

"Oh," Cavanaugh said, "that's another thing Jerry said. 'And you tell him, stay the hell away from Miller unless he really wants to write his own obit this year. No secret deals, no money, no nothing.' Meaning you."

"Fogarty's a whore," Barry said.

"Ianni's a whore," Cavanaugh said. "Makris's a fresh bastard and they've got a dirty file on him."

"No shit," Barry said. "The White Tornado, and they've got a dirty file on the guy? Son of a bitch." He began to laugh. "What is it, whips and stuff?"

"Jerry said the guy apparently had some trouble with his wife and made himself a goddamned fool over it, and now he's fooling around."

"So's Ianni," Barry said. "He's had a girl friend in Chelsea for years. Now there's a guy with class: gets himself a girl friend and sets her up in Chelsea, for God's sake."

"He better look out," Cavanaugh said. "Two guys that had girl friends got knocked off last year, one in the House and one in the Senate."

"That was funny," Barry said. "Costello I could understand. Him and his printing bill. I could never understand why one of those people that bought him for a fast five hundred on his 'I dunno how I'm gonna pay this thing' didn't turn him in a long time ago. 'I'm Senator Costello's wife, and I hope you'll vote for Mister Tierney.' The beauty was the Honorable Representative Walter Kilduff. 'Unlike Eileen Costello's husband, Walter has no opponent in the primary this year. But I do hope you'll give serious consideration to Mister Wapnold in November. Signed: Evelyn Kilduff.' Gorgeous. There's nothing like making an ass of yourself to get a man diselected."

"Well," Cavanaugh said, "it's not going to hurt Ianni anyway, because he's not important enough to throw mud at. Just get the money in the Everett Trust in his brother's name and forget about it. But Fogarty'd be a lot more comfortable if you'd kind of hang around and say something belligerent every now and then that'll keep the rest of us micks in our holes until he can lock things up. If it's all the same to you."

"What's Fogarty going to do for me?" Barry said.

"I asked Jerry that," Cavanaugh said. " 'Nothing, probably,' he said. No, he'll stay clear, or he'll back you, your choice, when you go for something else when he goes for governor."

"Five more years," Barry said. "Was it four more years somebody or other was talking about?"

"Plus two more, on and after, for lying about it," Cavanaugh said.

"Out of sight," Barry said. "Out of mind. Working for Gericare, Judicare, Medicare, and Denticare. Worrying about cranberries when babies're dying and people that always worked can't find jobs, and just by way of no harm, we're giving the wheat away to the Russians. So they'll like us. Shit."

"Yeah," Cavanaugh said.

Barry came back from the window and sat down. "We've really got to get this thing going," he said. "There isn't any choice. If we don't, and Teddy doesn't go, we'll have to get somebody that can beat them on Watergate, and then'll come in and stall around and horse around just like they do, except he won't steal."

"Sam," Cavanaugh said, "whaddaya want to be when you grow up?"

"President of the United States," Barry said.

"Never happen," Cavanaugh said. "How about the Fire Department?"

"How about, instead, special counsel to the President for domestic affairs?" Sam Barry said. "If we do this thing right, we're going to have two new Congresses and a damned good chunk of a new Senate, full of progressive people, if we can drape Gordon Liddy around their necks like I think we can, and it's going to be a Hundred Days when we can turn the whole country around in 1977, right on its pivot. I wouldn't mind that."

"That's what Jerry said," Cavanaugh said. " 'But first he's going to need a President, for that.' "

"So," Barry said, "get me a President, goddamnit. At least get me Jess Richmond and some other people. Go up to Maine and see if Joe Marsh's fed up with playing rustic sage. Stop in Boston next time and visit Harold. Talk to Senator MacIntosh. Find some money. I want my own President."

"Jess is tired," Cavanaugh said. "He's getting old."

"Get him young," Sam Barry said. "This is important."

"Louise comes in here now and then, you know," Sarah said in the Oak Bar at the Plaza. The residue of late afternoon light lay low in Central Park under the tall awnings over the windows.

5

"I imagine she does," Cavanaugh said. "She's gainfully employed. She can buy her own drinks."

Two men in silvery suits stood at the bar behind Cavanaugh. "He's a nice kid," the one in aviator eyeglasses said. "You know his father. I've known him all my life. He was at my bar mitzvah and I was at his; and we were at Cornell together. I've known Jack all my life."

"Jack Isaacs?" the second one said. He wore a wig.

"Jack Isaacs," the first one said.

"We had a condominium on the same floor, last year," the second one said. "He is really a sweet guy. Laura and his wife didn't get along so good, but what the hell. . . ."

"I always liked Joan," the first one said. "I used to go out with her, before she met Jack. Not a bad lay in the old days, if you want the truth from me."

"We used to see a lot of them in the mountains," the second one said. "Her and my Edith became very close friends, so naturally now, she sees me with Laura and it disturbs her."

"You can't blame her for that," the first one said.

"Naturally not," the second one said. "My Laura's best friends with his Sherry, that I guess he dumped over."

"He did," the first one said. "Last year, he did that."

"You can't blame him for that," the second one said.

"Hey," the first one said, "it's the right thing to do. We should've done that, you and me. Life'd be a lot simpler."

"Where do they get these people?" Sarah said.

"Where do they get us?" Cavanaugh said. "Maybe they belong here, and we don't."

"Simpler," the second one said, "not as nice."

"Easier," the first one said. "Simpler is easier. Running around, the coats and the presents coming out of the business, making the excuses at home: I'm getting old, Eddie. In my life now, it's the simple things I like. I'm mellowing. No problems: I don't like problems no more, complications and that. I used to love problems. I used to thrive on them. Not anymore. No more complications, if you please. I want to have my drink. I want to do my business, make a little money, have a little fun, take a vacation now and then, and be happy, go home and see my family in the evening. That's what I want to do. The simple verities. I can look at the cakes on some child now and it doesn't matter to me. I've been reading *Walden*, you know? He's got the right idea."

"He really has," Eddie said. " 'Simplify, simplify.' "

"I love this," Sarah said in a low voice, "minding other people's business."

"Why are they letting us do it?" Cavanaugh said.

"They're not letting us," Sarah said. "They're forcing us. They're having fun, putting out their pearls for us to see."

"Well, this kid," the first one said, "he got out of college, and he didn't know anything, and Jack called me up and said: 'Do me a favor, all right?' And of course I love Jack. Jack says: 'Do me a favor,' I'd do him a favor if it meant I hadda take the food outta the mouths of my kids. 'Do me a favor,' Jack says, 'and take the kid on. I bring him in over here, he's never going to know anything, always he'll just be my son, and I took him in. It's not good.' I took the kid on.

"Eddie," the first one said, "I thought it was me, doing Jack a favor. Let me let you in on something: I was doing *me* a favor. The kid can do things that I never thought of. He can do things which if I thought of them to do, I wouldn't do them, because they're impossible. Only I wouldn't think of them. He thinks of them, he does them, and he makes money. I called him in. The first two quarters he was there, he was doing things and he's a great-looking kid. I had to keep him. I said: 'Terry, I dunno. I thought I was doing your father a favor. I took you on. He was doing me a favor. Tell me, I'm paying you twenty-one, what can I do for you?' You know what he says?"

" 'Make me a partner,' " Sarah said.

"Forty?" Eddie said.

" 'Make me a partner,' " the first one said.

" 'I did it,' " she said.

"I did it," the first one said.

" 'It was the best thing,' " she said, " 'ever happened to me.' "

"I never did anything," the first one said, "made me feel any better."

" 'I love Jack,' " she said.

"I love Jack," he said.

" 'But I love the kid more,' " she said.

"But I love this kid like he was my own son, which I never had," the first one said. "It's breaking my heart, what's happening to him. He's not married. He goes out all the time, he doesn't go home. I said to him: 'Terry, you should get yourself married and go settle down. You're making almost seventy thousand dollars a year. You can afford a nice family, a wife, a few kids, and have a nice life and be a great man. You're not even thirty.' "

" 'He wouldn't listen,' " she said.

"Does he pay attention to me?" the first one said. "He does not. Does he listen to me? No, of course not. Twenty-seven years old, he's got all the answers, knows everything. You know what he does? He gambles."

"What're you doing in town?" Sarah said.

"Some work for Sam," Cavanaugh said. "Also getting in trouble, I hope."

"Oh," she said, "you're getting in trouble, all right. If you think you're going to get out of town without getting in trouble, well, you better take yourself down to Doctor's Hospital and check yourself in for a while. You going to see Louise?"

"She's in Chicago this week," Cavanaugh said.

"Oh," Sarah said, "that's that *Playboy* thing that Springer's doing. You know what I bet? I bet he discovers that *Playboy*'s actually exploiting women's naked bodies."

"Is that what it is?" Cavanaugh said. "Don't the girls in that book have any clothes on?"

"Scarcely a stitch," Sarah said. "I've seen it. Oh, a little gold chain around the middles sometimes, but mostly what you see is tits and ass."

"No kidding," Cavanaugh said.

"And pubic hair, too," Sarah said.

"I got to get a copy of that," Cavanaugh said. "I'm very partial to the real thing. I bet I'd like pictures of them too."

"You want to be careful," Sarah said, "might make you horny."

"Not me," he said. "I've got iron self-control and stuff."

"It's the stuff that interests me, right at the moment," Sarah said. "There's two things I don't understand about Louise, which don't bother me very much because I don't like her, the way she's turned out. One of them I won't mention, because you're modest and you'd blush, and the other one is how she can work for Springer."

"He pays her good money," Cavanaugh said, "and she does what she wants."

"That's what I mean," Sarah said. "I don't understand how she could want to do what she does for him. He does women's rights and he does black consciousness and he does encounter groups and radical chic and the population explosion. He's just so goddamned slick, and *au courant*, and just the fact that he's there, occupying space, means that somebody who could really tell you something about those things that you'd really like to know doesn't get the chance. There's only so much money and so much program time, and what he uses up on superficial stuff is gone, and I don't see how Louise could've gotten so she'd like doing that. She used to be the kind of a girl who knew the difference between things that were good, and things that were just crap, and now she's cranking out the crap and being regal about it at the same time."

"She's successful," Cavanaugh said. "She likes being successful. She was never sure she was going to be. It's a nice feeling, and she appreciates Springer for giving it to her."

"He's easy to appreciate," Sarah said. "It's not that I don't like the guy. He's very personable, particularly if you're the kind of person that doesn't have anything hanging down between your legs. Very unthreatening to women. And even if you're a man, he keeps that business entirely separate from his projects and his company. There's just nothing about the guy that's oppressive or intrusive, but God, the man never took a chance in his life. Well, maybe the first time he discovered what he really wanted was a lollipop, but that was long ago. All he does now is be polite, and charming, and put together those lovely, glossy packages, and make huge amounts of money. I think if you rubbed Ed Springer, some money would come off. Working for him is like having a key to the bank. Not like that jerk I'm with."

"Is Michael political at all?" Cavanaugh said.

"This week he isn't," she said. "Last week he was more or less at loose ends, and he called me up one night when he was stoned and started muttering about something that sounded like it might turn out to be politics, if I listened long enough, but I was almost asleep and I told him I was entertaining a friend and couldn't talk. Next week he might be political, but this week he's sort of veered off into Zen archery and whether you can use the same kind of thing to beat everybody playing tennis. He plays tennis every day."

"He hasn't done anything for quite a long time, has he?" Cavanaugh said.

"He hasn't had to," Sarah said. "He made a bundle off 'The Major Grapefruit Comes to Shea,' booked them when they were so obscure not even *Rolling Stone* acknowledged their existence and everybody said he should forget Shea and hold it in a phone booth, and then they came up with 'Murderous Fancies' and people got trampled, trying to get in. He's living on that. Michael doesn't do anything when he doesn't have to, and he hasn't had to since June."

"What do you do when he's like that?" Cavanaugh said.

"Anything I want," she said. "If he's not in, I don't go in either. I made an afghan."

Cavanaugh began to laugh.

"I did," she said. "I read a book. I actually read *The Winds of War*, all the way through. I lost eight pounds."

"You look great," he said.

"You don't have to flatter me," she said. "You know I'm, what is it?"

"Putty in my hands?" he said.

"More like randy as a billygoat," she said, "now that I know Louise isn't in town. Is that why you decided to come up here this week, because she wasn't here?"

"No," he said.

"Shit," Sarah said. "Now I thought I was going to feel all warm and cozy because Hank Cavanaugh came up to see me just as Louise went traipsing off someplace else. I could've gone around humming to myself for a week or so on that. Haven't you any notion of how to let a woman be wily with you?"

"As a matter of fact," Cavanaugh said, "now that I've dropped the ball . . ."

"Never mind, never mind," she said. "I'll probably start to languish as soon as you leave, but I'll choke back the tears and be brave while you're here, never letting you see how you've hurt me. Men are so insensitive."

"I had to go to Boston," he said. "I had to go to Maine first, and then I was in Boston Tuesday and today, and I was going to fly back. But then I decided, Sam wants me to see Senator MacIntosh, and I figure sooner or later he'll want me to see Hobie, and I got this idea also, there was a minor possibility that you might be wandering around aimlessly, in search of a considerate escort."

"So you did come a little bit to see me," she said.

"Yes," Cavanaugh said.

"Nope," she said, "I don't buy it. You're just trying to work your way out of a mistake, and I'm not going to let you. For the rest of the night I'm going to be dancing with tears in my eyes. My feelings are still hurt. Where we gonna fuck, anyway?"

"I hate to tell you this, my precious," Cavanaugh said, "but I have an unfortunate war wound which prevents me from consummating the sexual act with any woman whose feelings are hurt. Course, hurt feelings are common. Even the President has them. He thinks the Committee's out to get him."

"Can't fool the Trick, can you?" she said. "No, sir, he knows a cat when he sees one. 'That looks like a cat to me,' he says, quick as you please. He wasn't born yesterday. Are they going to impeach that bastard?"

"Why, Sarah," Cavanaugh said, "impeach the President? Think of the rent that would make in the fabric of society. Why should he be impeached?"

"Because I don't like him," she said. "He's so damned icky-poo and nasty, and he hasn't got any class. He's so

damned tight-asshole and, and *creepy*. That's what he is:
he's creepy. He makes my skin crawl when I see him."

"I thought Julie was great," Cavanaugh said.

"Oh come on," Sarah said, "for standing up for her
father? That makes her a champion? Bullshit. What the
hell kind of girl wouldn't go out and give everybody the
finger that was after her father? That just shows it, what
a crummy state we're in, when everybody goes gaga about
something that any decent person would've expected, because it's a relief to say something nice about somebody
with that last name, it makes us seem so fair, and besides,
you get sick of cheap gloom even if cheap gloom's all that's
available. We're so hungry for classiness now, we'd eat up
Capone if the guy wasn't dead."

"Ah, you New York girls," Cavanaugh said, "why can't
you dance the polka? What in the world has happened to
the traditional values of American life?"

"I was in Jimmy's after the Liberal Party thing the
other night," she said. "Horace told me those goddamned
churchgoers ripped off at least sixty million dollars with
that sideshow they were running, and McGovern couldn't
pay his phone bill."

"They admit to over forty," Cavanaugh said. "I heard
Liddy had fifty Minoltas. Can you imagine that? What the
hell were they doing with fifty cameras? They must've had
Cubans coming up in battalion strength."

"Take pictures of us getting laid and them going to
choir practice and prayer breakfasts," she said. "Goddamned shakedown artists: that's all they are. Michael was
right. 'It's the same fucking thing you've got to do when
you want to park a truck someplace,' he said. 'The first
thing you do is palm somebody a five so you can rent one
with brakes that work. Then you get somebody to drive
the truck, and that's hard because you want a guy that'll

drive the truck where you want the truck driven, instead of stopping off someplace while his buddies take six or eight thousand dollars of your sound equipment out of the back. Then when he gets the truck there, you start asking around until you find the guy you've got to pay off so you can park the truck and unload the equipment, and you better have fifty bucks handy for the kids who watch the truck while he's taking stuff up, because if you don't, he's not going to have very much stuff to take up when he comes back for the second trip. It's the same thing. No difference at all. Just another goddamned hustle.' "

"How's Dan?" Cavanaugh said. "Speaking of hustles."

"Now, now," she said. "Very fine, actually. He really likes private practice, and he's so relieved he's not married to me anymore. . . ."

"With your insatiable sexual desires," Cavanaugh said.

". . . with my insatiable sexual desires," Sarah said, "and so his head's in much better shape now. If Dan could've felt this good, married to me, he'd still be married to me, and I think I'd probably even still be married to him. But of course Eldridge Cleaver was right: I was part of the problem, not part of the solution, and I couldn't *stand* him the way he was, that I made him. You ought to hear him when he gets started on John Mitchell. 'That bastard'd make a snake gag.' "

"I heard Louise was seeing him," he said.

"I didn't," Sarah said. "That'd make things nice and round, though, wouldn't it?"

"It doesn't matter," Cavanaugh said. "I'm not entirely sure Dan's what she needs, but it'd be all right if she was."

"Look, Hank," Sarah said, "you know, I, it's not like I didn't know and everything, or I didn't want to see you."

"I know," he said.

"But I was at Putney with Louise," she said.

"I know," he said. "I meant it. It really doesn't matter. I mean that. What she does is her own business."

"It's not that we're friends or anything," Sarah said. "I don't mean that. If we were friends, I wouldn't care how much you steamed up my glasses, I wouldn't go near you."

"I know," he said.

"I don't even *like* her anymore," she said. "But, I'm kind of jealous of her, I have to admit that. She's got a great thing, working for Springer, and she can get it down, and that gives her lots of money, about double what Michael pays me, and I love plenty of money. Three or four times I damned near accepted the General's offer to come home to my old room and my teddy bears and my checking account with four figures left of the decimal. And Louise is, look, I put this on because I was seeing you, right? An actual dress. I wear Levi's all the time otherwise, even when Michael's genuinely doing something and we're working twenty-eight hours a day, trying to get enough coke and smokes for eight or ten crazy musicians and their friends with sleepy faces and staring eyes and trying at the same time to keep the silly bastards from getting good and busted so we have to refund all the money. I hack around, and I hack around some more, and she's always dashing off here and dashing off there, she's always so well got-up and having lunch at Lutèce, and I envy her. I admit it."

"Actually," Cavanaugh said, "she's fairly disorganized."

"I didn't mean organized," Sarah said. "I'm *very* well organized. I just look like hell a lot of the time. Because I decided a very long time ago that there were only so many things I could do, and a few that I really wanted to do, well, and being Dan's version of the Princess von Furstenburg just wasn't one of them. One of the ones I couldn't do, I mean, and that was important to him."

"Never mind," he said. "You can make afghans."

"That ain't all I can make, sonny," she said. "Rrrrr."

Cavanaugh laughed.

"Another thing I decided," she said, "well, two things, actually, I decided two things. I decided I wasn't going to go around with a dirk in my purse, looking for a clean shot at the back of the woman who's got the deed to the man I want."

"You were the one that was talking about flattery," Cavanaugh said.

"Never mind," she said. "If it makes you even hornier than the thought of my fantastic body by itself, it's perfectly all right. I know just the thing for that condition, and we can repeat the treatment as often as necessary until you feel much, much better.

"But I decided," Sarah said, "I'll take what I can get. If that's dalliance, well, I never had anything against dalliance. And you fall off the branch, well, don't you worry, my friend, I'll catch you before you hit the ground. But I'm knocking nobody off no branch. When you're ripe, you'll fall, and if you never get ripe, well, I'm a big girl now, and I knew what I was getting into."

"So to speak," Cavanaugh said.

"So to speak," she said. "The other thing I decided was that I am not going to be one of those disgusting harpies that fly around this town making fools of themselves cutting up their ex-husbands every time the poor bastards go out and get laid. I'm very relaxed about my Daniel, now, much more so'n when I was married to him. If he's getting his rocks off, it's all right with me, although I do think he ought to provide the names of three male friends or an instrument suitably shaped to any normally healthy woman who becomes involved with him. So, if my Daniel and your Louise're being naughty, I'm the worst person in the world to ask about it, because I'm just chock-a-block full of charity for all of them, and malice toward none. Okay?"

"Okay," Cavanaugh said.

"Now," she said, "on to more important things."

"Like some more Jack Daniels," Cavanaugh said.

" 'An Irish queer,' " Sarah said, " 'likes women better'n booze.' Where're you staying? What I really mean, is, are we going over to my loft again because you're at the Commodore like the last time, like some goddamned salesman?"

"Now that isn't fair," Cavanaugh said. "I had to stay there. I went to Boston on the plane and we couldn't land, and I came back and there weren't any seats on the train, and the Commodore was the nearest place to check into. You're not going to beat me up for a snowstorm, are you?"

"Just so you know," Sarah said. "I'm a respectable young woman. I went to Bennington and my mother tells me I was well brought up, and the likes of us do not engage in adulterous liaisons at the Commodore."

"Nobody expected you to," Cavanaugh said. "But for appearance's sake, I thought I ought to leave my bags somewhere, and at least register. Louise hasn't got your sense of delicacy, my dearest. She's mentioned your name in sharp tones to me, once or twice, and I fear she might prove very strident indeed if it turned out I was snowbound at your place instead of barging in on her roommates, full of airline booze and apologies."

"I don't know how she can stand that," Sarah said, "living with those women. How the hell can you get laid?"

"She's always lived with Tenley," Cavanaugh said. "Ever since I can remember, at least. Her husband's never around. He's in Teheran with Anglo-Iranian Oil. I think she got pregnant by Telex. The other one, I don't know. I never met her, and I've got no desire to."

"The last time I had a roommate was in college," Sarah said, "a mean little vixen who used to go through my underwear, and I knew it, and I caught her at it one day, and I said: 'All right, Mary Beth, you little shit, what're you looking for?' 'Shampoo,' she said. 'I don't keep shampoo with my panties,' I said," Sarah said. "I know what she was looking for. She was looking for my diary, which she knew I must be keeping, and using to record the most intimate details of my personal life, because I truthfully assured her that I never kept one. She conked out by ten thirty every night, and she used to complain about the light, and I'd tell her I wasn't tired, and I was going to stay up and read Dylan Thomas, or William Butler Yeats, or whoever it was that I happened to like to be reading at the time, which was true, and that's how she knew I was keeping a diary and probably sliding down the drainpipe to get material while she was resting her complexion and preserving her hymen. She married a kid who looks just like a pear, just exactly like a pear. A pear-shaped math PhD from Yale named Louis. Never Louie. Louis. 'Louis and I went to the Paradise,' and 'Louis and I went to the symphony,' and I didn't think you were supposed to dislike people then, so I only thought of him as Gaspar the Magnificent, and I never called him that, to her, and Louis got on the faculty at MIT and Mary Beth had seven children and they all live in Andover and have people in for sherry. I was in her wedding because I was being polite, and all the time I was in it I was thinking: 'I will never have a roommate again, as long as I live, unless it's a man with an enormous cock.' Daniel met half of the specs. And I never have. Which brings me back to it: where are we gonna go to fuck?"

"I'm staying here," Cavanaugh said. "Your place or my place, doesn't matter to me. I'd like a little dinner first, the jug of wine and the customary loaf of bread before thee, but the house dick's tolerant of everything short of currency changing hands for services rendered, so you can choose."

"Perigord East," she said, "and here. I am really impressed. I'm going to have dinner in a real restaurant, and I'm going to get laid at the Plaza. You know I never got laid at the Plaza in my whole life?"

"Sarah," Cavanaugh said, "this may surprise you. No, I didn't. But then neither've I, so we start off even, at least."

"I got laid in a Porsche once," she said.

"*That* surprises me," Cavanaugh said. "Those things're small. How'd you manage it?"

"It was my first time," she said. "A sixteen-hundred Spyder. And I didn't manage. I was managed. Have you got a suite?"

"Hey," he said, "I work for the government, remember? I get twenty-five dollars a day for travel. It's costing me forty-three just to stay here. You think I'm made of money or something?"

"When Dan was with Anti-Trust," she said, "we came up here and stayed at the Biltmore, and we couldn't afford that, even. No, I can see that. You wouldn't have a suite."

"They gave me a small linen closet," Cavanaugh said, "into which some evil genius has contrived to put a bed. It's painted light green and I can't shut the radiator off."

"Never mind," she said, "it's better'n the park. The nights've been getting chilly."

"There hasn't been a helluva lot to recommend the days," he said.

"Bad shit?" she said.

"Ahhh," he said, "I saw Jess on Nantucket a couple weeks ago. I saw Hobie this afternoon. I'm seeing people because, I think when you get right down to it, because Sam has me on the road trying to make wishful thinking into thinking, and seeing Hobie and Jess only makes me sadder."

"Hobie's all right," Sarah said. "I haven't seen Jess in a hundred years, but Hobie's got a townhouse and a place at the Hamptons, and Elaine's positively radiant these days. I hate Elaine. Did I ever tell you I hate Elaine?"

"No," he said, "but I don't know Elaine, so it wouldn't matter."

"Goddamn her," Sarah said. "Elaine looked good when she was pregnant, the bitch. And then she had the baby, and one week later, *one fucking week*, I went out there —this was long before I knew you, darling—with this Englishman named Thomas who practically put me in a coma, he was so tiresome, and I went skinny-dipping at Rachel Osgood's party and got rid of him, and Elaine was on the beach in a bikini and she looked marvelous. I hate her."

"Is there any way," Cavanaugh said, "you can wear a bikini and still not have some white on your tits if you've been out in the sun a long time?"

"How big a bikini?" Sarah said.

"Doesn't matter," Cavanaugh said.

"Sure it does," Sarah said. "You could have a real little one, that'd probably get you arrested if you wore it on a beach, and if you had real big aureoles, or whatever they are around your nipples, you might not."

"Assume small nipples," Cavanaugh said. "Moderately small nipples, anyway. Regular-size nipples."

"Um," Sarah said. "No."

"That's what I thought," he said.

"I just got somebody in trouble, I think," she said. "Not that I mind."

"I called up Jack," the first one said. "I called him up. I said: 'Jack, tell me what to do. I don't want to do nothing I shouldn't. I don't want to skip doing something I should. Am I telling you something I shouldn't be?'

"He says," the first one said, "he says: 'No, how the hell can you be telling me something you shouldn't, you didn't even tell me anything? Tell me what you want to tell me.'

"I said: 'Jack,' " the first one said, "I said: 'At first I thought it was the gambling. I tried to talk him out of it.'

"He says: 'Mel, do me a favor: don't talk him out of it. Kid made close to a hundred grand the last year, gambling. Leave him alone. I used to wish he was taller. He's not a bad basketball player when he's a kid. Now I'm glad. Couldn't make anywhere near what he makes, he was Bill Bradley, he makes what he makes on the gambling.'

"I said: 'Jack, you gotta listen to me. Nobody wins all the time, gambling. He's gonna start losing, he'll clean me out. What do I do?'

" 'Some people gamble and win,' Jack says to me. 'Leave him alone. He gets enough so he can buy you out, sell out. Come down here. Play a little golf. Live like a human being for a change.'

"That was two and a half years ago," Mel said. "I been as nervous as a pregnant woman ever since. All the time I was thinking, he's gonna be in the cash accounts. He's gonna take customers' stock and sell it. He's gonna do this, he's gonna do that. I watch them books like a hawk, like I never did before, and I watched those books before.

"You know what I did?" Mel said. "I cut over nine thousand dollars a year out of overhead, watching those books. I got myself a two percent increase in profits, watching that kid. He's buying, he's selling, I'm scared to death he's gonna get accused of churning accounts, he's on the phone all the time, in the past year, in the past two years, since I called Jack, the book value of the business's gone up over a hundred and forty thousand dollars. A hundred and forty. Because I did the guy a favor, when he asked me. In April, we got it all planned out, the kid's buying me out. He's got the financing, I'm getting two-point-eight for it and I never thought it was worth over one-and-a-half in my whole life. I'm gonna retire ten years before I expected. I'm gonna have a nice time."

"You wanna retire, already?" Eddie said.

"No, I don't," Mel said. "But I wanna be rich when I do. He can't keep this up, the kid. Sooner or later, I know human nature, he's gonna take a bath and it's gonna take the business to get him out of it. The business I built, with my own hands. I'd rather, it was his when it goes, and I'm rich and in Florida all the time, it was mine and it went and I hadda be poor up here. He used to take out my Lisa. I didn't encourage it, I didn't discourage it, I made it clear to him, doesn't make a bit of difference to me, you marry her, you don't. Business is business. And she's a difficult kid. I told him, we signed the papers? Because I love that child. I said: 'Now on, Mister Jack Junior, stay away from my daughter, all right?'

" 'All right,' he says, 'but I can ask you: how come?'

" 'My daughters,' " Mel said, "I told him: 'My daughters, I love. Can't refuse them things, they ask me. I don't want Lisa coming around, five years from now, telling me I got to sell out myself and her mother, cover your losses.'

" 'Never happen,' he says. 'It'll happen,' I said. 'It always happens.' I love Jack. Jack don't agree with me. 'You don't agree with me. It's all right. I still think I'm right. I been around a long time. Do what I say.' And he did."

"No," Cavanaugh said, "you didn't get anybody in trouble. It's just a matter of finding out what happens to people, and I'm doing it. But sometimes, I don't like it."

"All right," Cavanaugh said, "I'll start near the border and work my way down, if that's all right with you."

6

Sam Barry leaned back in his chair and steepled his fingers. "First tell me," he said, "is there any good news, is there going to be any good news in this?"

"All information is valuable," Cavanaugh said. " 'It's a fact of history that there is such a thing as bad news. In the reign of a tyrant, the messengers who bring it are killed. In a democracy such as ours, I remain confident that its transmission is a service. I have bad news for you tonight. We are still in Vietnam. Shall the people who report that, as the bad news it is, be silenced? Or shall we return to Washington to put a stop to the arrogance of power which creates that news?' "

"I suppose I asked for that," Barry said. "I didn't like it all that well when Steve put it in my mouth. He has a tendency to be florid. But I have to admit, it got a big reception at Faneuil Hall."

"All right then," Cavanaugh said. "There being no such thing as bad information, I have some information for you."

"Let me put it another way, then," Sam Barry said. "Is there anything I'm going to like in what you've got to tell me, or did you blow five or six hundred bucks to pick up a lot of stuff I don't want to hear?"

"I think it's probably closer to four hundred," Cavanaugh said. "I was only gone four days, you know, and I was awful busy. I didn't really have time to run up a good voucher."

"Yeah," Barry said. "Well, all right, would you do me this much of a favor? Would you make something up so I can feel good? If it wasn't for bad news around here this week, there wouldn't be any news at all."

"What the hell happened?" Cavanaugh said. "I talked to Ellen and Sylvia every day, at least twice. They didn't say anything."

"Ahh," Barry said, "it's nothing. And it's a combination of everything. After coitus, all animals are sad. I don't know. The country's getting screwed. It's just being neglected, and nobody seems to be capable of or interested in doing anything about it. All you hear is impeachment. That's all anybody ever thinks about, it's all anybody ever talks about. Dawson's Most Favored Nation amendment bill came up in committee Tuesday, and she's really busted her ass on that thing. LaSallette's against it. He says it'll beat the daylights out of about six major industries, and four of them have plants in his district. They've both got sound reasons for their positions. I love to hear Jane when she's worked up about something; she has the measurements down to micromillimeters, and she can tell you anything you want to know about it, even if it's what'll happen to the humpback whale population if we do it. Roland's an old fart, of course. . . ."

"I was going to say," Cavanaugh said.

"Where we really went astray, he thinks," Barry said, "was when we didn't make George Washington king. But he's a smart old fart, and he's just as honest as you can be.

" 'Fellow came in to see me a couple weeks ago,' Roland said," Barry said, " 'foreign fellow. Comes from Spain, I think he said. Spain. Said I ought to visit Spain, was what he said. Take a look at the place. I should broaden my outlook. Said I ought to do that. Don't want to become *provin*cial, was what he said. Said I ought to go there.

" 'They make,' Roland said, 'quite a lot of shoes in Spain,' " Barry said. " 'I'm told that, at least. I understand they sell a few of them in Indianapolis. Why, they may even be selling them in Detroit. Perhaps the Congressperson would care to address herself to that point.' "

"Which serves Jane right for beating that feminist rug of hers when the Draft bill came up," Cavanaugh said.

"He's never called her anything else since," Barry said. "Oh, he's an old curmudgeon if there ever was one. 'Then, I think it was about a week ago, another foreign fellow came in to see me.' Of course he's got State all in a lather with his foreign fellows. Every time he says that in public, they call him up, because of course the foreign fellows take umbrage at being called foreign fellows, and call State about it, so State calls Roland. They should know better. There's nothing he'd like better than America for Americans, no foreign fellows here and no foreign aid going out over there, all American cars and American textiles and American hardware. He loves goosing State. He still thinks Dean Acheson was a dupe of international, atheistic, godless Communism. Could not understand, when I first came down here, how somebody from Richard Cardinal Cushing's archdiocese could advocate 'appeasement' of those Communist devils. 'Look at Drinan,' I told him.

"He went to the funeral, you know, the Cardinal's funeral? LaSallette went up to that and sat at the back of the cathedral while the very humble priest of God was uttering the obsequies. No publicity, no nothing. They cranked the old man's hat up into the rafters with the tassels on it, and every politician in the known world was there, including myself, and on the way out, there was Roland, sitting at the back, and his eyes were wet.

"You've got to look out for Roland," Barry said, "he's mossbacked and close to a fascist, but he's perfectly sincere and he's not scared of anything. He does things because he believes in them. There's no percentage in a Congressman from Nebraska going to Boston for the Cardinal's funeral unless he's doing it for publicity, and Roland did it so I don't think anybody but me knew he was there. And he wouldn't look at me when I saw him.

" 'A gentleman from Italy, it was, and he wanted to take me to lunch,' Roland said. 'At Sans Souci, where all the swells hang out, I am informed, but I told him I preferred my usual noonday repast of tomato soup and a common cracker, and invited him to state his business on the spot. Well, it appears that they also make shoes in Italy, along with automobiles, some of which find their way to these shores, to compete with our domestic products.' "

"Good Lord," Cavanaugh said, "does the Cadillac Division know they're building Ferraris over there, and shipping, say, a hundred or so of them here every year, for people who wouldn't touch a Cad with a stick?"

"I think it was Fiats that worried him," Sam Barry said. "Fiats and shoes with brass hardware on the insteps.

" 'It was only a day or so later,' Roland said, 'when a caller from Taiwan waited upon my convenience. He had barely departed, somewhat downcast, I might add, when a trio of visitors from Japan arrived to solicit a few moments of my time. All of them addressed themselves to the problems of electronics manufacturers who make products in their countries and ship them to our country, for presumable retail sale. I gather that they simultaneously contrive to return great profits, high employment, and remarkable prestige to these nations, while existing in a gravely precarious economic situation which will put them out of business if the United States of America obliges them to compete on equal terms with Motorola, Zenith, General Electric, and a host of other firms which pay minimum wages set by this Congress over my strenuous objections, upon which the recipients are obliged in their turn to pay taxes levied at what I believe to be nothing short of confiscatory rates.' "

"The last time I looked at my Magnavox," Cavanaugh said, "I think I saw something about how it was made in Hong Kong, or someplace."

"Oh, of course," Barry said. "Roland exaggerates shamefully what helps him, and somehow overlooks what hurts him, and he's been here so long he's become convinced that he's the reincarnation of the prairie Pericles, so he has to talk like he lived in Charleston, South Carolina, all his life, sitting out between the mansion pillars on the veranda, reading Gibbon to improve his mind. But he still has a legitimate point there, and Jane knows it. And Jane's got very heavy artillery on balance of payments and currency devaluation and how we're getting our tails whipped on the West German mark and the Swiss franc, and Roland knows that. And we all know that sooner or later we're going to have to tackle the thing, and we better start now, so we're ready to listen to them, and we ought to start sharpening the issues so we can finish in a couple weeks, make a little progress on this, and report out something substantial that people can get their teeth into. Like we did with War Powers, the first time. Let's get the sense of the Congress. Never mind which way it goes. Let's have forward motion.

"I came out of there," Barry said, "and I was going over to play a little handball with Homer, and I ran into Godwin coming out the other door. Gale'd just heard the same things I'd heard, and the first words out of his mouth were: 'The guy's really in bad trouble with those tapes, Sam.' Now Gale's a Republican, and he's running in a firm Republican district, and if it turned out the Beast of Buchenwald was actually a card-carrying Republican, it wouldn't hurt Gale. And he's a genuine, legitimate guy that doesn't agree with me on a solitary thing and couldn't be more gentlemanly about it. If that's all Gale can think about, we're sure not going to get very far with some of the others. Most of the others."

"Sam," Cavanaugh said, "nobody said you've got to like it. But you might as well come to terms with it. It's the first thing anybody asks you when you sit down with them, and when you try to talk about something else, it's like trying to discuss cryogenics with a whorehouse madam on a busy night. They keep coming back to the business at hand. I saw Brilliant, Monday."

"He wasn't on the list," Barry said. "Not that I object. I should've thought of him."

"He was up seeing Marsh at East Harbor," Cavanaugh said.

"I thought Joe was in Portland," Barry said.

"Joe's teaching in Portland," Cavanaugh said. "That's the theory, anyway. He goes in not very often. He's up there freezing his ass off already in a winterized summer house that his wife's family owns, and what he's really doing is writing a book and living off them and fifteen thousand a year from the university that doesn't care if he shows or not, so long's he's on the faculty in the Government Department. Brilliant was visiting Joe because Don's got an advance that he already spent to write a book of his own and he's kind of short of ideas. 'So he's up here trying to raid my brains,' Joe said, and Don said: 'I'm up here loafing. I've been here a week and I could pick your brains clean in an hour and a half.'

" 'I came up here,' Joe said, 'I drove across the bridge at Kittery and I thought to myself: "Now I have got it wrapped, I am going to be a goddamn authority, I'm going to think large thoughts and write prose that'll make students come in their pants. Not since Alexander Hamilton was there anything like Joe Marsh for explaining the American system." '

" 'Well,' Joe said, 'what I should've done was hang about forty pounds of gelignite on those pilings and blow that goddamned bridge sky-high, and then go out in a lobster boat and yank all the nuns and cans so nobody in boats could come in here, because I have had nothing but callers since I arrived. Here I am in this godforsaken place, and all I get's a continuing stream of visitors come to drink my booze and keep me up late and I haven't had a minute's peace since I got here, for Christ sake. It's no goddamned wonder Paul Travis wanted to be President, he was living up here and people're bugging him all the time. Must've spent a winter here sometime. I'd run in Uganda if I was in that position myself. I'm going back to New York.'"

"What does he think?" Barry said.

"He thinks it won't work, he's not a bit sure that it should work, and he doesn't plan to waste his time on it," Cavanaugh said. "I think that about covers his reaction."

"In other words," Barry said, "he's washed up and he likes being washed up."

"Look," Cavanaugh said, "Joe went down the line a year ago, he went down the line in '68, he did exactly the right thing when Bobby jumped in. He's a hundred and ten percent on what he's done already. You can't knock Joe."

"I can knock anybody I want," Barry said. "Happens, I don't want to knock anybody. I'm not even mad at John Dean and the rest of them. All I'm saying is, we can't spend the next three years discussing whether Nixon called Kleindienst a cocksucker. There's enough people wasting their time on that stuff as it is, and while they're doing it, the days are going by. What difference does it make if they can prove it? If they start hating him in Des Plaines like they hate him in Cambridge, and finally even Roland's got to vote to throw the bum out, what'll that get us? Jerry Ford, to gum things up the same way he's doing, and that'll give us a choice between Jackson and Ford. *Which I do not want.* Joe shouldn't want it, either, and if he does, he's not the same guy I used to know, that made those miners in West Virginia vote for a goddamned Catholic because all of a sudden somebody told them about their responsibility to the country instead of telling them how they were all going to make a thousand dollars a week because somebody was for the working man. I'm going to call him up." Barry pushed the intercom button on his phone.

"Sam," Cavanaugh said, "don't call him up. It's not like

he had a monopoly on what he thinks. Don Brilliant said the same thing. 'I'm glad I was up here, interfering with Joe when you came up to interfere with Joe. Saves you asking me. I agree with Joe.' "

"And you put it to Joe in those terms," Barry said.

"I did," Cavanaugh said, "and he put it right back to me. He doesn't have the slightest complaint about your position that somebody needs to do something, that whoever it is should get started now, and all the rest of it. He just says Travis is not the man now, he isn't going to be the man in '76, he can't be, he shouldn't be, and he won't be."

"Who else, then?" Barry said. "Did you ask him that, to suggest somebody else?"

" 'You know what I haven't done?' he said," Cavanaugh said. " 'I haven't even thought about it. And I'm not going to think about it, either. I'm going to get my work, *my* work, not somebody else's, done. For a change. Anybody that's making up a small party to go to Jerusalem this year's going to have to accept my sincere regrets, because I'm not coming. I'm not packed, and I'm not packing, either.'

"Then I went to Boston," Cavanaugh said, "and I saw the estimable Mister Fogarty, the Right Honorable Secretary of the Commonwealth."

"Fogarty too," Barry said.

"Fogarty also," Cavanaugh said. "Fogarty was worse, actually. He's so damned nebulous about everything, and he's got two ways of dealing with people and I don't like that. In the North End all he talks about is Truth in Labeling and he'll stop the Port Authority from expanding the airport, by God, and making those airplanes fly over all those beautiful Italian-American children so they can't sleep. Then he goes down to the Policemen's Ball and says mean things about the Mafia, and he's bound and determined to do everything *he* can to protect them with the finest equipment and pay scales in their courageous war against crime in the streets. On the way to see them, he stops off at the vault and tells the Wasp bankers how he'll crack down on welfare cheaters when he's AG, they can be damned sure of that, and the next day he's speaking to a small group of militant women at the African Methodist Episcopal Church in Roxbury and telling them there's no excuse for malnutrition and intolerable living conditions in a country as rich as ours, and furthermore, nobody better short-weight the black homemaker when he gets in office, he'll guarantee that. In the suburbs he's very concerned about narcotics and very much opposed to the anti-snob zoning law, and he can easily understand that there's not a smidgeon of bigotry and bias in the way they feel, they're just understandably concerned about property values and the rising real-estate tax. But the guy thinks that he's going to be AG in '75, and he plans to be governor in '79, and when I look around, I'm not sure he's wrong."

"He's very adroit," Barry said.

"Mike Fogarty walks between raindrops," Cavanaugh said. "You go to his old pals in the House and you won't find one of them that's willing to budge in any direction until they find out which way he's going. It's the same with the guys in the Senate. He's got his buddy Leon Donnelly absolutely entrenched as Senate President, and he's got his tame black, Casper Mellon, waiting right behind Lennie for when Lennie gets his judgeship, all ready to become the showcase mealy-mouthed bastard he's always wanted to be."

"Casper's an ebony nonentity," Barry said. "If he were white, he'd be out of work and badgering people to remember all the times he fetched doughnuts and coffee and picked up the laundry for them and drove their wives places, so they should give him a clerkship in Dorchester District Court and pay no attention if he didn't show up for work."

"Yeah," Cavanaugh said, "but try and get Casper to do something Mike wouldn't like. Casper calls Mike before he goes to the bathroom, see if it's all right with Mike, and if Mike said it wasn't, Casper'd figure he didn't really have to go anyway. In the Secretary's office they genuflect when Mike comes in, and they tug their forelocks when he leaves."

"I know it," Barry said. "When he wants you on his side, he's mild as milk. When he gets you where he wants you, and you know you can't get out, he acts just like Caligula. Linda's uncle introduced himself to Mike when he took over as Secretary, and he said Mike looked at him and said: 'As long as you do your job, it won't matter who your niece's married to, and if you don't do your job, it won't matter then, either.' He pretends he invented integrity, when all he is is a natural-born prick that cultivated his congenital advantages."

"The ACLU doesn't trust him," Cavanaugh said. "Nobody trusts him, really. I talked to Courtney and he said the ADA's not ready to do anything yet, until they decide if there's anybody in the state who can beat Fogarty. 'And suppose you find somebody that maybe can do it?' I said. 'A maybe's not good enough,' Courtney said. 'It's got to be a guy that we *know* can do it, for sure. Otherwise we either go with Fogarty, which of course means we're probably stuck with Walton for governor for another four years, or we stay out of it entirely. Which of course also means we can look forward to another four years of industrial development, mass transit improvements, and aid to higher education that won't attract five manufacturers, build eight miles of subways, or complete a single campus that wasn't started six years ago. And the *Globe*'s in the same box we're in.' I didn't run into one single person who liked Mike."

"Must be you didn't talk to Mike, then," Barry said.

"I did talk to Mike," Cavanaugh said. "We had lunch in his office. I suggested the Charles, just to see what he'd say. Or the Parker House or Dini's. Goodness no, he was way too busy. Things to do, promises to keep, miles to go before he sleeps. Besides, he's not sure if the Mayor's really serious about not running, yet, and he doesn't want to be seen with me until he finds out."

"Is Kevin?" Barry said.

"I hope not," Cavanaugh said. "He couldn't beat the other guy in his own backyard three years ago, and I don't think he can beat him next year, either. Nothing's changed that much."

"Rich Williams's been calling me," Barry said.

"He told me that," Cavanaugh said. "See, I wasn't going to let Fogarty keep me in the closet, and I wasn't getting anywhere with him and I still wouldn't leave. He got very fidgety, because everybody in the world could see I wasn't getting anyplace, and I was still there, and finally he said he had an appointment, and I asked him where, and he said down on State Street, and so I dreamed up this extraordinary coincidence that I had one on Franklin Street myself and I'd walk him down there. 'Who with?' he said, which is the kind of mousetrap you get yourself into when you spend all your time scheming and believing everybody else's scheming too, and I said, having set him up: 'Hey, Mike, these things're confidential. You know that. You wouldn't want me telling everybody I was seeing you, and what about.'

"He got it down," Cavanaugh said. " 'Hell, Hank,' he says, the good-fellowship bit, 'I'm out in the open. I appreciate your discretion, but don't worry about me, you know.'

"So," Cavanaugh said, "I was a little late meeting Mahoney, but it didn't matter. Especially after I told him how come. And on the way down to State Street, who do we run into but Rich Williams, coming out of the Golden Dome. Oh, you should've seen Fogarty then. In the office he wouldn't tell me if the sun was out, or even if he was in favor of the sun coming out. But when we saw Rich, well: 'Here's my old buddy, Cavanaugh. I love him better'n my mother.' "

"Did you talk to Rich?" Barry said.

"Just 'Hello' and 'How are you?' and I also threw him a 'Good ta *see* ya,' which Rich thought was funny but Mike thought was normal. 'I didn't see ya at Donovan's time,' Rich says. 'I was down at the bathhouse,' I says, 'the annual get-together for the Knights and Ladies of Saint Finnbar, dere was dancin' dere till two A.M. and da pastor was joinin' right in wid da rest of us, we all went ta Benediction before, and we had us some drinks and a small collation. It was a grand time. Nobody brought dere dogs.'

"Mike got it then," Cavanaugh said. "He didn't like it a bit, either. Making fun of the old tads: he don't approve of it."

"Mike ought to talk to the tads sometime," Barry said. "No, listen to the tads sometime, instead of firing them up all the time to be hating the niggers. They think it's great."

"He's too jumpy for that," Cavanaugh said. "Like as

not, somebody'd come along and catch him having a good time and start a lot of talk. So Rich says: 'What're you doing in town? Stealing something?' 'Singing and dancing Sam's way into your hearts,' I said. 'Good,' Rich said, 'have the bastard return my call when you see him. That'll go a long way toward it.'"

"So I suppose that means I've got to call him back," Barry said.

"It wouldn't be a bad idea," Cavanaugh said. "Pretty soon, too. 'Sam must've been awful busy lately.'"

"Yeah," Barry said. "Jesus, what do I tell him? I think the world of Rich. If Rich wanted me to come out for Stalin, I'd have to give it some serious thought. But that car dealer? I don't know."

"Rich doesn't like Walton," Cavanaugh said.

"Ingrate that he is," Barry said. "The governor made his idiot cousin a judge and the guy's been a conspicuous fool ever since. Can't understand why Rich feels that way."

"He also doesn't like what he sees winding up to run against Walton," Cavanaugh said, "and he was on the Governor's Council long enough so he hasn't got very many illusions left about what you can do with the regular party. Maybe he's right. He does have his enthusiasms."

"Albright's attractive enough," Barry said. "There's no question about that. And from what John Clancy tells me, he has good recognition, for a guy that never ran for anything."

"What've they got?" Cavanaugh said. "Another Becker Poll coming out?"

"Yeah," Barry said. "It'll be in Monday's *Globe*. Kevin looks a hell of a lot stronger'n he did a year ago."

"That's the Vice-Presidential thing again," Cavanaugh said. "Jesus, for a guy that was excused through no fault of his own from going down with the ship, he sure got a lot of good out of it."

"And Albright's only two points behind him," Barry said.

"Goodness gracious," Cavanaugh said. "Does anybody know what he stands for besides more highways?"

"Sure," Barry said. "Same thing as everybody else that never ran for anything before. Good government. What else?"

"Watergate, Watergate, who's got the Watergate?" Cavanaugh said.

"You know," Barry said, "when I first heard it was Vatican money that built it, I was kind of amused. Then the Vatican sold it, and I was scared. They're always acting like they're plugged in on a hot line to God. Maybe they are. Maybe they know something I don't, and they're unloading fast on account of it. Well, now I've got it, and everybody else that ran before, and won, has got it, and I'm beginning to think I should pay closer attention to what Monsignor Lally writes in *The Pilot*, and maybe subscribe to *L'Osservatore Romano*."

"Or else," Cavanaugh said, "call Rich. Maybe he's right. Maybe his guy can actually win."

"Tomorrow morning," Barry said.

"Tonight," Cavanaugh said. "He works late. You have to work late to drag in the kind of money he does. For the kind of candidates he drags it in for."

"Now, Henry," Barry said, " 'there is nothing so powerful as an idea whose time has come.' "

"Particularly," Cavanaugh said, "when the idea in question's got Rich Williams and his squadrons of fifty-dollar givers who don't expect anything from the guy except decency and hard work."

"True," Barry said.

"Maybe Rich'd like to put a little heat on Fogarty, too, if you called him," Cavanaugh said.

"I doubt it," Barry said. "For a vestryman at King's Chapel, he's a surprisingly aggressive fellow, but putting on heat's just not something Rich does very well. No, I'll call him, and let him do what he wants to me, because he insisted on me doing what I wanted to him, and that's fair. Now let's have the rest of the bad news."

"Harold Mahoney says we're in the wrong line of work," Cavanaugh said. "I saw the place he was in and I had to agree with him."

"You've got to have a hell of a practice for an office like that," Barry said. "I couldn't spend that much time cuddling up to old ladies and railroad executives."

"Office, hell," Cavanaugh said. "I'm not talking about his office. I'm talking about his new little hideaway."

"What happened to the place on the Hill?" Barry said.

" 'I got sick of living with the rats,' he said," Cavanaugh said. " 'The Swedenborgians're nice people, but they don't really approve of people coming and going at all hours of the day and night in their building, even if the people are coming to see you in your apartment. And the back was full of rats all the time. When it got dull, I bought an air-pistol, one of those Crossmans that runs on CO_2, and I'd plink at them. It wasn't bad fun. But I figured, sooner or later, one of those rats is going to learn to climb stairs or run elevators, and he'll teach the rest of them, and then Billy Raymond'll get a ratbite on the ass when he's up here some night poking some bimbo. I did it for Billy, and also for me and the firm. I run a dignified operation. I can't have my litigator standing up all the time because he's got rodent bites on his ass, when you ask him to step in and tell some discombobulated woman why she can't sue her estranged husband for divorce on the grounds that he refuses to take out the trash.'

"He's got about fifty-five rooms in the Commonwealth Towers," Cavanaugh said. "And it's done up like, I never saw anything done up like it is before. It's beautiful. He has a wall that looks like, I don't know, he told me what it was, polished bronze plates, I guess, and you sit there with the real city fifty floors or so down and the skyline and everything, and that's on your right, and on your left, you're sitting in these Eames chairs, the leather strato-buckets, there's this wall and there's the skyline in gold. It's gorgeous. No wonder Billy makes out up there. The Hunchback of Notre Dame could make out in that place."

"Billy's stood up remarkably well," Barry said.

" 'Someday,' " Cavanaugh said, "Mahoney said: some-day he's going to make a movie. 'If it's a dirty movie,' he said, 'Billy's going to be the chief stud. If it's a political movie, he's gonna play the senior Senator from New York. If it's about priests, he's going to be the Cardinal Arch-bishop from San Francisco.' "

"He never did that," Barry said, "until he made the try and lost. When I first knew Billy, I was in knee pants, and he was straight as the Anti-Saloon League."

"That's what Mahoney was saying," Cavanaugh said. " 'Can you imagine the torment it must've been for him to keep his pants zipped when he thought he might be AG? It's a blessing that he lost. He'd have prostate trouble long since if he hadn't.' "

"Is Harold with us, at least?" Barry said. "You tell me he isn't, and I may kill myself on national TV tomorrow."

"Harold is with us," Cavanaugh said. " 'Oh sure,' he said to me, 'I'm just like Billy's girls. All you have to do is ask me politely, and I'm yours until death do us part. Or at least for tonight, anyway, since I got to go to Syracuse tomorrow to get somebody else's hat blocked.' "

"Well," Barry said, "that's a help, at least."

" 'Not that it's going to help you much,' " Cavanaugh said, " 'having me with you. Twenty years ago, when Sam's dad and I had the Commonwealth pretty much to ourselves, it might've done you some good. But I'm just an old warhorse these days, and I'm seldom invited to the Tavern Club for lunch anymore.' "

"He's right," Barry said. "He was really all through when Paul Dever died, although I guess both of them thought they could survive it. Then Raymond's brother got himself indicted, and that really did them in. Even they knew it, then. When he went to Danbury, they were sunk. They might as well have gone down there with him, sorted mail and played softball for two years. My father, at least. That just about broke his old heart. I think it did break his heart."

"What'd Raymond's brother do, anyway?" Cavanaugh said.

"I never really knew Bruce," Barry said. "My father wouldn't talk about it when I was old enough to see that something must've happened, and I was too young to understand it when it was going on.

"It was an embezzlement of some kind. I gather he was executor of an estate, or part of an estate, anyway, and the beneficiary was a widow who lived in Connecticut whose husband'd been very successful with investments in Boston. Bruce was one of his lawyers, and he probated the will in Massachusetts and took care of things for her when she wanted something done. Then I guess she went a little dippy or something, and Bruce was conservator for some of her property, and he started, bit by bit, converting it.

"Stocks and bonds, I think it was, one of those damned trusts that I could never figure out, had land and corporation shares and bonds and everything so complicated that the only way in the world you could possibly enjoy it is to be the one who puts out his hand and takes the money it makes, and let somebody else spend all his time burrowing through the papers. Well, Bruce'd take the certificates out of the safety deposit box, and he'd clip the coupons the way he was supposed to, and send them in, but then when he went back to the box, he'd leave some of the certificates on his desk. He was selling them through some ferret-faced weasel in New York who got away clean, because they were bearer certificates and there was no way anybody could prove he knew they didn't belong to Bruce. But it wasn't tough to pin it on Bruce. Interstate transportation of stolen property. Sneaking down there on the Owl, ducking people he knew when they saw him at Back Bay Station with his briefcase.

"And the funny part of it was," Barry said, "nobody could ever quite understand why the hell Bruce did it." He got up and began to pace. "He had plenty of money of his own. The Raymonds bought stock very shrewdly in the twenties, and sold it just as shrewdly in 1928, and they owned land and gold and sat pretty while everybody else was auctioning off their Duesenbergs. It seemed to be just something he thought he was entitled to do, convinced that the rules didn't apply to him. He told my father that the dead fellow always intended to make Bruce a partner as well as his lawyer, and there was considerably more in the pot than the old lady'd ever need, no other heirs, so it wasn't hurting anybody and Bruce was only taking what would've been his if the guy hadn't died before he gave it to him. I think he was using it to buy up land on the Cape and he made himself land-poor, so he had to use somebody else's money along with his own.

"Quite a lot of it, too. I think it was about three, I don't know, three hundred thousand dollars, by the time the CPAs got through comparing what was actually in the box and what was supposed to be in there. They got a lot of it back, selling off the land, but it was forced sale, and everybody knew it, and I guess Bruce was, he'd been so obsessed with buying up everything that he didn't bargain like he should've, and paid a good deal more for what he got than it was actually worth. So I think after he sold everything he had, and paid his lawyers—he had Mortimer Haskins, and ten or twenty of Mort's associates, and it was a long trial and Mortimer didn't cross the street even in those days for less than thirty thousand dollars—he was still about seventy-five or eighty thousand dollars short.

"So," Barry said, "that was when Harold Mahoney and my father paid their dues for being made successful men by the Raymonds. Harold made up most of it; my father was on the bench then, and he really didn't have the kind of money that he made when he was in practice, which would've been enough, what he'd accumulated, to keep him comfortable on a judge's salary. But he insisted on kicking in, too, because he said they put him where he was and his troubles would've been their troubles if he'd ever had any, and so theirs were his.

"It wasn't only Bruce that lost property on the Cape in that transaction," Barry said. "And they disbarred him after he got convicted, Bruce, which wasn't a bad idea but it wasn't always the practice then. They had a really hard-assed prosecutor on the case and he wouldn't let Bruce up even after the money was paid back, and when he came out he was just another sad old man, and so were all his friends. It was like a blight. But I'm still glad that Harold's aboard."

" 'You can count on me for my usual contribution to hopeless causes,' he told me," Cavanaugh said.

"Twenty-five thousand dollars," Barry said. "Well, that's fine. It'd be finer if it was the old Harold that was giving it, because then it'd pry up some of the floorboards in some of the other countinghouses in this country, but it's not, so we'll take it for something we can count on that's a hell of a lot better than nothing. Unless Harold dies."

"He looked healthy enough to me," Cavanaugh said.

"Well," Barry said, "we won't ask him for it unless we can line up something a little heavier'n what we've got. There's no use taking advantage of a man just because he's softhearted."

"Then we're not very close to asking him," Cavanaugh said.

"MacIntosh was not impressed?" Barry said.

"He was able to contain his enthusiasm," Cavanaugh said. "Hobie the same. Young or old, it doesn't make any difference. They're all retired into private life, making their money, griping about Nixon, gloating about his problems, making smart remarks and having drinks, and sitting contentedly on their behinds.

"I saw Hobie in Costello's," Cavanaugh said. "Steve said since I was going to be in New York anyway, I might as well make time to see Hobie. He's representing Michael Tarza."

"That nutcake," Barry said. "Who's he supporting, Jane Fonda?"

"He's not planning to do anything for us," Cavanaugh said.

"Did you meet him?" Barry said.

"I saw him one night on Cavett by mistake," Cavanaugh said. "That was my sole glimpse of the gentleman. I guess he's a pretty successful guy, but he was talking ragtime and he looked like he styled his hair by sticking his dick in a live electrical outlet."

"I met him at a Coalition meeting," Barry said. "This was back in '68. What the hell he was doing there I don't know. Of course it was never entirely clear to me what I was doing there, either, but there wasn't a single rock group in the place. I take that back: John Lennon or McCartney or somebody was there. Andy Williams was supposed to've been there, but I didn't see him. They were all just the kind of people you'd expect to find at a Coalition meeting, the gawkers and the gawkees, and they were all saying just exactly what you'd expect to hear people saying at a Coalition meeting. John Lindsay came in around the end of it, I heard, and here was this guy trying for some reason I could never understand to do an impossible job, so everyone was very ostentatious about not being impressed. No, what we were doing was demonstrating conclusively to Hubert Horatio Humphrey that the antiwar sentiment among the best people was so profoundly *right* that he was bound in conscience to go tell LBJ to get laid, and this meeting was going to do it. And some enemy of the people introduced me to this Tarza fellow, and he told me in all seriousness that the relative positions of Saturn and Mars, and something in the Moon's Second House, or the House of the Rising Sun, or something, made Humphrey's election inauspicious, and assured that Sargent Shriver would be President by Easter.

"I just looked at him," Barry said. "You meet the goddamnedest people, going to those things. 'You,' I said, 'are a damned nuisance. You're the kind of jerk that gives peace a bad name.' Tony Restic was there with me, and he heard that, and he came over. He was going to calm everybody down. Well, you couldn't've excited Tarza that night with a cattle prod. He was off in some galaxy of his own. Perfectly serene and placid. Didn't ruffle him a bit. He just explained that he didn't *like* the idea of Sargent Shriver being President. He brought it up because he wanted to interest the Coalition people in running Joseph Alioto."

"Tarza gave McGovern fifty thousand dollars, I understand," Cavanaugh said.

"Nobody gave George McGovern fifty thousand dollars," Barry said. "They gave it all to the Republicans, for a retirement fund."

"Well anyway," Cavanaugh said, "he's not giving us any money. Hobie won't let him. 'None of my clients're giving you a nickel, if I've got anything to say about it,' he said. 'I could be censured and up on charges for advising people to do that. Michael's a kindly soul, and I can't have people skating around on his vanity, taking his money away from him.' "

"On some street corner in this world," Barry said, "there's a small group of people who remember, standing around with their hands in their pockets, waiting to go back to work."

"We need a new map, then," Cavanaugh said. " 'No hard feelings, you understand,' Hobie said, 'but I think this is a fool's enterprise. This whole thing is too important to go riding off in all directions now. We've got to conserve our assets and find somebody who can win, along with being somebody that we want to win. I like the Senator personally, but I just don't think Sam Barry or anybody else can make him the President of the United States, and that is what we need. This year, we lie low.'

"Then I saw John MacIntosh," Cavanaugh said. "Now, I am not the best choice you could make for a guy to go see John MacIntosh. That much I did gain from the experience."

"What'd he give you," Barry said, "the drummer boy?"

"Not to mention the bugler," Cavanaugh said. " 'I enlisted with my brother's birth certificate in 1917,' he said."

" 'I am not the youngest veteran of the First World War,' " Barry said, " 'although someday soon, if my health remains to me, I may be the oldest.' "

" 'I told them that at Colorado Springs,' " Cavanaugh said. " 'Of my own personal knowledge I know, young man, of a fellow that forged his own birth certificate and enlisted at thirteen. He is the youngest, young man. He's sixty-nine today, and I am prone to speculate whether the youth of this country today would do such a thing.' "

"You've got to hand it to the old bastard, though," Barry said. "No education to speak of, retires a full bird, makes himself a fortune, starting out at sixty, and sits in the Senate of the United States."

"You don't have to hand him a damned thing," Cavanaugh said. "He'd take your fillings if you left your mouth open long enough. 'When I retired I had three thousand and fifty dollars in the bank, to show for a lifetime career.' Yeah, and a pension that pays him more for breathing'n I get for working, I bet."

"I don't know," Barry said. "He worked for the country for forty-five years or so. You ought to get something for that. I can't stand the old walrus myself, which is why I sent you, but he's completely honest and he's the only bird colonel I know about that had the common rocks to come out and start complaining about the bombing."

"Some of the people," Cavanaugh said, "that bought

condominiums he was touting, they might have some quarrel with that stuff about complete honesty."

"He was just the man out front on that," Barry said.

"He was the man out front on that because he looks like everybody's granddad," Cavanaugh said. "He could get away with saying things that those sharp bastards in back of him would've been hooted out of town or put in jail for, if they said them. 'America's Favorite Retiree' my ass. He must've made close to a million, shilling for those thieves and peddling Arizona sunshine and bad plumbing and thin walls to suckers. I dunno, Sam. He strikes me like the kind of guy that took his opportunities where he seen them. I think he's an old faker, not that it matters since he isn't joining up."

"Really firm?" Barry said.

" 'Your man,' " Cavanaugh said, "try this and tell me what you think: 'Your man is politically dead, as far as I'm concerned. I won't help you, and I won't impose upon my multitudinous friends to help you, either. In fact, I'll go out of my way to convince them to the contrary, to stay out of this. The mood of the country is changing, young man.' I don't know how he can tell that from living on Park Avenue, which I made the mistake of saying, but apparently he can. 'Young man,' he said, 'I have traveled extensively throughout the world. I was with the Second Cavalry Trick Riding Team, stationed at Fort Ethan Allen in Vermont. When I retired, the promotion board wrote a report: "How can we replace a man with his breadth of knowledge and insight?" I know whereof I speak. As a member of the board of Oral Roberts University in Tulsa, Oklahoma . . .' "

"Oh my God," Barry said, "he's gone soft."

" 'I have many times, though I am without the benefits

of higher education, myself, expressed apprehensions about the progress of our society which have all too frequently, I am sorry to say, been borne out by events. With the opportunity to acquire a formal education, who knows what I might have accomplished?' " Cavanaugh said.

"He thinks he would've been President of the United States, of course," Barry said.

"No shit," Cavanaugh said. "Well, I was getting a little impatient, and I said to him: 'I had one of those idiot letters too, the one where they took your name off the mailing list of some seat-cover manufacturer and you're invited to send them a hundred bucks and then they ask you what you think about permissiveness? Is that the one? And they tell all those kids that play basketball and're going to be missionaries that you're dead-set against premarital inter- course and they should keep their drawers on?' "

"Uh huh," Barry said. "Well, at the time I hated the idea of seeing him so much, I figured it wouldn't do any harm to send you. That'll teach me to be selfish. Oh my God."

"That was his personal choice," Cavanaugh said. "He puffed up like a blowfish and told me to start thinking about the hereafter, and I didn't tell him the W. C. Fields joke, although I wanted to, and then he said the only way we're going to get this country straightened out is if we stop making pornographic movies and return to Jesus."

"If I thought the convention'd nominate Him," Barry said, "I'd drop what I'm doing and sign up with Mac- Intosh. But I don't think He's well-enough known to carry the big industrial states; He'd never carry Illinois."

"Sam," Cavanaugh said, "you ought to go into politics. 'Senator,' I said, you still call a guy *Senator* when he was appointed to the thing because a guy died and they didn't want somebody that could make enough out of three years to win it himself, don't you?"

"Oh sure," Barry said. "Where MacIntosh comes from, you call a man *Senator* if he once visited the Capitol."

"That's what I thought," Cavanaugh said.

"Particularly if you want money from him, or support," Barry said, "or something which there is no way in the world I am ever going to get from him now. But I suppose it probably pleased him at the time."

"Right," Cavanaugh said. " 'Senator,' I said, 'Jesus ain't running, and what I hear out of Washington, He's a registered Republican, anyway, or so the President says, being in frequent communication with Him. And the guy I came here to talk with you about's not all that hot for it either. We just need him.'

"He looked at me," Cavanaugh said. "All of a sudden he was just a confused old man that people've been using for a long time by catering to his ego. He wants to do his duty, but he's too old now. He had his headquarters in the saddle . . ."

"When it should've been his hindquarters," Barry said, "yeah, yeah."

"I felt sorry for him," Cavanaugh said. "I felt sorrier for us, but I had some left over for him. 'See my lawyer,' he said. 'I never do anything anymore without asking my lawyer.' "

"Who's his lawyer?" Barry said.

"Dan Stoner," Cavanaugh said. "He was at Justice when I was with the *Post*. Ran a big flap about all the ferocious things he was going to do to that plastics company in West Virginia or Pennsylvania, wherever the hell it is, that the Mob took over to own their airplanes and their casinos in Freeport, and then he never did a damned thing about it.

Sort of a Makris in the big leagues, but no carry-through."

"I don't know him," Barry said.

"Well," Cavanaugh said, "I don't know. I guess you'd say I know him, more or less. He's sort of a friend of the family, I guess you might say."

"See him?" Barry said.

"I saw him," Cavanaugh said. "I didn't mean to see him, but I saw him."

"What is he?" Barry said. "Is he another one of those old bastards that's stealing Amtrak blind or something?"

"Uh uh," Cavanaugh said. "He's about our age. I ran into him down at the Turk. MacIntosh gave me his address, but I lost it in the wastebasket on the way out of MacIntosh's office, and then I took a friend home that wiped out on me about one in the morning, and I was too restless to sleep, so I stopped there on my way back to the hotel. I was drinking with Freddy Morse and we ran into him. Sort of."

"Who's Freddy Morse?" Barry said.

"Horror-show Freddy," Cavanaugh said. "Friend of mine from college that won two hundred bucks taking a shit in Times Square on New Year's Eve. Without getting arrested. While you were watching Guy Lombardo, he dropped a roll of quarters and squatted down with everybody else and took a shit. Clean profit of one hundred and ninety bucks. Put a 7-20-4 cigar in one of the cylinders of the Tampax machine when he was tending the heads and sweeping out down at the Gray Gables Inn when we were in college. 'What if it was her last dime?' I said. 'Or her first time?' he said. 'I shouldn't've done that.' Went to law school and turned out to be the world's leading genius on corporate taxation. Makes about four million dollars a year now, goes in at seven, comes out at eleven, starts looking around for someplace to drink, never got married and doesn't intend to. Every time I go to New York, I drop by the Turk and look for Freddy, and every time I do, he's there. Not a single bit of clout, can't do a damned thing for you and wouldn't if he could, doesn't give a shit who's President, who isn't, or even what the policy is in the Internal Revenue Code. What he can do is manipulate it. I think he wishes they would change it. More of a challenge.

"So," Cavanaugh said, "we ran into Stoner, and we had a brief chat, during which I didn't mention Mister Mac-Intosh, Senator Travis, or anybody else, and then I went home."

"Well," Barry said, "it wouldn't've hurt to at least ask the guy."

"Sam," Cavanaugh said, "you know what I think? I think we're hollering down a well."

"I don't," Barry said.

"Sam," Cavanaugh said, "Hobie, all of them. It doesn't matter whether you like how they're behaving. It doesn't matter if you think they're wrong. They're acting this way, and that makes them right. We're either wasting our time, or else we're spending our time too early, and that's a lot like the same thing, to me. One way or the other, it doesn't matter. This thing is not going to work."

"Hank," Barry said, "I told you: I know what you think. I don't agree with you. This is a democracy. What I say, goes. This is worth doing. At the very least, it'll start people thinking about what ought to be done. This is the beginning."

"This is jerking off," Cavanaugh said.

"Steve's been around a long time," Barry said. "He doesn't seem to think so."

"Steve needs a job," Cavanaugh said. "He was six feet from the kitchen at the Ambassador the night Bobby got it, and he still believes if he hadn't stopped to talk to somebody, he would've been there and knocked the guy's gun up and Bobby'd be President today. He's had four jobs since then. He had his wife run away from him and he didn't even realize it for two weeks after she did it. He's been all over the district, because he figures if he leaves, something might happen and he wouldn't know about it before it was in the papers. And besides, where does he go? Where do you go when you've been here? What do you do? He's stuck and he knows it. If somebody offered Steve a GS15 to plant turnips, the first thing he'd want to know would be if it was here, and if it was, he'd take it and plant turnips. He's beaten up and discouraged and he doesn't want to leave Washington. He wants to sit here and get a check, and dream, and wish Bobby never got shot, and Jack before him, and when he drinks he talks about how he's going to write a book. Then he cries. Then he goes home. In the morning he goes to work, and he had an affair with Sally Overshoe last year and she went around telling everybody he's got a problem getting an erection, and premature ejaculation when he does."

"Sadie Overholt?" Barry said.

"Sadie Overholt," Cavanaugh said. "The guy's all through. He doesn't think anything. He just does his job, and he waits for the ever-present, faraway fellow in the bright nightgown."

"There're people who do think, still," Barry said. "They'll be with us."

"Who are they, Sam?" Cavanaugh said. "Where's the Senator? Is he around? He wants to blush maidenly for the press when they ask him, fine. But where the hell is he, while I'm clattering around the countryside taking guff in your name? Is he interested? Never mind interested. Is he alive? Where are all these people?"

"It's just a matter of finding them," Barry said.

"All right, Sam," Cavanaugh said. "Never mind where they are. What kind of people are they? True believers, like you? The South will rise again? Enough money so they can set up an office with a broken-down advance man to run it, and tell themselves: 'Look, the cause isn't hopeless, it can't be, we got an office'? That kind? We've both been around, Sam, and we've been through things. You can't cheat an honest man, and you can't bamboozle the mean-tempered bastards that show up when you've really got something nailed, come in, take their coats off, and go out and knock heads and get something done, instead of being polite on the phone and moping about their ex-wives all the time. Where the hell are they? They're someplace else. They're hiding out. They're not around."

"They're waiting to be shown," Barry said. "That's the way they always are. First you get a band, then you get a wagon. We're the vanguard. That's what our job is, to show them. Just like McCarthy did in New Hampshire. Nobody was with him, either."

"The kids were," Cavanaugh said. "Where're the kids? They vanished. They're raising families now. They went to work for the John Hancock and the American Can Company."

"There're other kids," Barry said. "They're out there. All we've got to do is give them a reason to come in."

"Sam," Cavanaugh said, "they're gone. The new ones're in coed dorms, and they're drinking beer again when they're not doing that. And McCarthy didn't win, Sam. He lost. It just looked like a victory. And look what happened to him."

"He dumped Johnson with that," Barry said.

"Where is he now?" Cavanaugh said. "He's not around anymore. He wasn't around anymore when he was still around, theoretically. The guy in there now? He's already dumped. It's been done. It's over. You haven't got anything to be against anymore, that'll inflame people enough so that what they're for looks like it's feasible. They heard all the stuff that you're for. They agree, but they're full of ennui. They don't want to listen anymore. They want to go home. They want to play games. They want to develop the kinds of careers they put off the last time. It's too soon. It's too late. It's too damned much trouble."

"Do you know Matt Dennison?" Barry said.

"I heard of him," Cavanaugh said. "That's about all."

"Make arrangements to talk to him," Barry said. "That's what I want you to do next."

"Would you mind telling me," Sarah said on the phone, from New York, "what the hell happened between you and Dan, and what caused it?"

"I certainly would," Cavanaugh said, in Washington. "It was an affair of honor. Between gentlemen. One gentleman. One asshole. No offense, dear."

"You were both drunk," she said.

"I can't speak for Daniel," Cavanaugh said. "I was certainly drunk. I was blind drunk. I was not blind drunk. I retained my remarkable coordination. I didn't have time to get blind drunk. I was only there forty minutes or so, and before that I spent most of the evening committing unspeakable acts. I was as mad as hell, though. That I was."

"He says you insulted him," she said.

"Sarah," Cavanaugh said, "it's after three thirty. It looks like it's after three thirty, at least, and it certainly feels that way, and I've got a plane to catch in the morning."

"Where're you going?" she said.

"Southboro, Michigan," Cavanaugh said. "I've got to meet a guy in Chicago, and then I'm flying to Michigan."

"Who's the guy?" she said.

"At this hour," he said, "I don't remember."

"Does she have brown hair or is she one of those crummy bleached blondes you always go apeshit over?" Sarah said.

"The first one's over fifty," Cavanaugh said, "and he's black, and he claims to know something that'll help Sam. Now maybe he does, and maybe he doesn't. I've got to go talk to him. The other one's well over sixty, and he's one of those old dinosaurs that's done so many things he can do anything he damned well pleases. Sam says I've got to talk to him, and I work for Sam, so Barkis is willin', and that's what I'm going to do. Now what the hell's the matter with you, waking me up at this hour?"

"I was lonesome," she said. "The hairbrush had a headache. Come up to New York right away and mistreat me."

"I was sleeping," he said. "Shut up right away and let me go back to sleep."

"I was at Clarke's," Sarah said, "and Louise came over and offered to scratch my eyes out. I think that was what she was going to do. Maybe she was going to pull my hair. She was mad at me."

"Before you ask," Cavanaugh said, "I didn't tell Louise a fucking thing."

"That wasn't what was bothering her," Sarah said.

"What the hell were you doing in Clarke's, for Christ sake?" Cavanaugh said.

"Oooh," she said. "Are you jealous?"

"What difference does it make?" Cavanaugh said. "I haven't got any money, and I'm married."

"You're definitely jealous," she said. "At long last, you've flattered me. Are you in bed with somebody else, and she's doing things to you and that's why you're being so nice to me, to get rid of me?"

"Henry Kissinger," he said. "You didn't know that, did you? We're hot for each other. That's why Sam's on Foreign Relations, because I'm on domestic relations."

"Did you punch Dan because of me?" she said.

"No," he said. "Dopey as I am, in the middle of the night, no, I didn't. I don't think I did, anyway."

"You did punch him," she said.

"He looked a lot like he was setting up to punch me," Cavanaugh said. "So I took the precaution of punching him, a couple of times. Now, you better watch your ass, because I'm starting to wake up. What're we talking about?"

"About how you punched Daniel, because of me," she said.

"That's not right," Cavanaugh said. "Daniel tried to punch me, because of Louise, and I guess technically he did."

"I don't understand that," she said. "I understand it, but I don't like it."

"I didn't like it, either," Cavanaugh said. "Is there any way I could call you tomorrow night from Southboro, Michigan, and we could talk about this like mature human beings?"

"No," she said. "By then you'll be in the mercenary

embrace of some heartless trollop, and you will've spent a whole day thinking up a plausible story. I like this much better." She began to sing: " 'Tell me, where are the simple joys of maidenhood?' "

"Oh, shut up," Cavanaugh said.

" 'Where are all those delightful, laughing boys?' "

"Your former husband," Cavanaugh said, "is a total toad."

" 'Where's the knight pining so for me, he leaps to death in woe for me, oh where are a maiden's simple joys?' "

"He was making a big pain in the ass of himself," Cavanaugh said, "and he got on my nerves, and he saw he was getting on my nerves, and he was feeling more oats'n he had, and he invited me outside."

" 'Shan't I do the simple things a maiden should?' " Sarah sang. " 'Shall I never be worshipped and adored?' "

"I was simple," Cavanaugh said. "I was ready to go home anyway."

" 'Shall two knights never tilt for me, and let their blood be spilt for me, oh where are the simple joys, harmless delightful joys? Where are the simple joys of maidenhood?' "

"You're ineligible," Cavanaugh said. "You can't pass the physical. You're not so hot at singing, either. I went outside with the son of a bitch and I cold-cocked him."

"Fighting over little old me," she said. "I'm going to call Martha Mitchell. Son of a bitch."

"How's your twat?" he said.

" 'Shall I not be on, a pedestal,' " Sarah sang, " 'worshipped and competed, for? Shall I not be carried off, or better still, start a little war?' Soaking wet."

"That's what I thought," Cavanaugh said. "You want to call me when you're through?"

"No," she said. "This's what's going to get me through. Why'd you sock my Daniel, my former Daniel?"

"Your former Daniel," Cavanaugh said, "is a lying bastard, and he's insulting, too. Just as rude as he can be. And he wants to fight when somebody catches him out."

"Oh," she said, "I knew that."

"I didn't," Cavanaugh said. "So I made the mistake of catching him out. He's got a very nice tan, your former Daniel."

"He was on vacation," she said. "It was his first vacation, poor dear, in umpteen years."

"And where was he on vacation?" Cavanaugh said.

"He was sailing," she said. "Ever since he made some dough, he's loved sailing."

"Because he's supposed to love sailing," Cavanaugh said.

"Sure," Sarah said. "Nobody ever actually loved sailing. It's the same thing as that silly game you men play with little racquets and hard rubber balls. You do it because you're supposed to. We have our little lunches and our little chats and our little dresses and our little hats, and you have your little bars and your little cars and the New York Knicks."

"I don't have the Knicks," Cavanaugh said. "It would never occur to me to go to a professional basketball game. Why on earth anybody wants to pay to get into those is something I cannot understand."

"Well," she said, "it's the same thing. Everybody's the same. That's why you harps buy boats and that's why Dan goes on boats. You lower orders think we've been up to something all these years. The joke's on you. We were bored stiff too."

"The surroundings were a little nicer, I've found," Cavanaugh said.

"Much nicer," Sarah said. "Just don't get to thinking they're a new kind of roses that the bloom doesn't wear off, and you'll be perfectly fine."

"I'm perfectly fine now," Cavanaugh said.

"I'm not," Sarah said. "I could use one of those delightful things you gave me last week, right about now. What'd you call it?"

"A dash in the bloomers," Cavanaugh said.

"That's it," she said, "one of those, please, to go. Does the Metroliner run at night?"

"No," he said, "and it's too late for the shuttle, too. Or too early. Something."

"Shit," Sarah said.

"That's what I said to your Daniel," Cavanaugh said. "I asked him where he got his nice tan, and he said he was out on *Terpsichore's Darling*."

"That *is* a lot of shit," Sarah said. "He was on *Celerity*. He was on *Celerity* for almost a month."

"How is dear David, not to mention dear Jenny?" Cavanaugh said.

"Dear Jenny, I think," Sarah said, "had it sewed up a long time ago, on the reasonable theory that she had enough to bear and she was afraid it'd get her in trouble. Anyway, it never got her in fun, that's for sure. But the hell with her. I never met David and I don't want to, either. From what I've heard, he's precisely the kind of guy I never want to know."

"Well," Cavanaugh said, "as near as I can make out, David runs a regular little floating colony of loose women and irritating men there, and that's all right with me if everybody has a nice time. And Louise was on that boat and she liked what she was getting on it better'n she liked what I could give her, and that was your Daniel. Which is also all right with me."

"You're not in much of a position to complain, my sweet," Sarah said. "And I must say, I find that remark about loose women distasteful."

"Yeah," Cavanaugh said. "What is not all right with me, though, is having my nose rubbed in it when he's through with it, and that is what your Daniel was up to when I found it necessary to sock him. The son of a bitch was baiting me. Everybody in the Turk knew he was on *Celerity*, including the girl who checked the coats, and who he was on *Celerity* with, and what they were doing, and he's going on and on about what a great guy Tenley's father is, and what a great boat Tenley's father's boat is, and what a great girl Tenley is, and all the grand times they had for themselves, out on the bounding fucking main, and everything he said was the absolute truth except you had to know it was a different boat and a different girl that's technically married to me, he was talking about. And everybody did, too."

"Daniel really shouldn't drink," Sarah said. "When he drinks he thinks he's a B squash player because he's a superb natural athlete. Not because he's smart and he plays squash all the time in the same courts. Did you hurt my former Daniel?"

"I hope so," Cavanaugh said. "I certainly did the best I could to hurt him. He started back with one of those long haymakers that guys who never fought in a saloon before in their lives like to try, and I belted him twice in the guts before he could throw it. Which made him lose interest. Also his dinner. In the gutter. So he hit me on the shoulder, I guess you could call it, on his way down, but it wasn't much of a punch. I thought about picking him up and doing a little more to him, but then I thought: 'What the hell's the matter with the guy anyway, makes him act like this, going around and getting in fights?' And I didn't."

"It was probably always something he wanted to do," Sarah said. "Daniel was always very neatly arranged, with every button buttoned, and I thought that's the way he was. But he wasn't. Inside he was really quite angry at something, and it cost him a lot to be diffident and calm. The only clue was, when he was at Justice he used to holler every so often that he was getting nineteen thousand dollars a year to go up against lawyers that billed at least five or six times that, and it pissed him off. I used to laugh at him. The things I did that I thought would make him feel better, I guess, were wrong. 'Never mind, Danny boy, when you've been around as long as they have, you'll be known and be making as much.'

" 'I'll be known,' he'd say, and I remember, when he was getting ready to leave Justice, he really got a little weird. He was going to show everybody, something or other. That he was just as good as they were. And he did start making some money, and it made him feel better. So much better, he started wondering about all those other neat things he never tried, because he was afraid to try them, and maybe he'd be just as good at them as he was at making a lot of money, and one of them was sneaking around and fooling around.

"Well," Sarah said, "he wasn't very good at that, nowhere near as quick at picking things up as he'd been when it was how to make money he was picking up. I met a couple of them, and heard about two or three more. We got married before we knew what the hell we were doing anyway. I was just sick and tired of hearing the General recommend promising young captains, and I don't know why Daniel did it."

"To get your pants off," Cavanaugh said.

"As you ought to know, my prince," Sarah said, "removing my pants has never been a difficult chore for someone I found really attractive. And nice."

"You told me," Cavanaugh said, "I was your one true love."

"And you are," Sarah said. "If you weren't, I wouldn't be calling you now. I'd be out someplace, getting this huge pair of antlers off. But you are not my first true love, true love. So I told him: 'Look, this is embarrassing me. I don't care what you do,' and that was what really frosted him, that I'd say I didn't care if he did it, 'although I am surprised to find out you've apparently got such an appetite for it, considering how many nights I've had to make do with a carrot.' I wasn't mad about him screwing. I was mad about the way he went at it. And he got himself up on a very high horse and told me he'd do as he pleased, with anybody he wanted, and I said: 'Take a hike, you fucker.' Which was what he wanted to do anyway, even though he didn't have the balls to know it, much less the balls to admit it to anybody else."

"Does he know anything he shouldn't know?" Cavanaugh said.

"Oh, sure," she said.

"Ah," Cavanaugh said. "What the hell made you do that?"

"I didn't do a goddamned thing," she said. "That's another thing I decided I'm not going to be: one of those abject creatures who goes out and fucks and then calls her ex-husband to tell him she can still find a cock somewhere to put between her legs. I don't go around showing my diary to people. But I assume he does. Doesn't Louise know?"

"I got no idea," Cavanaugh said. "She doesn't labor under the impression that I live in a monastery and abide by the rules, but it's not like we compare notes or anything. When we're together, then we're together, and when we're not, we're alone."

"Because," she said, "Daniel isn't much fun when he's happy, you know."

"He's even less fun when he's stiff," Cavanaugh said. "He is a royal son of a bitch when he's half in the bag."

"He's got to be riled up before he's good for anything," Sarah said. "He really doesn't know how to behave, and he knows he doesn't. So he's really very quiet in a new situation until something happens to take his mind off it. Then he can be a very interesting guy to have around."

"*Interesting* is one word for it," Cavanaugh said.

"Does Louise like it quiet?" Sarah said.

"I married Louise the day after Bobby beat Keating," Cavanaugh said. "Nobody'd been to bed for a day and a half, although Louise and I'd been there several times earlier. But it was the end of something, and we'd gotten to like each other, and it seemed like a shame that I was coming back down here and she was going back to Springer's office and the excitement was over, at least for a while. So we drove down to Maryland and got married, and then we came here, and she stayed for three days and we didn't go out. I'm not sure if we actually had any clothes on for the whole three days. Then she went back to New York and got some clothes and flew to LA to see a guy at Universal about something, and I went in and presented a suitable excuse for my absence to the austere gentleman in charge of my comings-in and my goings-out and I didn't see her again for five weeks. All in all, except for the stop in Maryland, it was a marvelous idea.

"Then I met her in New York," Cavanaugh said, "and

we went up to Connecticut together and I was presented to her father, who was positively apoplectic. So I took it for about three hours, twenty minutes of insults, half an hour of stony silence, then about an hour of wrath, and I got off my best behavior and started mentioning some old family recipes and stuff like that. Things you can do and fun you can have with your fingers and other organs. Come to think of it, he wanted to fight me too. She was as happy as that pig we all heard so much about. I wonder what the hell it is about her that's so special that every man I meet wants to fight me because I've supposedly got her.

"Then we went up to Randolph," Cavanaugh said, "and my father kissed her but my mother asked her if she was Jewish. Outside of that it was a lovely weekend. She took the plane back to New York, and I took the plane back down here, and we've talked a lot on the phone since then. Also, I've seen her about two or three times a month, on the average, except when she was someplace else. Or I was."

"Then Louise must've told him," Sarah said.

"Well," Cavanaugh said, "somebody must've told him something, to make me need to remember Sergeant Manning's homely maxims on the manly art of doing something to the other guy before he gets in a position to do something to you. What'd Louise say to you?"

"Louise was with Tenley," Sarah said, "and Tenley was with that complete bozo she's been seeing for a hundred years, I can never remember his name. I doubt he can, for that matter. And I was there with Bob Rush, and Bob's a sweet guy. He was telling me how his wife still doesn't understand him, even after two hundred years of couples therapy. And I was being patient with Bob, and telling him over and over that the answer was still the same: No. And Louise came over to where we were sitting, we were in the back, having steak Diane. I bet Bob's bought me a whole steer by now, trying to get me to screw him. And she said: 'I was wrong about you.'

"I thought she was talking about Bob," Sarah said. "So I didn't answer right off. Bob thought she was talking about Bob. 'Louise, for Christ sake,' he said, 'I haven't seen you in years.'

" 'Not you,' she said, leaving out: You asshole, which she obviously was thinking, 'your little friend here. The brown wren.' "

"Nice talk," Cavanaugh said.

"Hank," Sarah said, "I know my limitations. When I was thirteen I noticed that there were girls in the world with boobs that were bigger'n mine, and when I was nineteen, I was resigned to it. On my good days, on my really good days, sometimes I almost look cute, but it takes an awful lot of work, and I don't go through it that often. Certainly not to meet Rush for dinner.

"She was really mad," Sarah said. "Her eyes were flashing and she had her shoulders all hunched, and she was absolutely spitting. 'Why, Louise,' I said, 'what's the matter? Your vibrator shorting out or something?' "

Cavanaugh laughed.

"Always ready with a tactful remark," Sarah said. "I get in more trouble that way. 'Everybody knows what you are, you tramp,' she said. 'Louise,' I said, 'this is really not the sort of conversation we were trained in school to conduct. Now if you can't be ladylike, well, of course, no one will expect you to be. But I certainly hope you're not going to make an absolute spectacle of yourself.'

" 'Don't you dare patronize me, you cheap little tart,'

she said. She thinks I'm cheap because I didn't screw my Daniel out of any money or anything. 'You common whore, you can do what you like. Why don't you go down to the Bowery and make the bums feel better?' And mind you," Sarah said, "this was when she was warming up. When she got to the point, she got nasty. 'Louise,' I said, 'it distresses me terribly to see you behaving like this. It's very unrefined, I must say, and I do hope you'll make an effort to control yourself.'

" 'If you want to get back at Dan for walking out on you,' she said, which I thought was rather unkind, not to mention grossly inaccurate," Sarah said, " 'get back at him yourself, if you can. Don't be sending Hank around to pick fights with him.' "

"I was having a peaceable drink with a friend when that started," Cavanaugh said.

" 'You can get your warped little pleasures any way you want,' she said. I didn't know what the hell she was talking about. 'But if that happens again, well, Dan's too much of a gentleman to do anything about it himself, but I'm not, and I'll fix you.' Then she stamped her feet. She actually stamped her little feet and shook her little fists, and I said: 'Louise, I do believe you're having an actual tantrum.' And she stalked off.

"I had to get it from Bob," Sarah said. " 'What in the world is the matter with her?' I said. I like Bob. He's very nice. He looks so wistful when I won't go to bed with him. 'You got something going with Hank Cavanaugh, must be,' he said. 'What if I have?' I said. 'Cavanaugh hit Danny outside the Turk the other night, I heard,' he said. So that's why I called. Where were you, my darling, by the way? I called you at quarter of two and you didn't answer. Were you out being naughty?"

"No," Cavanaugh said, "I was out being ripped off. I was at the police station."

"Who'd you hit this time?" she said.

"I was making out a report," Cavanaugh said. "Some boogies stole my car."

" 'Boogies,' " she said. "Is that any way to talk about blacks?"

"Blacks behave themselves, like whites," Cavanaugh said. "They go to work, and they take care of their families, and they mind their own business, just like harp, that're Americans. It's not the same thing. People with black skin that steal your car are boogies. And coons. If it was harps that did it, they'd be goddamned micks. Fucking bastards. This is the second time this's happened in six months, and the last time they did it they took the seats and the tape deck and the radio and the wheels. I'm getting sick of it."

"How do you know it was boogies, you should pardon the expression," Sarah said.

"I know it was boogies because they got the monopoly down here," Cavanaugh said. "It was boogies, all right."

"I hope you get it back and it's all right," she said.

"I don't," Cavanaugh said. "I hope I never see the goddamned thing again. Look, if they don't steal the train, when can you come down here?"

"Uh," she said, "I can come down Sunday, if you like."

"And how long can you stay?" he said. "I really need to see you. Want to see you."

"Isn't that nice," she said. "That's very nice. I like that. Are you going to fight me?"

"Wrestle," he said.

"Thursday," she said. "I told the General I'd come for the weekend and listen to the General's Wife practice on me. She, ah, well, she disapproves of my life style. She thinks I should be at onement with God."

"Ask her to explain Haldeman and Ehrlichman," Cavanaugh said.

"Gumdrop," Sarah said. "Lollipop. All-day sucker. See you."

The phone rang again before he was completely wrapped in the blankets.

"Uhhh," Cavanaugh said.

"Nice try," Louise said. "Who the hell were you talking to, at four o'clock in the morning?"

"My broker," Cavanaugh said.

"My," she said. "You must own a lot of stock to have to talk to him so long. You must be doing very well. Who's your broker, Horn and Hardart?"

"Where are you, my devoted spouse?" Cavanaugh said. "Have you come to our nation's capital, to ease my troubled mind?"

"I'm in New York, my precious," Louise said. "Just like Sarah Clendennon and her ex-husband're in New York tonight. Were you chatting with Miss Clendennon, by any chance?"

"Why, Louise," Cavanaugh said, "what would I be doing, calling Sarah Clendennon at this hour of the morning?"

"What were you doing, then?" Louise said. "I've been trying to reach you since midnight. At first I couldn't get any answer, and then the line was busy."

"Actually," Cavanaugh said, "my original plans called for me to go to sleep. But when I came out of the Monocle, my lovely car was not where I left it, and I came away with the impression that, well, somebody must've swiped it, since I've never known it before to go off on trips by itself. So I spent the rest of the night talking to some cops about the crime rate around here. One incident in it, anyway."

"Have they found it?" she said.

"No," he said, "and actually, I hope they don't. I hope it's gone for good. What I really hope is that the bastards totaled it and killed themselves, but you can't expect just good luck in this world. I expect they'll find it, all bitched up and stripped like the last time, and then I'll sell it, or take the insurance if it's completely ruined. Those things're like a lot of things. Once they get damaged, even a little bit, they're not worth a damn anymore. They're just not the same."

"Hank," she said, "I want to see you."

"Okay," Cavanaugh said, "let me think. I'm going to Michigan in the morning, but I should be back Thursday night. Saturday I'm supposed to go up to Boston, and then I've got to get myself right back here because I've got one bitch of a week next week. Can you come down Thursday? Unless I get trapped in Detroit, of course, and have to lay over. Maybe Friday'd be better."

"You couldn't come here?" she said.

"Not this week, really," he said. "Not next week, either, unless—I could go shuttle to shuttle and meet you in La-Guardia instead of flying right through from Boston."

"This is ridiculous," Louise said. "Have I really got to apply in writing when I want to see you?"

"Well, Louise," Cavanaugh said, "your interest in my movements is very unusual. When I agree to see people that my boss wants me to see, they more or less expect that I'll be where I say I'm going to be, when I'm supposed to be there. There's no percentage in running around getting everybody all pissed off, that I can see. Now if you want me to, I can come up a week from Friday, and we can have the weekend."

"We've got to talk," she said.

"We're talking now," he said.

"Not like this," she said. "Not at this hour of the morning, and not on the phone."

"Well, I went to law school nights," Cavanaugh said, "and I guess I just don't notice when it gets late and people call me up for the first time in months and stop me from getting any sleep."

"Are you sure you're alone?" she said.

"Lemme check," he said. "Yup, I'm alone all right."

"I heard about your fight tonight," she said.

"You were misinformed," Cavanaugh said. "I didn't have any fight tonight. Not until this charming discussion began, anyway."

"You had a fight last Thursday night," she said. "What's the matter with you, going around starting fights? Have you gotten stupid?"

"Once in my life," Cavanaugh said, "I started a fight. I was as drunk as an owl, I was stupid drunk, and I was twenty years old and I was a summer Marine and I selected a big old cop to spar with, a two-hundred-and-ninety-pound Shore Patrol guy, outside a bar in Norfolk. I think he wanted me to come with him. 'To the brig,' I think he said, and I was very impolite: I told him to go fuck himself. I think you could say that I started that fight. It was the first one, and he got a very quick decision, and I learned a lot from that, Louise. I haven't started a fight since."

"I was mortified when I heard about it," she said. "And if Sidney ever hears about it, he'll spend the rest of his life ruining you in this town."

"You tell Sidney Kafka," Cavanaugh said, "that if I pick up one thing that even makes me think that somebody might be bad-mouthing me, anywhere, I'm going to hold him responsible for it, and the next time he goes a-court-ing, he'll have a nice picture of himself and the young lady in question in the newspaper the next morning. Like I said, I gave up starting fights, but I never took any vows I was going to let people piss on my boots, and you can tell Danny Stoner for me that if he wants his profile changed, all he's got to do is hand me another ration of shit and I'll save him the bill for the rhinoplasty."

"Shut up, Hank," she said. "You don't have to treat me to your truck-driver's bravado."

"Or else you can tell him," Cavanaugh said, "keeping in mind that you called me, and I think I can stand the heartbreak if you hang up on me, that it's one thing if he wants to fuck you. If you want to fuck him, that's between him and you. But from now on, he better get his punching jollies with guys that can't fight any better'n he can, or he's going to get very badly hurt. The other night I was mad and half-drunk. The next time I'll put the little prick in the hospital."

"Are you telling me how to live?" she said. "Am I really hearing this, from you, the way you run around?"

"I'm telling you and any playmates that you might want to pass the word on to," Cavanaugh said, "that you better learn some manners. It's obvious you haven't got any judgment, so your life depends on you being polite. And if you can't manage that, then have him go get his contact lenses changed so he can at least learn to tell the difference between a hundred-and-sixty-pound wise-ass boy friend and a guy that weighs one-ninety, doesn't want any trouble from people, and gets mad when they give it to him anyway."

"Do you think you will've calmed down some by Friday?" she said.

"If I don't get a new supply of foolishness from you in

the meantime," Cavanaugh said. "Or any additional lip from your boy friends."

"I'll fly down on the shuttle," she said. "I'll have to go back the same night, though. Saturday I'm leaving for LA again."

"I'll meet you for dinner," Cavanaugh said. "Meet me at the Jockey, at, how about seven?"

"Can't you pick me up?" she said.

"How the hell can I pick you up if I don't have a car?" Cavanaugh said. "You can't get a cab in this town after four. No, I don't know, I haven't got the book here. I know I'm supposed to see Sam when I get back, and it'll take two hours, but whether that's supposed to be Thursday or Friday I don't remember. It'll . . . I don't know."

"Can I use your apartment to change?" she said.

"I don't see how," he said. "I had the locks changed a month ago when we started getting daytime callers again, and you haven't got a key."

"Could you leave one under the mat or something?" she said.

"No," Cavanaugh said, "actually, I couldn't. That mat's never in the same place at night that I left it in, in the morning, and there's so many wire scratches on all the mailboxes here you can barely read the numbers. I'm out a Corvette this week as it is. I'd really like to hang on to my camera and color TV if I can."

"Okay," she said, "I get the message. Haven't got time to clean up the bathroom from your overnight guests, is that it?"

"It's not that," Cavanaugh said. "It's just that since, well, I've been deprived of your kind ministrations, I've been reduced to dressing up in order to get my rocks off, and I know that you'd start looking for the instant coffee the minute you came in here, and find my lingerie behind the false panel that opens when you rap the third board from the left at the back of the closet in the bedroom, and you wouldn't believe it was mine. You'd probably think I'd been having women in here."

"I'll see you at the Jockey Club," she said. "Try the best you can to stay out of trouble till then."

"Give my fondest regards to Mister Stoner," Cavanaugh said.

"Subject as it must be to revision," Judge Ronald Franklin said, "my assessment is this: the people who were with him the first time will not be with him again. He was a bitter disappointment to them then, and they have experienced many more disappointments since then. In a sense, I believe, they reason, many of them, that had he proven successful with the assistance that they tendered him, subsequent disappointments would have been prevented."

They sat in the Admirals' Club at O'Hare International Airport and drank Chivas Regal on the rocks, in the paneled silence.

"It wasn't his fault," Cavanaugh said, "those other disappointments, really."

"Certainly not," Franklin said. "It was probably not

properly any culpability of his that so arranged matters as to make him so grave a disappointment. They supported him because they perceived him as a good and decent man. 'Lincolnesque,' I believe the adjective was. Certainly that quality, as it generally does, attracted them, for some reason." He smiled.

"He is a good and decent man," Cavanaugh said.

Franklin nodded. "A man from humble beginnings who worked hard; also, compassionate and obviously of high intelligence. On the whole, unobjectionable qualities for a prospective President of the United States."

"Were then, and are now," Cavanaugh said.

"But, by themselves, insufficient," Franklin said, "as we learned, to our sorrow, the last time. What we desire now, if it is not simply to be let alone, and if we know what it is, in definable terms, is someone slightly harder, still compassionate, yet stronger, better able to cope, and at the same time, sensitive as he to the realities of actual suffering and yet firmer in the implementation of his kindness."

"A tougher guy," Cavanaugh said.

"I mean no personal disapproval of him," Franklin said.

"Sam's aware of that," Cavanaugh said.

"He may very well be tough enough himself," Franklin said, "the Senator. For all we know, he may have, by this time, a character case-hardened by the experience he has undergone. But that, as you see, is precisely the problem: *for all we know.* He is perceived as weak. Perhaps not necessarily weak, or even indecisive, another characteristic of which we in Illinois have had some proximate exemplars, and again were disappointed. He is not perceived merely as charitable, if that is the right word: he is also perceived as one easily dismayed, as it were. Vulnerable, in a way that is appealing and somewhat distressing. A tougher guy, as you say, is probably what is needed, notwithstanding the regrettable fact that the Senator may be that man, but unable to convey his condition persuasively to those who must become convinced of it."

"Suppose," Cavanaugh said, "and just grant me the proposition that it's so, suppose he could project a meaner image the next time. Would that do it?"

"Considering that," Franklin said, "let me seem to digress. He now confronts a problem which he did not face the last time."

"I'm not sure of that," Cavanaugh said.

"Again let me emphasize," Franklin said, "that we speak not of things as they are, but of things as they are perceived. Our practice obliges us to satisfy the semipublic and public predilection for selecting real leaders by comparison of the height, breadth, and symmetry of the shadows they cast, and not upon the assessment of their actual stature. To win—and we must return at least partway to the serviceable understanding that winning is pretty much everything, in politics—we must carefully choose the man who casts the most formidable shadow, without controlling reference to the relative substance of two or more competitors of equivalent philosophical acceptability. Much of the shadow is the emotional preference of the person perceiving it. The last time, the people, more or less reluctantly, acceded to the self-denial of their emotional preference, perceiving the object of it as beyond their grasp."

"Chappaquiddick," Cavanaugh said.

"Chappaquiddick," Franklin said. "Time has passed. A great deal has happened. That perception is no longer the consensus. The emotional preference survives it. It may be that the current consensus, which supplanted the old, is incorrect. But that does not matter. They do not perceive things in that way anymore."

"Jesus," Cavanaugh said, "if the guy runs . . . It scares the living daylights out of me. There's sure to be some crank out there who'll go for the hat trick and try to blow his ass off."

"I share that emotion," Franklin said. "But things as they are do not exist for our purposes, Sam's, yours, or mine. Things as perceived are all that there is. As they are, a disappointed people believes that there may be a Restoration, and what would be restored is something for which they have a poignant and profound nostalgia. In large part, what they seek, and crave, is insubstantial, impalpable, and thus their craving for it is irrational. But much of life is irrational, and we do well to recognize that.

"Your man," Franklin said, "is not the candidate of that choice. He does not represent that consensus, and he cannot ignite it to move in his direction. The choice has commenced to seem of surpassing importance, much more so than it did before. This time, I think, they will vote as though their lives depended on it, as they were urged to do, but presumably did not, in 1972, because their livelihoods *do*, and that is a readily understandable concept, soon apprehended as surpassingly important. All it takes is a little privation."

"Which, of course, is why I'm here," Cavanaugh said.

"I wish I could proffer more encouragement," Franklin said. "There's altogether too much cruelty in life as it is, and I'd prefer to reach out for the gentility of assurance that, yes, he is the man, and he can and will be elected, and if elected, as I expect any consequential candidate to be, he will have the influence upon the Congress necessary to turn the country around, and get it moving again. You note my choice of words."

"We're not against him," Cavanaugh said. "Not by any means. If he goes, we'd welcome it. He's perfectly acceptable. But we're convinced he won't go."

"I'm not convinced he won't go," Franklin said, "which affords me much less freedom of movement than your conviction permits you. And the people are not convinced either, as I am not, so their prophecy, mistaken when made, may become self-fulfilling. Should it not, your man is among a fair number of second choices who must be re-examined in the light of the issue of who is best among those available. And I have no doubt that he will be."

"Could I ask you this?" Cavanaugh said. "Who else do you see?"

"Several," Franklin said. "And I have no franchise to exclude anyone from the most thoughtful consideration. So I am sure there are men whose names would not occur to me, because I have not seriously scrutinized them for myself, and to state any names now would render them a serious disservice. The problem here, Hank, is that you are premature. Until the issue of the preferred candidate is resolved, you are premature."

"What we're trying to do," Cavanaugh said, "is make it as sure as we can that when—and if—it turns out the preferred man's not available this time either, our man is positioned correctly."

"A reasonable effort," Franklin said.

"Sam's very loyal," Cavanaugh said. "I didn't mean to suggest otherwise. But he's also very committed, and he has to be sure he's doing all he can to make sure that from 1977 until 1981, we're not still just treading water on things that really have to be done and really should've been done in 1970. That's what he's trying to guard against: just replacing one stand-patter who's a Republican with another stand-patter who's a Democrat. The crooks're through. The question now is, who's the most progressive guy we can get in, that can deliver? That's what Sam's doing, and he thinks: Travis."

"He may have undertaken an impossible task," Franklin said. "The mood of the country may be such that a stand-patter is the only candidate who can be elected. There's another dimension to the proposal that you make, and I think it has not had the attention which it deserves. It seems not to have had, at any rate. While as a human being, and a black, I deplore the direction which the Administration has taken on racial issues, as a politician I am constrained to remark that even so marginal and grudging a program, much of it regressive, has severely chafed the lower white middle class. They have, of course, always enlisted precipitously in the armies of opposition to our progress, to do the dirty work at wages so low that no one secure in his wages and livelihood would be tempted in the least by the incentives. But they are not secure, of course, and tend to grab for things, like everybody else. Then too, the chafing has been, I think, artificially induced, or the flames of it fanned, by the incumbent and his gang of bullyboys and henchmen. We are recent people. We waited a long time. Ten years ago, I would not have found myself hospitably received in this club."

"Club?" Cavanaugh said. "This isn't a club. This's a high-priced private waiting room. All it takes is twelve bucks if you work for the government, twenty-five if you don't, and for the comfortable chairs you get to pay the same price you pay in the air for a drink you can stand up and buy, down the hall, for half. Maybe two thirds."

"You ring the buzzer," Franklin said, "and they let you

in. Ten, fifteen years ago, they would've let me in, but I would not have been admitted cheerfully, or welcomed hospitably. Today most of my people lack the twenty-five bucks, although the government does work for them, in that it provides them with the little that they have."

"Not the government," Cavanaugh said.

"No," Franklin said, "the taxpayers. The taxpayers provide it. They give nowhere near as much to the poor as they allow the rich to keep for themselves, which in the abstract seems much the same thing, but the Congress is an elective body, and the Internal Revenue Service chiefly does as the Congress tells it, and not as the White House tells it, for which we might all be reasonably grateful, and if that is the sense of the country, so be it. Were I running the country, things would be different, and that may be why I am not running the country."

"Nobody's running the country," Cavanaugh said.

"Not at the moment," Franklin said. "And the country is available to be run. But its availability is conditional, and the conditions are that the man who wants to run it must either be the beneficiary of an uncritical emotional response, in which event he can do as he wishes, depending on the strength of the response, or else he must articulate well the abiding attitude of the majority of the voters on substantive issues, and hope devoutly and successfully that he is not contending with the beneficiary of an emotional response. Assuming, of course, that the substantive issues are presently identifiable, and that somebody knows what they are."

"I've got to go to Detroit in twenty minutes," Cavanaugh said, "and I've got to walk most of the way, just to reach the plane. I've got a strong feeling that you're trying to tell me something, right?"

Franklin laughed. "When I first met Sam Barry," he

said, "he had this bomb-thrower with him. Fellow by the name of Richmond. Do you know him?"

"Good friend of mine," Cavanaugh said.

"The first symptom of senescence," Franklin said, "inquiring about the obvious. They were out here, uttering dire threats against anyone who might even consider opposing Jack, and it was totally unnecessary, we were all for him anyway, but their loyalty was infectious. Two or three weeks after they had gone where they were going anyway, I think it was Wisconsin, I was still admonishing the fainthearted to reflect carefully before they made less than a complete commitment. I asked Sam, and Richmond, why an experienced politician such as I should accept, not guidance, really, but outright commands, from two novices such as they, and Sam told me: 'Because the novices are going to run this country, and if you want a piece of the action, you're going to have to have your cards.' Except for the sniper, he was right. Oh how I wish he'd been right without exception."

"Was he right?" Cavanaugh said.

"He was right," Franklin said. "I have no monopoly on wisdom. Sam and I are old friends, and I admire his dedication. But it was politics then, and it's politics now; the admiration is a dividend for friendship, but the wisdom, if there is any, is the gravamen of politics. Sam invokes politics now, and in that I must use my own judgment. We practice the art of the possible, and right now I'm uncertain about what is possible. I am less perplexed, though still unsure, of the opposite: what is impossible. But, provisionally, I think that what Sam has in kind now is impossible. I think it unlikely, at very least, gravely unlikely, and thus to be reserved. Not shunned. Reserved."

"The Mayor?" Cavanaugh said.

"The Mayor keeps his own counsel," Franklin said. "He invited me to breakfast this morning. I went, and I listened attentively. He accords Sam the sort of respect that any pragmatist of any moment vouchsafes to any ideologue of accomplishment, however incomprehensible."

Smiling, Cavanaugh said: "Thank you, Judge."

"How old are you?" Franklin said.

"Thirty-three," Cavanaugh said.

"And before this," Franklin said, "what did you do?"

"I was a newspaperman," Cavanaugh said. "I was a Marine. I've got a law degree, but I've never practiced."

"You were not always in politics, then," Franklin said. "I'm fifty-six. My mother was the unchurched wife of a sharecropper in Copper Bend, Missouri, and one day the sharecropper didn't come home. I was very young when this happened, even as was she. I think she must have been about fifteen or sixteen. After several days when he did not return, she became convinced that he'd been lynched. There were nightriders in the area; she may have been right. She may have acted simply because she was afraid, and went and told someone equally ignorant, of her nameless fear, and that person, being older, may have functioned only to put a name on her fear, and frightened her away. She was not a stupid woman then, and she is not a stupid woman today. She made it all the way to Chicago with an infant, carrying her second child in its third or fourth month, with money that she begged from people she suspected to have murdered her husband. Whites, that is. All whites.

"So I came here when I was a baby," Franklin said. "I'm not a baby anymore. I sat on the bench, and I've practiced law, and when Lyndon Johnson came here, I shook his hand, with deep pleasure. There was a picture of us, in the *Sun-Times*, which my mother saw, and she refused to speak to me for three days, because the President was a Southerner.

"Now I'm getting old," Franklin said. "I'm not old, but I'm getting old, and many of the people I've cherished are dead, or very old. The people I told you about, who were disappointed, have been using up their days as inexorably as those who never even hoped, bearing the burden of the illusion that things in this country are of infinite perfectibility, and the weight, heavier still, of the knowledge that they acted upon that illusion, expecting better things, and did not get them. Just like you, and Sam."

"I don't know about me," Cavanaugh said. "Sam, certainly, yes."

"I shook hands also with Frank Nitti," Franklin said. "When Al Capone was a legend, I was a boy, and I saw nothing particularly reprehensible in him. When I was a man I began, dimly, to see something wrong, but I was never able to work out to my own satisfaction what made so especially wicked his murderous successfulness in monopolizing all the wickedness that equally murderous men of less resolution would have committed independently had he not existed. Would there have been no cribs, no rotgut, no gambling, and no bribery in Cook County, if Greasythumb Guzik had been smothered before the umbilicus was cut? Or substantially less? I doubt it. Because I believe now, and had then the glimmerings of the same belief, that people may as well have what they want, because they will get it anyway, and there is no cognizable possibility of preventing them.

"It struck me," Franklin said, "recently, to be sure, but it struck me, that there was no essential difference between what I have wasted a life on, which is politics, I am guilty of that, and what honest cops waste their lives on. There are practical differences, mammoth practical differences."

"My father's a cop," Cavanaugh said. "A retired cop, but he's still a cop."

"There are habits from which a man cannot retire," Franklin said. "My daughters, when we see them, still venture on occasion the view that I never say anything without first reflecting upon what a higher court will think of it. The cops stifle whatever disapproval they may feel, the honest cops, for much of what their superiors direct them to do: close bordellos, raid bookmakers, whatever. Some of them minimize the effort required to accomplish the stifling by not carrying out the directives, very often. Because, without accepting a dollar, or even sharing the appetites, they perceive that the people will have what they want, ten thousand laws and a million cops to the contrary. But they do that at great expense to their own mental comfort, because they are professionally or occupationally committed to the converse, and it does not help them that they know it to be false.

"I proceeded upon the presumption that the function of my primary profession, of government, is to give the people what they want. I never had any misapprehensions of serious moment about what they want. I knew, I knew well enough: steady work, meat on the plate, a car, a chance for advancement which can be realized by hard work, an annual raise if advancement is not really possible, no military draft, and no bullshit.

"The government, of course," Franklin said, "cannot deliver those desiderata. And that, I confess with some rue, is a cognition embarrassingly fresh in my philosophical progress. It cannot, because the government consists of men, and the only ones in it who can do anything titanic are those who have passed through the fire of election under the most intensive competition.

"That competition," Franklin said, "does not conduce to the attraction of men who will do what the people want done. It rewards those, instead, who advocate persuasively to the people that the government can provide what they desire, which it cannot, and that those provisions will be forthcoming if the advocate's elected, or else it elevates those who are absolved from the manufacture of such false promises by their capacity to generate a feeling. The people respond to feelings. A yearning for greatness. A sense of common purpose, unity, and spiritual consensus.

"None of those intellectual-emotional phenomena is an adequate substitute for side meat and greens in decent quantities," Franklin said. "Each will do to distract the people from their inchoate perception, struggling for generations to emerge, that what they chiefly want is for the government to leave them alone, and not interfere, and six or eight hours of overtime a week, in the month before Christmas. I'll tell you something: government never did any good for any person. It has served society well enough, fighting its wars, punishing its criminals, when they could be caught, and with a great deal of creaking and groaning, putting a floor of civility under relations between social groups which are irrationally disposed to hate each other, hobbling if not eliminating the superior abilities of the top dogs to visit routine calamities upon the underdogs. But that is just another way of saying that government, at its best, has never managed more than a marginally survivable diet for those who would otherwise starve, hasty and meager medical treatment for those who would otherwise die a little sooner, perhaps without pain, without treatment, moderately efficient sewage disposal, garbage removal and excellent fire protection, and a few circuses to amuse those alert enough to seek out or invent their own amusements. There is no limit on the amount of misery. You'd better not tell Sam that."

"What do I tell him?" Cavanaugh asked.

"Tell him," Franklin said, "that I want a candidate who can generate the inspiration that will get him elected without depending upon the unlikely completion, within three years, of the herculean task of making dominant that inchoate consensus, that what the people really want is to be left alone to make themselves happy in the best way they can."

"If I do that," Cavanaugh said, "he's going to make me call you. Sam's a very hopeful man. He doesn't savor delicacies. He likes meat, and potatoes."

"Tell him," Franklin said, "tell him I said: No. Tell him to go home and tend to his family, and do the best he can, without worrying about it. We'll all muddle through, same as always. We're tired. We want to go home."

"That place is a whorehouse," Cavanaugh said. **9**
"It's an out-and-out whorehouse."

"I take it you scored," Sam Barry said. Steve
Hamner sat on the sill of the window overlooking the
courtyard, and laughed.

"Sam," Cavanaugh said, "I've got to take you aside. You
don't score in a whorehouse. You score on a press bus, you
score at a party, you score when you visit an office and
strike up a carnal attraction with somebody of the opposite
sexual persuasion."

"Also in bars," Hamner said.

"Look, Steve," Cavanaugh said, "there's bars and there's
bars. What I'm talking about is technically a bar. The guy's
a novice, all right? You bring him along slowly. The finer
distinctions we get to in good time.

"Now a whorehouse is this, Sam," Cavanaugh said, "and keep it in mind, all right? So I don't have to tell you ten times, as usual. A whorehouse is a place where you go and you pay for a service and the service is rendered. Now in this place that I'm talking about, I paid for no service and no service was rendered. Neither did I strike up a meaningful relationship with some broad that wanted to get laid, same as me. Had I accomplished the latter, I would've scored, provided I paid no money. Very difficult task in a place like that.

"In college," Cavanaugh said, "we used to go up to Dottie's. Dottie ran a whorehouse, a plain, unprepossessing, run-of-the-mill, cost-effectiveness whorehouse. For five bucks you got blown, for ten bucks you got laid. Fast, but you got laid. Around-the-world was twenty-five dollars. It was a big old house in Brighton that I suppose some molasses baron built in 1851, and you could tell it was a classy joint, so to speak, because they washed your dick in PhisoHex and nobody made a lot of noise.

"In my youthful innocence," Cavanaugh said, "I supposed that Dottie's place was typical of whorehouses. In other words, if you went to a whorehouse in Norfolk, Virginia, roughly the same things would happen to you, and so also in Racine, Grand Rapids, Laramie, Denver, and maybe even Fall River. Well, I was in Fall River, but I didn't go to a whorehouse there, and although I was somewhat startled when the goddamned whore supplied the rubber in Norfolk, I decided that perhaps the volume of business there militated against the preliminary ablutions I had come to expect, again so to speak, at Dottie's. In Tijuana I was indisposed, by reason of observing a dirty show in a bar where a fat broad jiggled out wearing only high heels and permitted a sailor to eat her by thrusting her private parts over the rail, shouting all the while: 'No bite, no bite,' and he did, and she screamed, and he spat on my foot, so I did no personal research. But I was in with bad companions, and I have reason to believe that the commerce of whorehouses is pretty much the same, the world over."

"Is that international relations?" Hamner said.

"It's hearsay," Sam Barry said.

"The both of you," Cavanaugh said, "shut up. When you get an authority in, don't interrupt the bastard to show him how much you know. Let him show you how much he knows.

"From this diligent, if intermittent, study," Cavanaugh said, "I formed the impression that whorehouses are invariably metropolitan. I know, I know: the Chicken Ranch. But I come from metropolitan antecedents, and I guess I thought the farmers worked it out on the sheep or something. Otherwise, how all them wholesome farm girls?

"Nevertheless," Cavanaugh said, "I gradually became aware that there are as many varieties of whorehouses as there are of, say, restaurants. There are middle-class whorehouses, there are roadhouse whorehouses, and there are fancy whorehouses that look like nifty apartment buildings and you never see the madam 'cause she lives someplace else and lets Ma Bell let the members do the walking."

"Very *good*," Hamner said.

"I've often said," Cavanaugh said, "your greatest asset is your appreciation of my humor, Steve."

"You, Hamner," Sam Barry said, "are in serious trouble. If that's true."

"Moving right along here, folks," Cavanaugh said. "At first I was bewildered. I was first bewildered in the Marlinspike Motel in Hyannis, Massachusetts, one foggy night after many drinks and the rejection of sundry clumsy advances committed by your obedient servant upon a veritable claque of honeys in the Hu-Kee-Lau, just down the road. I was covering the President, for Christ sake. Women should've been falling at my feet. What the hell was going on? I wasn't drunk enough.

"My companions," Cavanaugh said, "had the good sense to go to bed, if alone, or the good luck, if accompanied, but I was young and in my prime, and I was damned and determined that even if I couldn't do it all the time, I was at least going to do it enough times so I could lie when I was old, with a bad conscience. I repaired to the Spinnaker Lounge at the Marlinspike, for more vodka gimlets.

"There I found, all but alone," Cavanaugh said, "by which I mean to indicate that the bartender was in there, greatly vexed by a customer who wanted vodka gimlets, a maiden of not more than thirty-five summers, with a certain glint to her eye that presaged an inclination to indulge in sexual intercourse.

"I struck up a conversation with her," Cavanaugh said. "Now, I worked for a fairly small newspaper at the time, and that was a good way to wind up at seedy motels, because the paper didn't go for reporters traveling better cabins'n editors, and the editors were all guys that were members of, or married to, the family that owned it, and when they traveled, their idea of extravagance was renting Dollar-a-Day cars. Hertz was out of the question, because that profit-and-loss sheet at the end of the year was how they calculated their goddamned income. Accounting always made your reservations for you, when some story suddenly developed minor local overtones, like: 'Local Man Elected President of U.S.,' and if it'd been that, 'Staff Reporter' who wrote the story, instead of AP, would've stayed in some fleabag in Richmond to cover the Inauguration. And then they would've led with Merriman Smith of UPI and used 'Staff Reporter' for a sidebar, probably: 'From Our Correspondent in Washington,' with no byline.

"A complaisant lover, she was," Cavanaugh said. "I approached with impeccable *politesse*: 'Wanna fuck?' I said.

" 'I suppose so,' she said," Cavanaugh said. "She looked at me and she looked at her watch. There's something about clothes you buy off the rack that gets you a special price in any place that does business on volume."

"You see, Sam?" Hamner said. "That's what I told you. Don't change. The way you look's appealing."

"I've never been to a whorehouse in my life," Sam Barry said.

"No shit," Cavanaugh said.

"No shit," Hamner said. "Sam's never been to a whorehouse in his life, Cav."

"I heard him say that," Cavanaugh said.

"I never would've believed it of you, Sam," Hamner said.

" 'It's late,' she said, in her dulcet tones," Cavanaugh said. " 'Look: ten bucks and lemme go home, all right? Give him five.' And she indicated the bartender by moving her head. Who would have given *me* five bucks if I'd've promised to clear out without ordering more vodka gimlets, or at least switch to bar Scotch and water. And that was when I began to learn that there were other kinds of whorehouses.

"Now this place in Southboro," Cavanaugh said, "was a whorehouse of the Marlinspike genus, but of a more refined species, and what surprised me about it was it never would occur to me that you could set up a whorehouse in Southboro, Michigan. There's nothing out there but flat land and runways and airplanes. Dottie's had people around it, a whole city full of guys that wanted to get laid. But there's nothing in Southboro but approach lights. And yet here're all these old bastards with their twenty-five-dollar whores, maybe fifty at the outside, and there must be a million of them. Where the hell they come from, I'll never know."

"How was Matt Dennison?" Barry said. The light from the courtyard was strong in the office.

"He said he was a little tired," Cavanaugh said.

"What'd he say?" Barry said.

"He said he was a little tired," Cavanaugh said. " 'I'm going up to Flint tomorrow,' he said, 'to see my brother who's dying slowly, painfully, and courageously of cancer, and taking an inexplicably long time to do it. He can't do more than moan. He does that from the pain, and when he moans, that gives him further pain. I suppose it's growing up in Hurley that makes you fight things you can't possibly beat.' Then we had a little discussion about tough towns in the world, and he thought Hurley was tougher'n Iron Mountain, Michigan, but he never got to Juarez, Singapore, Marseilles, or Casablanca, and the only one I knew about was Juarez, so we were a little handicapped. And he said: 'I'm sixty-seven years old. The day after tomorrow I'm going to see a man in Lansing, and then I'm going back to Madison. What I should be doing is going back to Hurley. The place's tamed down a lot now. They leave old men alone. And I should spend my days in the Dells, going after muskies and telling lies when I didn't catch any. This is ridiculous, me sitting up in places like this with people like these, at my age. How the hell old is Averell Harriman? He ought to sit down and stop embarrassing us young fellows and leave us alone with our angina.' He said he was with FDR. 'I had some energy then.' "

"He did, too," Barry said. "He was in Tommy the

Cork's office. My father used to talk about Matt. He used to drink martinis at the White House with the imperial presence himself, and he was no court jester, either. Matt made a million dollars in the Depression."

"With what?" Cavanaugh said. "A printing press?"

"One of his aunts died," Barry said. "She left him five or six thousand dollars, and he took it and quit managing the feed store, or whatever he was doing, and started trading agricultural futures. Hog bellies, winter wheat, corn, alfalfa: he had all these waybills and invoices and grain elevator receipts flying around, which if he'd kept any of them would have had him swamped in food he couldn't eat, sell, or give away, and he just kept buying them and selling them for about three years. When he got through, he had a million dollars, and he took half of it and bought silver futures, puts and calls, I think, and he cleaned up again when we went off gold.

"Meantime," Barry said, "there wasn't a farm in Wisconsin that some bank didn't have up for foreclosure, and Matt took the other half and went around buying up mortgages, cheap. Only, Matt didn't foreclose them."

"Ah," Cavanaugh said.

"Sure," Barry said. "My father went to Matt's mother's funeral. My father and Matt were very close friends. In fact, Matt came to my father's funeral, and that was about twelve, fifteen hundred miles he had to travel, piston engines, too. It took him a long time, and he had pleurisy then, too, but he came. I thanked him. 'It's all right, my young friend,' he said. 'I remember how I felt when your dad came out.' Well, Dad was in Chicago when Matt's mother died, and he just got on a train and went up there. He never got over it. He had to get a man to drive him to Hurley, and it was a long ride through the woods, fifty, sixty miles or so, and he used to tell about how you'd come down these long hills with a curve at the bottom, pitch blackness, and the headlights'd hit the trees at the curve and there'd be three or four wolves, 'with their eyes red as coals,' and then you'd be gone. 'Not a good place for a flat tire,' Dad said. Then he got there, and gas was rationed because it was still in the middle of the war, and yet here were all these old buggies out there, falling apart, and some of the people'd come two or three hundred miles to pay their respects. My father said it was amazing, this frontier town, all these big, rawboned bastards, long lines of them, hair like straw, and their women, and they all came up to Matt 'like they were shaking hands with the Savior,' my father said, 'and maybe they were.'

"These were people," Barry said, "whose sons were fighting on Kwajalein and in North Africa, and dying, and getting wounded, and here was a man that was very high up in the Administration that was sending them out like that, and yet even the Germans, the Lutherans and the Bavarians, they were at the wake too. My father said he told Matt it was an inspiring thing, an inspiring thing to see, and Matt said they were just his friends. That was all, just his friends."

" 'Now, my friend,' he said to me," Cavanaugh said, " 'you tell me about my young friend Sam and how he's doing.' I told him about War Powers. 'I heard about that.' I told him about your attitude on the wheat deal, about milk supports, depletion allowances. I think I left out your views of leash laws for Georgetown, but I put in everything I could think of that he might be interested in. And I was right: he was interested, interested enough so he already knew all the stuff I was telling him. Matt Dennison takes a little pride in you, Sam."

"I know it," Barry said.

"Meantime," Cavanaugh said, "all the old buffaloes're pawing their honeys, and Dennison's making one small shot of Jack Daniel's last longer'n I would've thought possible, and I knew I was boring the ass off him, and finally he said: 'Linda, have you seen Linda?' I told him I saw Linda couple weeks ago. 'Is she all right?' I told him she was absolutely Grade A, Number One. 'And Sam,' he said, 'is Sam all right?' I told him you were even better, if that was possible. I didn't mention about how you're always going to whorehouses and have to take a million units of penicillin a day just to keep the chancres in control."

"That was decent of you," Barry said. "I'd hate to have the old man disillusioned."

" 'That's fine,' he said," Cavanaugh said. " 'What does Sam want me to do?' So I told him."

"What'd he say?" Barry said.

"He said: No," Cavanaugh said.

"Oh," Barry said.

"Jesus Christ," Hamner said, getting off the windowsill, "we've got a real barn-burner going here, haven't we, folks?" He turned around and looked out the window. "There was a guy I knew in Harrisburg," he said, "that I think was worse off'n we are. I'm not sure, but I think so. Did very well, and then the abortion thing came up and he made one hell of a speech. I even called him up, when I read about it, but it wasn't the speech I read about. Next day this broad that works for the radio station holds her own press conference, and she says she can't understand how come the Senator's so dead-set about legalizing abortions. 'I mean, after all, he paid for mine,' and she waves the canceled check. 'I had to go to Cincinnati.' He said he thought she wanted the money to visit her aunt. But at least people were paying attention to him, for a while."

"Calm down, Steve," Barry said. "I said this'd take time. I didn't say it'd happen tomorrow."

"Look," Hamner said, turning around, "I'm a German. I'm like one of Matt Dennison's Germans. I take orders. You tell me something's not going to happen tomorrow, I believe you. But you ask me to go to work for you again, I respect you, I develop this notion that it is gonna happen. Sometime. Things that're gonna happen sometime, start to happen. This isn't starting to happen. I've got three kids and a housekeeper to feed, plus a large dog I bought when the kids asked me to, and a house that I'm sentimentally attached to and the bank's financially interested in. And I like Rockville. I shouldn't, I know, but I do. What the hell happens to me if nothing happens?"

"Did he actually say: No?" Barry said. "Tell me exactly what he said."

" 'Sam should know better'n to send you to ask me that,' " Cavanaugh said. " 'He really should know better. I'm amazed that he'd do that.'

"I took that to mean: No," Cavanaugh said.

"I better call him up?" Barry said.

"He's not mad at you," Cavanaugh said. "At least, I didn't get the impression he was mad at you. He was just surprised. 'I was with him the last time,' he said. 'I gave my word. He was the best man available. By far, the best. Paul Travis is a credit to American politics. He wasn't good enough. And this time, I hope and pray, well, I have somebody else in mind.' So I asked him who it was. It's always the same guy, and it's the same guy with him. But, nothing doing. 'Sam knows where my loyalties lie. I don't have divided loyalties. If I can't have what I want, I'll take what I can get. But I think maybe this time I can have what I want, and if the country wants him too, I'm going to see that they get him. And if they do, I'll retire. And if they don't, I'll retire. But that's it. If it's Sam's man they want, I'll give all that the statute allows for Sam's man. But not until I'm convinced that it can't be my man. You tell Sam that.' And now I have," Cavanaugh said.

"I'll go this far with you, Steve: we're not getting a whole lot of encouragement," Barry said.

"Then there was Judge Franklin," Cavanaugh said.

"The Honorable Ronald C. C. Franklin," Barry said. " 'Unfit to serve,' but savvy as hell."

" 'Unfit to serve'?" Cavanaugh said.

"Sure," Barry said. "He was a Kerner man, and they went to a new system of picking judges out there. I don't know whether they'd been electing them, and they were going to start appointing them, or it was the other way around. But the guys that were in under the old system were going to get grandfathered into the new one, and the only ones that were mad were the ones that had the thing lined up under the old system. Well, the bar association inherited testicles or something, and put them on, and the next thing you know, they had enough heat going so all of a sudden you were going to get grandfathered, and stay on only if you were all right. Which was a substantial change in things. So they had a study, and the Honorable Franklin was one of most that they found unfit to serve."

"Jesus," Cavanaugh said, "he sure didn't sound unfit to me. I only went to Northeastern and GW Law. I had trouble keeping up with the guy."

"He was a Rhodes Scholar," Barry said. "I think he was a Rhodes Scholar, anyway. If he wasn't, he should've been. He just played the game like it was always played, and then the U.S. Attorney came in and started raising hell, and he was one of the casualties. He didn't choose his friends carefully, once or twice, and when they came after him for it, he showed he was at least smart. Maybe not sensible all the time, but smart in the corner. And he quit. Issued a very dignified statement to the press, the gist of which was: 'I don't go where I'm not wanted.' Took the wind right out of their sails. Because I don't think he really did anything. He might've had a couple friends too many in Gary, but he didn't do anything. Or East St. Louis. But when he quit, it just took the steam out of them. Smart guy."

"He must be," Cavanaugh said. "He agrees with Joe Marsh, and Jerry, and Fogarty and all the rest of them."

"Oh dear," Barry said.

"I feel a cold wind blowing on the nape of my neck," Hamner said. "I can suddenly foresee a day when I will have to go to actual work."

"Steve," Barry said.

"Sam," Cavanaugh said, "we're shoveling shit against the tide."

"If this place is bugged," Barry said, "you're going to be very embarrassed when I hand the tapes over."

"You're overextended, Sam," Hamner said. "It's just a matter of trying to go too far, too fast, on a road you don't know."

"I know the road," Barry said. "I've been down it personally, not like you guys. I'm familiar with this, when it seems like you're out there all alone, and a long time, too, and then, slowly, very slowly, they begin . . ."

". . . twisting," Cavanaugh said, "twisting in the wind. Look, have you talked to the Senator?"

"Not recently," Barry said. "He knows what we're doing, but he's got to be included out or he can't touch a damned thing on the air, and if that's what's going to happen, who the hell plays Voice of Reason on things like bombing and impeachment?"

"Has it occurred to you recently, Sam," Hamner said, "that the net effect of what we're doing is stroking a guy's ego, and that's all?"

"No," Barry said, "as a matter of fact, Steve, it hasn't."

"Well, Sam," Cavanaugh said, "maybe it should."

"For me," Hamner said, "maybe it has to. How the hell do I pay the mortgage when this thing folds up and never went anywhere?"

"I didn't call you in to get the mortgage paid," Barry said. "You didn't come in and tell me it was the mortgage that interested you. You didn't ask my advice when you adopted two Vietnamese kids because your wife liked to do fashionable things, and you didn't extend yourself much to keep continuity when you decided you were all hot and bothered to work for the DNC instead of me, and I had to go out and get lucky real fast and get Hank. Which might not've happened, and you still wouldn't've done anything. What you're good at, Hamner, is making grand gestures, and no carry-through unless you're under the gun every day, and I haven't had time to keep you under the gun."

"Sam," Cavanaugh said.

"Never mind, 'Sam,'" Barry said. "You're the same as he is, in a different way. He's a traveling wizard, hooked on excitement, and you're completely indifferent, and the result is the same: zero."

"I tell you what, Sam," Cavanaugh said. "My wife's in town, and I'd like to go and have a shower and get cleaned up and have dinner with her. Can I do that?"

"Sure," the Congressman said. "Give her my regards. I'll see you tomorrow."

Louise wore a dark blue bodyshirt, turtle-necked, and tight dark blue pants. She wore a dark blue scarf on her hair, and a small platinum watch.

"You look like the cat burglar," Cavanaugh said, sitting down at the banquette with her.

"Now try not to be a bastard with me," she said, kissing him lightly. "You wouldn't let me change at your place, and I really didn't have much choice."

"I didn't mean it as an insult," he said.

They ordered drinks. The waiter had a very heavy Spanish accent, and seemed to have trouble understanding English. "I'm going to be very careful ordering in this place," she said. "Slowly and distinctly, or they'll serve you the front lawn." She put her purse on the table, opened it and took out cigarettes. There was a white business envelope inside the bag; there was no name or address on the front of it, and it was not sealed.

"The food's good, though," Cavanaugh said. "There's only about four or five places in the whole town where you can eat."

"That must be why the place's deserted," she said.

"It's the end of the week," Cavanaugh said. "It's for lunch anyway; nobody goes out to dinner at restaurants at night here anyway, especially not in this Administration. But they never did it much anyway. It's all dinner parties, delicate late-middle-aged manufacturers imitating Perle Mesta, enticing Senators to dine with anchor men, and being protective of Rose Mary Woods. It's like Anthony's and Jimmy's in Boston: they pay the rent on the lunches, and the nights and weekends're gravy. Sam told me, when Fogarty was Speaker up there, it's a wonder he didn't gain a hundred pounds. 'Eleven thirty? Right. Go out in the hall and scare up a lobbyist. I'm hungry.' And they'd go down to Pier Four. And they went down there one day, Fogarty's got this Jewish Rep from Brookline with him, and the guy ordered a steak or something, and Fogarty looks at him and says: 'Have a Thermidor.' 'It's a spider,' the guy says. 'It's a fuckin' arachnid, is what it is, a spider that swims. I don't pay much attention to them dietary laws, but I'm not eating no spider.' Fogarty looks at him: 'I don't care what it is,' he says, 'I like how it tastes.' The guy's name, the lobbyist, was Horace Bolster. The Rep looks at Fogarty: 'You'd eat four pounds of rocks if Anthony put them on the menu and whacked Bolster fifteen bucks for 'em.' Sam said you haven't seen eating unless you saw Fogarty and five or six of his pals scoffing up oysters at Jimmy's and washing it down with the bisque. It's the same thing here. It's like playing Monopoly in this town. Nobody's using real money. It's all a fight between expense accounts. The places that serve good food win the fights."

"Is that what you're doing when you say you're working late?" she said.

"Look," Cavanaugh said, "for me to get into that orbit, which doesn't happen very often no matter who you work for in the House, Sam'd have to be a lot more formidable'n he is. Rayburn's people got all the dinners they could handle, and McCormack didn't want to go out. He always went home. Albert goes out, and Ford did for a while. But Sam doesn't have the weight, really. He only gets invited to things that everybody gets invited to, when the Brazilians have everybody in for drinks because they're pissed off about the price of coffee or something. It wouldn't matter if Sam was the kind of guy that said witty things all the time. If you wanted to tell them to somebody else, you'd have to spend five minutes telling them who Sam is, so they'd understand that what he said was funny, and they ought to laugh at it, and that's too much trouble to go through. And besides, Sam's not witty. And he doesn't know anything, any secrets that nobody else knows, that he can pass on to the lady from the DNC sitting next to him, and if you don't have any tidbits, you don't get asked to come and glean somebody else's tidbits. He doesn't drink, and the only thing he reads is the Washington *Post*, and the New Bedford *Standard Times* and the other papers from home. He says he reads the *Congressional Record*, but he actually skims it, and he only reads the *New York Times* when I spot something and make him do it. He doesn't get his name in *Time* and *Newsweek* anymore because the war's over and he's just another Congressman who's outlived his issue: obsolete. Sam's just a nice, decent, hardworking Congressman from an obscure district that doesn't have any national publications publishing out of it. He isn't any fun. So, by extension, I'm no fun either."

"Oh," she said, "they don't know you like I know you, my love. Sam may go home to his adoring wifey every night, and dandle his adorable children, but you go out on the town and you howl, don't you, Hank?"

The waiter brought their drinks, and a brown pot of orange cheese. He moved Louise's purse to the corner of the table farthest from Cavanaugh. It remained open, the white envelope protruding slightly.

"Louise," Cavanaugh said, "I've been living on airplanes and eating food made from polystyrene for the past two weeks. If there weren't any calories in booze, I would've starved to death. I'm going to have some Maryland oysters and a few little crabs and a steak *au poivre* and a genuine salad with honest-to-God dressing on it, and I thought we might even have a bottle of wine that came all the way from France, on the other side of the American lake."

"Oh, I know, Hank," she said. "You've come a long, long way from Randolph, Massachusetts, and it's only natural you'd miss Leo's Drive-In not a bit."

"Leon's," Cavanaugh said. "Right on the spot where Doctor Kendrigan had his house, and my mummy used to take me as a tot to get warm oil put in my ears. And then cotton, little balls of cotton. One or two of which I could use nicely right about now, if what you came all the way down here to do is spoil my first dinner in a while. Because I'd much rather grab a hamburger at Leon's in peace than eat here with you in your warpath mood."

"Hank," she said, "I'm as mad as hell at you. I could've killed you when I got back from Chicago and the whole town was talking about that idiotic fight you had with

Dan. I had to have lunch yesterday at Caravelle with Britt Naismith and Jane Fletcher, and Jane's a real bitch, and the first thing she did when she saw me come in, with her bullhorn voice she said: 'Here's the queen of the schoolyard. Where're the boys fighting over your favors tonight, Louise, dear?' And Britt said she'd go and watch, if you were. For Christ sake, Hank, that's embarrassing. If you're going to get drunk and fight, you can do it down here, on your own turf. Stay the hell off of mine."

"How is Britt?" Cavanaugh said. "Still wearing her leather underpants?"

"Britt is a very talented, very confused girl," Louise said. "She's sexually disoriented."

"She's a screaming dyke," Cavanaugh said. "You got a lot of friends like that, haven't you? Double-gaited, limp-wristed guys, women that hold on just a little too long when they kiss hello; doesn't it get confusing sometimes?"

The waiter came back, and with great difficulty asked if they wished to order dinner.

"No," Louise said. "Go away. Bring us some more drinks."

"Please," Cavanaugh said to the waiter.

"You leave my friends alone," Louise said. "They're not my real friends anyway. I've known my real friends like Tenley since school. They're the ones I should've listened to. Tenley told me in 1968 that I was nuts to hang around with you. They've been a hell of a lot better for me than you've been."

"They're the salt of the earth, Louise," Cavanaugh said. "They know everybody, and do everything, and go everywhere, in pairs or groups of up to nine, and not one damned thing that any of you do's worth a pisshole in the snow, and you know it, and that's why you're all screwed up like you are."

"We care about each other, Hank," she said. "You wouldn't understand that. You don't care about anything. We've known each other, Tenley and I, since 1958, when we started at Smith. I've still got friends from Putney. Can you say that? Have you still got friends you made in high school, or where you went to college? No, you haven't."

"There's Freddy Morse," Cavanaugh said. "I was out on the town with Freddy just a week or so ago, I think it was."

"That imbecile," she said. "No, you haven't got any, really. You're just like that monster in the White House. All your friends are new, and cheap."

"I've known Jess a long time," Cavanaugh said. "I've known Jess since '61. And Walter, since '63. I think they're pretty nice."

"Jess," she said. The waiter brought the second round. "That drunk. All he's got's a little money, and no damned sense at all."

"He can get a reservation at Sans Souci," Cavanaugh said.

"He can get cirrhosis on the cobblestones, too," she said.

"Well," Cavanaugh said, "I have to admit, Louise, you've got me stumped. First I forgot all the guys I used to pick the dump with, and I'm a bastard for that, and now I don't forget the guys that did me favors, and I'm a bastard for that, too. I can't play ball with you if you're going to put a cover on the hoop, you know."

"You make me sick," Louise said. She finished her drink.

"Louise," Cavanaugh said, "you called me in the middle of the night because you were all upset, because I got mad when your boy friend got nasty with me, and then I didn't choose to flee when he had the poor judgment to apply for a fight, and you said you wanted to talk to me and I said: 'Okay.' You didn't say you were coming down here because you had it in mind to pick a fight with me yourself, and if you had, I would've declined the invitation. I don't like fights. They make me nervous. I don't like fighting women, either. I never actually fought one, but I'm sure I wouldn't like it, without even trying it.

"Now I've left you alone," Cavanaugh said, "and I've tried to mind my own business, though I never deeded you Manhattan, that I remember, and you've done what you wanted and I've done what I wanted and we've been reasonably honest with each other. Now if that has to be changed because Dan Stoner picked a fight with me, and lost, okay. If you want to clown around with me about how your career's ruined because I slipped his punch and threw in a couple of my own, my advice to you is: go clown around with the guy that started it, which is him. You've got lousy taste. That guy has no more class'n an empty toothpaste tube."

"I think you've got lousy taste, too," Louise said.

"That's your option," Cavanaugh said.

"She's just a flaky little thing that goes whooping around from macramé to witchcraft and then back to needlepoint and backgammon," Louise said. "She was second in the class at school, and then she retired her brain. I think Bennington does something to people's brains. The gray cells freeze, up there in the winter."

"Who's this we're talking about?" Cavanaugh said. "At this point in time, I am coming away with the impression that you are seeking to elicit an admission on a point of reference or a subject matter, if that is your question, on which I am not your best witness."

"Fuck you," Louise said.

"As they say on the Oscar show," Cavanaugh said, " 'May I have the envelope, please?' "

"What?" she said.

"The envelope," Cavanaugh said. "The one in your pocketbook. I assume it's for me."

"You ain't dumb, Magee," she said, and she smiled. She fished out the envelope and handed it to him.

"Do I open it now?" he said. "Or do you want the additional pleasure of summarizing the contents hereof?"

"Well," she said, closing the purse, "I'll tell you, Hank, it's this way: when you wouldn't let me use your apartment to change, I admit I thought at first you'd been setting up a little light housekeeping with somebody."

"That's probably why you kept asking me if I was alone then, I bet," Cavanaugh said.

"Very perceptive," Louise said. "It's sure hard to put anything over on you. Then I thought about it some more, and I began to think maybe it was just that you didn't want me in your apartment."

"It didn't occur to you," Cavanaugh said, "that it might just have been what I said it was, that you didn't have a key and there was no way I could get you one?"

"Actually," Louise said, "it didn't. Because it made so much sense to me, all of a sudden. 'If he's boffing Sarah in New York, knowing him, he probably *doesn't* have anybody living with him.' "

"Louise," Cavanaugh said, "you simply must stop accusing me of infidelity. It wounds me."

"And you're not going to admit it anyway," she said.

"I have nothing to admit, my dear," Cavanaugh said. "I do have some more advice for you, though: legal advice that you get for no—from, uh, friends, friends like Dan Stoner that happen to be lawyers also, is usually worth about what you pay for it."

"Danny's my lawyer," Louise said. "There's nothing between us."

Cavanaugh smiled. "I don't want alimony, Louise," he said. "You can do what you want, when, where, and with whom. With or without Polaroid pictures to preserve the memories."

"Thank you," she said. She moved the table forward and got up. "And now," she said, "if you'll excuse me . . ."

"I always wondered," Cavanaugh said, "what women did when they had to go and there wasn't any other woman around to go with them. Now I know: you go by yourselves."

"Nope," she said. "I've got a plane to catch. The last shuttle's at nine. If I miss that, American's got one at nine thirty, but otherwise I'm stuck, and frankly, my dear, this occasion's not all that delightful that I'd lose track of the time. See if I did, I couldn't go to your apartment anyway, could I?"

"Nope," he said. "No dinner?"

"Ah, the hell with it," Louise said. "If I'm not going to be staying with you, who the hell wants to eat with you? I'm going to LA on the Ambassador tomorrow morning, and I'll eat what they give me without any complaints."

"It's not bad food on that service," Cavanaugh said.

"I'm," she said, "well, I'm going to be out there most of the next year, for Springer."

"Does this mean," Cavanaugh said, "that we won't be *seeing* each other, Louise?"

"I'm afraid it does, Hank," she said. She sighed loudly.

"Well," Cavanaugh said, "that will be difficult to bear. All that'll console me is that you'll be able to keep your tan."

"Not all of it," she said. "The pool at the apartment's too close to the road."

Cavanaugh laughed.

"Am I going to be able to get a cab to the airport?" she said.

"For a prediction," Cavanaugh said, "probably. The hotel doorman's generally got two or three of them stashed in the bushes. He'll look like he's asleep. Wave a buck at him and see if the rustling rouses him."

"Well," she said, "okay. Good night then, Hank. Thanks for drinks, and not being too nasty."

"Hey, Louise," Cavanaugh said, "you could've sent me the damned thing. If we don't get along, at least you've got character. Happy trails to you."

When she had gone, the captain came up. "Zerr laddy wass opset?" he said.

"What happened to the other guy?" Cavanaugh said.

"Zer captain," the captain said, "weel tack ur or-dair."

Having changed his mind, Cavanaugh ate oysters and soft-shell crabs and prime ribs of beef, medium rare, and a salad with Roquefort dressing. He drank a full bottle of Nuits de St. Georges, 1970, and for dessert he had Irish Mist on crushed ice, and two cups of espresso. It took him two hours.

In the foyer he said to the doorman: "It's the blue Manta Luxus."

"Well," Sarah said, inside Union Station in Washington, "that's the end of us, then. A fuck- ing Opel?"

"It's a nice car," Cavanaugh said. "It's got crushed corduroy seats, and a four-speed shift, and eisenglass curtains you can roll right up, in case there's a change in the weather. And it doesn't have a soft top, which they can slash when they want to steal it, and they don't steal Opels anyway. Who the fuck'd steal an Opel?"

"Blue?" she said. She got in. He shut the door.

"Blue's what they had," Cavanaugh said, getting in on the driver's side and shutting his door. "These things're scarcer'n virgins. You don't like what they got, you can go nicely without. All of a sudden I began to develop very hot drawers indeed for a metallic blue Opel. Kind of makes you wonder, you know? Used to be, those Buick dealers had Kadettes and GTs bumper to bumper and row on row, and what you had to wait patiently for was a Riviera. Now everybody in our nation's capital's scrambling around for cars that're easy on gas, and they've got rows of Rivieras four deep at most places, and I started to wonder: how come? Maybe somebody knows something I don't? Those pants fit you good."

"Thank you," she said. "What're you going to do with the Corvette when you get it back?"

"I'm never going to see it again," he said. "My guess is, by now it's not white anymore. It's red or something, and some dentist in Darien that looks at people out of the corners of his eyes is telling his friends at the nineteenth hole that he got a hell of a buy on it from a guy that came into his office and started telling him about how he was getting a divorce and needed a fast four thousand. Good luck to him. They steal those things on order. Let him worry about it every night, is his the one they ordered."

"Speaking of divorces," Sarah said.

Cavanaugh drove out of Union Station and headed west, toward Constitution Avenue. "My," he said, "news travels rather fast in old New York."

"Well," she said, "I'm an interested party, you might say."

"I might not, too," he said. "That galloping shithead, no reflection on your juvenile taste in males, you understand, that she's screwing sent her down here with a lot of transparent devices for her to use to win a fight with words that he couldn't win with his fists. I hope you didn't say anything that could be used in evidence against me in a trial in a court of law."

"I said:" Sarah said, " 'Who? Huh?' and: 'Who's he?' I also said: 'Oh, gee, how awful for Louise.' "

"Good," he said. He rubbed her thigh. "It's one thing to do it. It's another thing to go around testifying in court about it."

"You think I'll get called?" she said.

"No," he said. "I don't think anybody'll get called."

"Nuts," she said. "Because, if it wouldn't embarrass you, I'd love it. I'd eat it right up. God, that'd be fun. 'And not only that,' I'd say, 'he used me cruelly, and he made me perform unspeakable acts. Wanna hear about them, Judge? This'll really grab you, Louise. See if he did this to you, what he did to me. It was awful. I came two quarts.' Then I'd be overcome with the shame of it all, and cover my face with my hands. And weep."

"Lemme think," Cavanaugh said. "Yeah, I think it would. I think it would embarrass me."

"Not when you saw what happened next," Sarah said. "You'd have women camping outside your door. You sure?"

"I don't want women camping outside my door," Cavanaugh said.

"Goodie," Sarah said, "at last you're learning your lines. Now see how nice I feel. You don't want women camping outside your door because you only have eyes for me, right?"

"Right," Cavanaugh said.

"Liar," Sarah said. "You men are such liars. You just don't want to be embarrassed, you liar. Are you going to use me cruelly tonight?"

"This afternoon," he said. "Then again tonight, and don't plan on sleeping through till noon. I've got work to do tomorrow morning, and I want a piece of ass before I leave."

"All right," Sarah said, "that will suffice. I just want to warn you, though: don't promise what you're not planning to deliver. I came all the way down here on the train, and if I don't get so sore I can hardly walk, I'll complain to the Better Business Bureau. What the hell's going on with her, anyway? All I got was this dreadful, smug, I'm-gonna-make-you-feel-good-and-guilty telephone call from Tenley: 'I hope you're satisfied.' I was going to say: 'I'm not, but after I get four or five days of competent screwing down in Washington next week, I promise you: I will be.' Instead I played dumb, and as a result I didn't get any information."

"Boy," Cavanaugh said, "if the General's Wife hears about this, well, I don't know."

"The General's Wife can go read *The Reader's Digest*," Sarah said. "The General's Daughter will see to her own devices."

"The long and the short of it is," Cavanaugh said, "she's going to divorce me. Springer's got some kind of rubdown going with Allied Artists, and it's going to take about a year, and she's going to establish residence in California and divorce my ass. And it serves me right, by the way."

"It certainly does," Sarah said. "Mother's right: in the end, everything works out for the best."

"Sometimes it seems like you've got to wait and hang around an awful long time though," Cavanaugh said.

"Is it going to cost you a lot of money?" Sarah said.

"It can't," Cavanaugh said, "because I haven't got a lot of money, and sooner or later I'm going to have to face the fact that I'm probably going to have less."

"Why?" she said.

Cavanaugh drove up 17th Street and turned left onto Wisconsin Avenue. "Any money I had," he said, "has always been salary, and I've always spent it diligently, lest the morrow come and they declare currency invalid, worthless, and of no legal tender, and go back to wampum.

"I've spent eleven years working," he said, "if you don't count the co-op jobs I had when I was in college, at the *Globe*. I've never supported a family and I never owned a house. I've had two MGs, three Triumphs, a GTO, a Firebird, the old Vette, the Vette that just got stolen, and now, this. I've worn out a good many South-wick suits and Brooks Brothers shirts, and cast them away when they frayed and raveled with never a second look. I've eaten a number of good dinners, consumed respectable quantities of *premier cru*, taken a few trips and bought a few other things.

"I've had to learn everything," Cavanaugh said. "I never had any concept at all of how to do things. I learn fast, but I've still spent a lot of time learning while the people I'm competing with were doing. The only stock I ever bought that really went up was Zapata Offshore, which I bought at fourteen and sold at twenty-three and felt very pleased with myself about until it went to eighty-five or so, split three or four times, and went up to one-twenty-one or so afterwards. I have an unerring ability to pick stocks at top price. When I become disgruntled, I rely upon my broker's advice, and he's just as reliable as I am. They don't always go down, but very few of them go up, and those that do, don't go up very far. I've made—I was lying awake Friday night because I'd put too much good dinner on my shrunken stomach, and it decided if it had to stay up, digesting the stuff, so did I, and I finally got out of bed and got a piece of paper and started adding things up. I was absolutely horrified.

"I've been working for a living since 1962," Cavanaugh said. "Eleven years. I figure I've grossed over a hundred and seventy-five thousand dollars. I've got ten or eleven thousand dollars in stock, about two thousand in savings bonds, my personal effects as I believe they are called, the canceled checks for my taxes, a sizable number of books, the gratitude of my parents for one RCA color console that's wearing out now, and some very expensive habits. Where it all went, I don't really know."

"But you've still got your job," Sarah said.

"I've got it," Cavanaugh said, "but there's two things wrong with relying on that. I'm not sure I should keep it, and I'm not sure I can keep it, if I could. Can. I can. I might have to do something, but I can."

"Tell Sarah," Sarah said.

"I had a hell of a fight with Sam yesterday," Cavanaugh said. "It's all right, because you're allowed to fight with Sam if you work for him. Not that I really needed it, after my delightful Friday evening, but I was in there most of yesterday, and the only thing you can say about working Saturday is that there's no trouble getting in and out of the garage. But I did it, anyway, and try as I might, there was just no way I could get Sam to believe that he's wasting his and my time, his money, and all of our energy. Steve's too, and everybody else that's finagled up in this thing to resurrect Travis."

"Travis is through," Sarah said.

"Of course he is," Cavanaugh said. "Even he knows it. He saw Steve yesterday morning when Steve was in the cafeteria in the New Building, and came over to him and said: 'Even though we shouldn't be seen talking, I want you to know, I appreciate it.' And Steve said he knew it. And the Senator said: 'Don't spend too much time on it, though, please?' And then he went away.

"Sam wouldn't listen to Steve, either," Cavanaugh said. "Not that Steve pressed him very hard, because if Sam listens, Steve's got this little problem about getting work that he's had before and really doesn't enjoy very much.

"I'm not as careful as Steve," Cavanaugh said. "Maybe when I've been through as much as Steve, I'll be more diplomatic. But I'm going to die someday, and I resent wasting my time, even if I'm wasting it in the service of a man who sees to it I get paid a princely wage for doing it. I never did have any sense. So I really laid it on Sam, and we had ourselves a nice shouting match, and it ended up about the middle of the afternoon with mild-mannered Sam notifying me that I can either get myself committed to this lofty enterprise, or get my ass out of his goddamned office."

"Goodness," Sarah said. "Sam Barry said that?"

"I can do," Cavanaugh said. "I can put on a convincing performance. But should I? Maybe that's part of my problem: I've still got my job, I know exactly what I have to do to keep it, at least for the next four or six years, and all I have to do is do what I know I have to do.

"That's the way I've always lived," Cavanaugh said. "On the assumption that I had my job, and there'll be a check next Friday, and it'll be a good one. I went from sixty-five hundred a year to what I make now, almost six times as much, without a whole lot of trouble, and I guess I think that's the way it'll always be: when I'm forty-four, I'll be making two hundred and twenty thousand dollars a year."

"Gee," Sarah said, "you wouldn't have time to get married this week, would you? Or do we have to wait for old Louise to finish?"

"Things shouldn't just," Cavanaugh said, "I don't know, but I'm beginning to think I shouldn't keep on, just letting things happen. I've spent my whole life that way. By accident. It's there. It looks good. I'll take it. Or do it. Or whatever. I took the co-op job at the *Globe*, bringing in bourbon and Camels for Milliken, because I was an English major at Northeastern and the job was nights and I used to like to go to Suffolk days and lose the money I was supposed to be making for school, picking horses the way I picked stocks. You wanted the favorite to win, all you had to do was have me bet on him, and I made two-twenty on a two-dollar bet, and if you wanted a longshot to lose, all you had to do was get me to bet on him.

"I got the job at the Blackstone *Record*," Cavanaugh said, "because I had all the qualifications for a job on the *Record*. I once worked in a newspaper, fetching things for the City Desk, and I was breathing, and had ten fingers, which meant I could perhaps learn to type, and would take it for seventy dollars a week, three of which were for working nights, covering the Marlboro School Committee without the foggiest goddamned notion of what in the name of God was going on.

"I went to the Hartford *Courant*," Cavanaugh said, "because Jess was with the *Globe* when I was a copyboy, and we had a few drinks back in '62 when JFK was relaxing at Hyannis Port and estimable Editor Billings had had enough of me clamoring around to do something interesting, and Jess told the guy from the *Courant* that I was a hotshot, and the guy believed him. He thought Jess was God. Jess was from the Washington *Post*, and Pierre Salinger talked to him personally.

"I went to the *Post*," Cavanaugh said, "because I got sick of Asylum Street, and I applied, and I was getting crafty by then, and I used Jess's name, and it still carried weight, and they never even asked him what he thought of me. I got down there, he was working with Bobby by then, and he ran into me, and I thanked him, and he said: 'For what?' Then he said: 'Why'd you come? You were set for life in Hartford. I saw some of your stuff.'

"I said," Cavanaugh said, " 'Where's Hartford? It's in the minor leagues. I'm a big-leaguer.' This was in the press-staff elevator. Jess began to laugh. Lovely man, Jess. I thought if you could get to know somebody like Jess, and work your ass off, your father was wrong, and screw the security: go for the brass ring.

"I went to law school," Cavanaugh said. "That's a pretty serious decision, right? I went to law school because Hap Schaefer and I were sitting around shooting the shit in the fish bar one night in Georgetown, and he told me law school helped him, even though he didn't finish, and he had a column and that's what I wanted, so I went. I didn't want to be a lawyer, I just went.

"I went to work for the Committee," Cavanaugh said, "because I got so I could get anything I wanted out of Senator Hammond, and he was a nice guy, and he thought if somebody could get something out of him, the guy must be good. I was making ten-six, and he was offering sixteen-six, so I thought that was my reward for going to law school, and I took it.

"All my accidents," Cavanaugh said, "have been happy ones. Most of them, anyway. But I don't really think it's sensible to think I can just keep relying on luck. On just letting things happen to you and being confident they'll be good things. I'll be very much surprised if I'm making a quarter-million bucks a year when I'm eleven years older, very much surprised indeed.

"I've been blind lucky, that's all," Cavanaugh said. "I recommend it. It's a great thing. My father used to say there're three ways of being born: rich, smart, or lucky.

'Take lucky. Makes up for the other two.' It does. When the Hammond investigation was over, Sam was looking for somebody to make more'n twice as much as what I went to the Committee for, and it just happened that Sam knew Jess Richmond, and happened to run into him, and tell Jess Steve was leaving to go to the DNC, and Jess recommended me. Because he likes me."

"I like Jess," Sarah said.

"Jess is a fine guy," Cavanaugh said. "Sam's a fine guy. He's a starry-eyed bastard, but he's a fine guy. But that's a precarious way to insure continuous employment, especially since Jess's in wet drydock up on Nantucket and he doesn't happen to run into Congressmen and Senators much anymore, and Sam's not going anywhere. And if he is, I'm not sure I can or ought to go with him."

"Is he in trouble?" Sarah said.

"Nope," Cavanaugh said. "He's just not going anywhere. He is where he is, and he works his butt down to the bone for the district, and he's sober, industrious, bright, and wise, and he don't run around on Linda no more."

"Did Sam used to run around?" Sarah said. "*Sam Barry?*"

"Don't you ever tell anybody that," Cavanaugh said. "He and Linda were engaged from the cradle, the way I get it. And they got married when they were in college. And then when Sam moved down here, when he first came down here, before she moved, I don't know, I guess it was the first time in his life that he, it dawned on him, there were loose women in this town and he was on the loose among them."

"Here we go again," Sarah said.

"No, we don't," Cavanaugh said. "And I guess he had a big time for himself while he was getting used to the idea that he was a Congressman, just like all the big kids. Then she came down here, and he just stopped doing it."

"Jesus Christ," Sarah said, "doesn't anybody behave themselves anymore?"

"Sam does," Cavanaugh said. "He's Straight Arrow now. He's just what the ads say, a devoted family man. He just had a little spell there for a while, and then he snapped out of it. Oh, I heard he had another little spell, a little, uh, adventure, during the convention last year, when he was in the same place as Dee Richmond at the same time down in Miami, there. But I was with him two days after the convention, and it sure didn't show if he did. No, Sam's all right. I just wish I was as put-together as Sam is, in my head.

"It's just that Sam," Cavanaugh said, "Sam's a dedicated man, and they're nice to have around if they're dedicated to doing the kind of things that not only ought to get done, but are feasible. Sam's fifty percent short on that scale. He's dedicated to doing things that ought to get done, and that's all. He's got this tendency, like a lot of them, that he thinks if it ought to get done, he can do it, and then they get their heads down and try to do it. And there just isn't any way in the world that you can persuade them that it doesn't make any difference how dedicated they are; it just can't be done. It's not there.

"He's got this semidivine serenity," Cavanaugh said. "He doesn't really mind if he fails. Oh, he minds. He doesn't like it at all. And sometimes he's very discouraged, and then the guy that's got my job, which right now is me, has to go in and boost him up. But he's realistic at the same time. He knows his ideals're much higher'n somebody else's, and he's resigned to it—that people're not always going to be good, the way he wants them to be. So he can slug away at something that doesn't even compress when you hit it, and bark all the skin off his knuckles, and when he's too tired, he gives up. And he goes home. And he broods. And the next morning he comes back in, and he's got another idea, just as wild and innocent and marvelous as the one he just gave up on, and you're off to the races again. Sam was the voice of one crying in the wilderness, when he ran the first time as an out-and-out dove, and he finally prevailed. The experience conditioned him. He thinks he can do it again, an infinite number of times. He thinks he can do it on rail transportation, natural gas, soybeans, and urban sprawl, and so he tries, on all of those things, and that means I'm tearing around all the time, always asking for something, never giving anything away because Sam's got principles, using up my life on things that haven't got a tinker's damned prayer of making it.

"Sam can take it," Cavanaugh said. "I can't. I'm just a kid from the woods that got lucky. Now I've got to get smart."

"What're you going to do?" Sarah said.

"Well," Cavanaugh said, "that's one of the reasons I wanted you to come down here this week. You thought it was just to screw, didn't you?"

"I was reading a book yesterday," Sarah said. "No, it was Friday morning. I was reading a book yesterday, too, but it was about Catherine of Aragon. Friday I was reading a book, before I went to see the General and the General's Wife, that was absolutely gross. Coarse. Vulgar. It was *dirty*. And did I get some ideas for this next week, my friend."

"We are not going to rig up a Chinese basket, if that's what you've got in mind," Cavanaugh said. "The ceiling in my place won't hold it."

"I get dizzy on swings," Sarah said. "No, no block and tackle. These're just *nice* things. I'm going to surprise you."

"Are you also going to help me figure out a way to tell Sam?" Cavanaugh said. "I thought of going in there with a handbag and a white envelope in it, but somehow, well, it's not rude, but it lacks the spontaneous touch that I'd like. Taste."

"Have you got something else?" Sarah said.

"Oh," Cavanaugh said, "I'm not going to do it until I do. But I want to get started on things, you know? I want a plan."

In Georgetown Sarah rejected lunch at Rive Gauche. "Since I can't have a Chinese basket," she said, "can I have, maybe please, some Chinese food later?"

Cavanaugh agreed.

In the bar in the basement of the Jared Coffin **12**
House on Nantucket, Cavanaugh sat with Richmond and a number of people who minded
their own business on a rainy November Saturday night.
"Back in '61," Cavanaugh said, "one of the things I had
to do was go up to the State House to get copy sometimes,
on Thursdays a lot, when the guys up there were putting
Friday AM's copy on the wire and getting Sunday stuff
out for early setting.

"John Clancy was up there then," Cavanaugh said, "and
I remember one night, he told me about Charlie Fraley's
cousin."

"'Sir Lancelot Fraley,'" Richmond said, "Senator
Fraley from Lawrence, the Thirty-third-Degree Knight."

"Fourth Degree, you fuckin' Prot," Cavanaugh said.
"It's the Masons that've got all those twenty-nine other

ones. No wonder you never amounted to anything in state politics. You guys don't know anything that's important."

"Fourth Degree," Richmond said, nodding. "He's going to a funeral of some goddamned Grand Knight or something, and he's got on the full regalia."

"Oh," Cavanaugh said, "everything. The tricornered hat and the white plume, the black cape with the red lining, the tuxedo, everything."

"And the sword and the shoes with the silver buckles," Richmond said, nodding.

"Comes out of the church," Cavanaugh said.

"And here's this Polish woman, probably fifty," Richmond said, nodding his head and laughing. " 'Oh, Senator, oh, Senator, save me please, they went and took my poor husband off to Danvers, you must go and get him.' "

" 'Fear not, Fair Maiden,' says Fraley the Other," Cavanaugh said. " 'I will miss the interment of my brother Grand Knight. . . .' "

"How come those guys never bury anybody?" Richmond said.

"Doesn't suit their dignity," Cavanaugh said. "You're your average harmless Christian, you get buried. The quality gets interred."

"Same way with my guys," Richmond said. "Sometimes I see in the paper, they have 'committals.' Is that better or worse'n interments, better or worse'n burials?"

"The guest of honor," Cavanaugh said, "generally doesn't give a nondenominational shit.

"Up goes Fraley to Danvers in his Ninety-Eight, of course," Cavanaugh said, "hell-bent for election and he's gonna save Pulaski from the shock treatments, or whatever it was. And the next thing anybody knows, the Senate President's getting the call."

" 'We got a guy up here with a plumed hat on and he's wearing a sword,' the superintendent says," Richmond said. " 'Says he's a State Senator, come to save a patient from a gross miscarriage of justice.' 'What's he say his name is?' 'Joseph Fraley,' the super says, 'Democrat from Haver-hill.' 'Never heard of him.' You know," Richmond said, "they were telling that story in Washington? 'I went up there to get a friend out,' Fraley said. 'Then they wouldn't let *me* out.' Oh, it was beautiful."

"I was starting to feel like I was getting ready to join Joe Fraley," Cavanaugh said. "I should've had the sword and the plumes and everything, I was gonna run around like I was doing. I mean, what the hell, it's been a lousy day and everything."

"It'll be a nice day tomorrow," Richmond said.

"Yeah," Cavanaugh said, "I wasn't complaining. There's nothing like a foggy day spent drinking. But I hadda get out. I told him. I told him why I was coming up here and everything."

"It must've been tough," Richmond said.

" 'Jesus Christ, Hank,' he said to me," Cavanaugh said, " 'it's only a year since I got reelected.' See what a dummy I am? I had to pick exactly one year after Election Day. 'Nothing's permanent, Hank, but I thought I could at least get a term out of you.'

"There we were," Cavanaugh said, "down in the tunnel. I always feel like I'm in, I'm going to prison when I'm in that tunnel, those goddamned government-gray walls. I didn't handle it very well at all. You know Paul Doherty?"

"Met him once," Richmond said. "Fine guy. Full of shit in the Bishop's behalf, and knows it."

"There you go again," Cavanaugh said. "The Cardinal Archbishop, for God's sake. That stuff matters. You better never go into politics, is all I can say, Richmond, not in this Commonwealth, at least."

"What Commonwealth?" Richmond said. "This's Nantucket. Everything else's America. This's where I live."

"Not for long, though," Cavanaugh said.

"You think so?" Richmond said.

"I think so," Cavanaugh said. "I didn't handle it very well, not very well at all. I was going over to the House to tell him Monsignor Doherty and the rest of the Right to Life group were going to be late, and he was coming back to Cannon, and I met him. 'All right,' he said, 'good enough. Now, next week, I want something good next week. I'm thinking about possibly offering an impeachment resolution of my own.'

"I said: 'Jesus Christ, Sam, are you out of your mind?' He said he wasn't," Cavanaugh said. "I said: 'Sam, leave it alone, willya? Let things take their natural course. You stay out of it. Firebrands we don't need, not now, with that gap in the tape.'

"Well," Cavanaugh said, "he wasn't going to stay out of it. And he was going to go the full route, too. Rise on a point of personal privilege, everything. Proceed to a vote. 'Sam,' I said, 'you'll lose, and that'll scuttle the whole thing.'

" 'Hank,' he said to me," Cavanaugh said, "I swear to God, the guy's next to impossible when he gets going on something, 'Hank, the guy's right. This thing's gone on long enough. If they haven't got the goods on him by now, too bad. They haven't got the goods on him. If they've got the goods on him, they've got to move. One way or the other, we've got to get people off Topic A and get them to start thinking about things that need thinking about. It's either got to be him, or it's got to be somebody else, but it's got to be somebody, we can't hack around any longer. Win, lose, draw: there're other things that have to be dealt with, and dealt with now. *Now.*'

"I said: 'Sam,' " Cavanaugh said, "I had this thing all planned out, you know? I didn't want to hurt the guy. I knew what I had to do, and from what I got from Rich Williams, I was pretty sure I had the way to do it. It was just a matter of meeting Albright and making sure we didn't hate the smell of each other, and . . ."

"What'd you think of Albright?" Richmond said.

"Jess," Cavanaugh said, "I didn't expect a whole lot. It's like coming down here this time of year. It's raining and it's so foggy even Air New England's worried? Well, you expect that. What I expected with Albright was one of those guys that makes his own television ads and jumps out of trunks and smashes windshields with axes and stuff like that. But I need the job, right? And the guy's got this job for me, if we can stand each other, and that's really all I was after. If I can get with MARAD . . ."

"I don't know what that is," Richmond said.

"Massachusetts Association of Retail Auto Dealers," Cavanaugh said. "On the payroll, at last. I'm a goddamned lobbyist. Where's the damned State House, you know?"

"Never been there," Richmond said. "Wait a minute. Yes I was. I was with the *Post* when JFK came up and gave 'The City on a Hill Speech,' and there was a lot of, say, discomfort around. I think it's up on Beacon Hill. Go into Dini's and ask around. There might be somebody in there, can help you. Maybe even call Mike Fogarty. I bet he knows."

"Also," Cavanaugh said, "he said that from time to time, they might want me to go to Washington. Being as I know a couple people down there."

"Gee," Richmond said, "you know people in *Washington?*"

"Not a single soul," Cavanaugh said. "But, I was genuinely impressed with the guy. What he knows about the way things really happen? Well, put it this way: he doesn't know as much as Sam, but what little he knows is right, and give him a year, he looks like a pretty quick study to me. I think the guy might actually turn out to be a pretty good governor, if he can get it."

"Suppose he can't?" Richmond said. "What do you do then?"

"He was very level with me," Cavanaugh said. "He said: 'Look, there's no use horsing around here. I've got a good business, and I didn't get it by going for less than the full skin, and Rich's told me about you, and he says that you're good and you're tough. Now, that means I have to assume you go for the full skin, because Rich says you do, and he does, so he ought to know. Hopes and dreams I'm not trying to get you on. I don't know what chance I have. I was the one who decided to take the chance. I'm not asking you to take my chance with me, when I can go back, selling cars, and you can go back, on relief. The job is real. We need another lawyer in MARAD. We'll still need one if everybody turns up his nose at me. I'm as liberal as hell,' he said, which he isn't, not by a long shot: he's still for lots of highways and stuff, and he says he's for mass transit, but there's no money for it."

"Not too surprising, for a car dealer," Richmond said.

"Yeah," Cavanaugh said, "but I think if he was governor, he wouldn't be a car dealer anymore. He'd be governor. He's right on corrections, he's right on tax reforms and incentives, and he's got some very good ideas on welfare reform."

"Which have the life expectancy," Richmond said, "of a snowball in hell, in the General Court."

"Well," Cavanaugh said, "that's another problem. I never said to anybody: 'What I want is a job with no problems.' A governor can do more'n a Congressman. It's just the way things're built. I think he's a good guy. He seems to think I'm a good guy. Rich's just as pleased as he can be, and the job pays twenty-five thousand dollars a year, American money. It's twelve-five under, but it's not in Washington, which I don't object to."

"Washington didn't do bad for you," Richmond said.

"Did great for me," Cavanaugh said. "Now, I'm through with it.

"I had it all planned," Cavanaugh said. "This was long before I came up here. Sarah and I worked out a whole game plan. Left nothing out and nothing to chance."

"I knew Sarah," Richmond said, "over a year before I realized there was a brain behind all that fun-fun-fun."

"Pretty unobservant, Mister Richmond," Cavanaugh said. "So it was perfect. I set the thing up, to come up here. I get everything arranged here, I go back down there and tell Sam. Nice and dignified. Someday, I'm going to do something in dignified fashion. I'm going to tell Sam: 'Look, it's time for me to get out of here. It's a logical time anyway. You should make a change, too. This thing we've got going? I haven't gotten anywhere with it. Steve's moderately hot for it. You get along fine with Steve. Put Steve in. Let me go, go back and see what a guy can do in a smaller pond.'"

"Is Steve really hot for it?" Richmond said. "I thought Steve had more sense."

"When he feels good," Cavanaugh said, "Steve's a believer. When he feels good. That's why he's holding down a six-month job as director of the search committee, and he thinks it's really, he thought it was really, a sure billet until business started in earnest in '75, '76. But it isn't.

"Well," Cavanaugh said, "it is. But it shouldn't be. Sam's got some, and he knows people with some, and they'll do what he says because they love him, and that includes writing checks. So Steve could've been right, if he wanted to be, but there was no way in the world that Sam could be right, and Steve knew it, and Steve's a decent guy. They'd never cut him completely loose. But it's silly. Steve belongs with Sam, and Sam needs Steve, so they can be visionary together. The Senator's a great man, but I can't find anybody who really thinks he can be revived."

"Because he can't be," Richmond said.

"Including him," Cavanaugh said. "And that's too bad."

"But that's the way it is," Richmond said.

"And that's what, that's the kind of thing that Sam and Steve can't stand," Cavanaugh said. "Oh, Steve can stand it better'n Sam, but neither one of them really likes it: the way things are. They don't like things the way they are. So much so that they convince themselves things aren't that way. It'd break your heart, trying to talk to them.

"So," Cavanaugh said, "that was the game plan. I'd pick a nice, peaceful time, and I'd say to Sam that I just wasn't having any luck with what he wanted me to do, and that I knew it was important to him, and the country, because it has to be important to the country if you want to get it past Sam, and I'd say: 'Look, Sam, I want to try something on the state level. This thing for governor at home, it's really shaping up into a war, and it's next year's war, and the earliest real war I can count on here's two or three years off. I can always come back. In the meantime, Steve can do what I'm doing just as well as I can, probably better, and the guy's good and you got along before. So let's see, we can get something started back there, and it's important, you know? "Massachusetts, the One and Only"? The kind of things that you and I believe in, if you can't start them there, well, if you can't start them in Boston, they can't be started.' "

"I think I'm going to barf," Richmond said.

"You been drinking all day," Cavanaugh said. "Sam wouldn't've done either."

"True," Richmond said. "That's probably why you're hanging around with Sam instead of me."

"Sam's a million laughs," Cavanaugh said, "if you like a steady diet of social responsibility. Kind of rough, if you've got a message about Paul Doherty and you meet him in the tunnel and he's set to go haywire and it forces you into things. 'Sam,' I said, 'come on, let's have a cup of coffee.' And we went into the coffee shop, and I told him."

"What'd you tell him?" Richmond said. "Did you tell him he's an asshole?"

"No," Cavanaugh said, "I didn't. Because he's not. But I didn't tell him what I was going to tell him, either, that I'd worked out so carefully. Instead, I chewed him out. I was mad. And the upshot of it was, he was, he's going to put Steve in my slot, and I'm coming up here, and he is very, very, very disappointed in me. Very disappointed."

"I'm not," Richmond said.

"No," Cavanaugh said, "I didn't think you would be.

"Now, this is the next prepared text. You want it the way we worked it out, or should I just flog you right out in front, the way I did to Sam?"

"Why don't you give it to me with the hair on?" Richmond said. "It's just as easy, and it doesn't take as long."

"You're tougher'n Sam," Cavanaugh said.

"Not that it matters," Richmond said.

"Albright can win," Cavanaugh said. "He needs help with issues and positions, and he needs just plain generalized savvy, and he needs experts. Which you are, and you've been stagnating out here long enough, and now you're going to come up to Boston and go to fucking work."

"For what?" Richmond said. "I don't work for love. I work for money."

"You also don't work for money," Cavanaugh said, "so you might as well work for love. You can duff around here, while it gets winter again, or you can come up to Boston and duff around, and either way you can clip the coupons and live on the dividends, and maybe the son of a bitch wins and you helped to shape him. And that'll discourage Fogarty from running for governor, five years from now, and Jerry says that'd be a super-keen idea, if we discouraged Fogarty."

"I don't see anything to argue with in that," Richmond said. "How's Jerry?"

"Jerry's fine," Cavanaugh said.

"He put you up to this," Richmond said.

"He did not," Cavanaugh said. "I haven't seen or talked to Jerry since the day after I left here the last time."

"Who did?" Richmond said.

"I shouldn't tell you," Cavanaugh said.

"Tell me anyway," Richmond said. "I'd like to know."

"Jess Richmond," Cavanaugh said, "Six-one, four-six, six-three. Down at the Jetties last summer. If you can lose to me, and then order me around, I can win and then order you around."

"You're going to make it, aren't you, Cav?" Richmond said.

"Yup," Cavanaugh said. "Already have."

"Okay," Richmond said, "I'll do it. You win again."

"That's a very graceful concession," Cavanaugh said. "I'll take it with equal grace."

"It's no concession," Richmond said. "I always had an interest in the government."

A Note About the Author

George V. Higgins has written three best-selling novels, *The Friends of Eddie Coyle* (1972), *The Digger's Game* (1973), and *Cogan's Trade* (1974). Formerly a reporter for the Providence *Journal* and the Associated Press, he published two widely acclaimed articles on the Watergate events in the *Atlantic Monthly* in 1974. For three years he was a lawyer in the Massachusetts Attorney General's Office, and later served as Assistant U.S. Attorney for the District of Massachusetts. Mr. Higgins now practices law privately in Boston.

A Note on the Type

This book was set on the Linotype in Janson, a recutting made direct from type cast from matrices long thought to have been made by the Dutchman Anton Janson, who was a practicing type founder in Leipzig during the years 1668–87. However, it has been conclusively demonstrated that these types are actually the work of Nicholas Kis (1650–1702), a Hungarian, who most probably learned his trade from the master Dutch type founder Kirk Voskens. The type is an excellent example of the influential and sturdy Dutch types that prevailed in England up to the time William Caslon developed his own incomparable designs from these Dutch faces.

Composed, printed, and bound by The Haddon Craftsmen, Inc., Scranton, Pennsylvania. Typography and binding design by Susan Mitchell.